The Earl's Wife

The Earl's Wife

Amy Lake

**Five Star
Unity, Maine**

Five Star First Edition Romance Series.
Published in 2001 in conjunction with Alice Picard Literary Agent.

Set in 11 pt. Plantin by Christina S. Huff.

Printed in the United States on permanent paper.

Library of Congress Cataloging-in-Publication Data

Lake, Amy, 1952–
    The earl's wife / by Amy Lake.
        p.   cm. — (Five Star first edition romance series)
    ISBN 0-7862-3035-5 (hc : alk. paper)
    1. Married women — Fiction.   2. Nobility — Fiction.
    3. England — Fiction.   I. Title.   II. Series.
PS3562.A374 E27 2001
    813'.6—dc21   00-049065

The Earl's Wife is dedicated to my family.

Chapter One

The bell on the draper's shop door tinkled, and Claire glanced behind her. A well-dressed man and equally well turned-out woman walked in, laughing. The man's head was inclined towards his companion, and the rich brown of his hair—Claire couldn't help but notice it—was in startling contrast to the almost white-gold of hers. Claire raised her eyebrows fractionally at the low *décolletage* of the woman's gown. A bit daring for an afternoon's shopping expedition, but she did look beautiful.

He was very tall.

Claire turned around before she could be accused of staring and returned to her careful examination of the basket of Haraldson's less expensive lace remnants. She allowed herself a small smile. The portly shopkeeper had spent the last ten minutes hovering over her, obviously anxious that she make a selection, but at the entry of *monseigneur et madame* he breathed, "Heavens, the Earl of Ketrick," and at once forgot that Claire existed. He hurried towards the newcomers as the woman with white-gold hair laughed, a throaty, musical sound.

"Edward, the one thing I *don't* need is another hat."

"Nonsense," came the man's voice in reply. "I know of not a single woman in London who believes she is the owner of an adequate number of hats."

"Oh, *hopeless,*" said the woman and laughed again.

"Here milady, this one surely cries out for a gentlewoman of your rank," said the shopkeeper, almost tripping in his haste to lift an enormous confection of turquoise satin and ostrich feathers out of its perch in the window. Claire caught a glimpse of the hat out of the corner of her eye. Good heavens, could that possibly be a *bird's egg* nestled among the explosion of feathers? Claire decided that indeed, it could, and she barely repressed a snort. What a toady the man was! And with poor taste, as well.

"Oh, no, my dear," the woman said, addressing herself to the shopkeeper. "That's much too grand for me."

It was the man who laughed this time. "Indeed."

"I should think . . ." The woman hesitated, and Claire felt rather than heard her soft, gliding steps as she moved around the shop.

"That young lady's hat is very fine don't you think, Pam?"

Startled, Claire looked around again. The man was staring at her, his deep blue eyes amused and speculative.

The nerve! Did he take her for a shop's model? Claire favored him with her coolest glance before returning once more to the remnants basket. She was uncomfortably aware of the sudden pounding of her heart. He was quite the handsomest man she'd ever seen. A strong nose and chin, with cheekbones that looked chiseled out of stone. His chestnut hair wasn't styled into any of the current fashions—"the Brutus" or "the Chevalier"—but was pulled back and held with a simple black velvet ribbon at the nape of his neck.

She told herself not to look at him again, feeling strangely uneasy. Perhaps it was time to move on to a different shop. The woman's voice stopped her as she started towards the door.

"Edward, my love, you are right as usual."

Claire glanced up to see an exquisite face, framed in white-gold curls and smiling reassuringly at her.

"That cloche is beautiful on you," the woman said. "Wherever did you find something so perfectly elegant?"

Claire had heard enough insincere compliments in the last few months to recognize a genuine one. But the feeling of unease returned as she considered the dangers inherent in any casual acquaintance with a member of the *ton*.

"Forgive me, ma'am," she said to the woman, surprised that her voice sounded strong and clear. "It was a gift from *mon frère*—my brother." She hesitated, then added, "He loves to keep secrets. *Bonjour*." Claire nodded to the lady and swept confidently through the door.

Once safely outside she forced herself to walk slowly away and to look straight ahead rather than back at the shop. So she missed the eyes of the man as they followed her exit, and the eyes of the lady, as they followed the man.

Edward Tremayne, the twelfth Earl of Ketrick, stared thoughtfully out the shop window.

"Who is she?" he asked. He was surprised to hear Lady Pamela reply, scarcely realizing that he'd spoken out loud.

"I don't know," said Lady Pam. It was an unusual admission for her. "Her French seemed impeccable, but then, we only heard a few words."

"Hmm," said the earl. He had turned back to the shopkeeper's latest effort when another thought struck him. "Her hat—it would have looked marvelous on Melissa, don't you think?"

"Hmm," echoed Lady Pam. Edward didn't see her roll her eyes.

"Pooh," thought Claire, ducking down the nearest alley

and making her way home in zigs and zags. "Telling fibs about a hat." Well, it wasn't all a lie, she reassured herself. Jody *had* found the feathers, and had helped her drag Grandmama Isabelle's old court dress out of a musty attic trunk. The heavy gold satin of the underskirt had been perfect for the simple silk-lined hat.

Jody's feathers, tucked into the satin at a graceful angle, bobbed up and down as Claire moved quickly through another alleyway. She held her skirts as high as she dared and wrinkled her nose at a particularly noxious odor coming from one of the doorways. A large rat scurried across her path, and Claire sidestepped it neatly. Their house, rented for the season, was in a respectable neighborhood, but it wouldn't do to tarry on some of the side streets nearby. The rent consumed almost every pound she had been able to scrape together, even at that. Claire heard the clip-clop of a hackney cab on St. James's Square and knew she was almost home. A few hours of rest would be welcome, and then it would be time to dress for Lady Pemberton's ball.

"I don't like it," said Jody.

Claire sighed. She and her brother had been having the same argument for days. It was remarkable how stubborn a fifteen-year-old boy could be.

"Major Trevor is too old for you. And that baronet is *much* too old. Besides, he's fat."

"We've been over this before," said Claire, patiently.

"*Je sais.* I know." Jody screwed up his face and did a passable imitation of his sister's voice. "An older man will be more likely to marry for his own pleasure"—Claire winced at the word—"and less likely to have family scrutinizing every particular of his prospective bride."

"The major and the baronet are both kind, respectable

10

men. I wouldn't marry a cad or a drunk—you know that, Jodrel."

It was Jody's turn to sigh.

"And it's not as if I'm planning to make a fool of my husband, either. I'd work hard to be a good wife, and he would never have cause to regret offering for me."

"I know that, too! Either one of them should consider himself incredibly fortunate to have you."

Claire smiled at her brother's loyal declaration.

"But," Jody added, "you don't love the major, and you *certainly* don't love the baronet."

Pah, thought Claire, it must be the French blood. They were both sitting cross-legged on the old four-poster in her bedchamber. The fireplace here had a decent draw, making it the coziest room in the house. She threw a pillow at her brother, resulting in a small explosion of feathers. Jody sneezed.

"*L'amour!*" she exclaimed. "*Quelle bêtise!* You're fifteen years old, what do you know about love?"

"I know as much as you do!" retorted Jody.

"Ha!" said Claire. "Well, it's a highly overrated commodity, I'm quite sure."

"Perhaps Sir Clarence doesn't think so." Jody, hand over heart, puffed out his cheeks in imitation of the baronet's ample jowls. " 'Oh, Mamselle Claire,' " he intoned dramatically, in an execrable Yorkshire-accented French, " 'vooz etts ler ploo belle, ler ploo magnifick.' "

Claire grabbed another pillow as Jody dove for a defensive position underneath the duvet.

" 'Ler ploo splendeed,' " came his voice faintly.

They both collapsed in laughter.

Jody considered the possible outcomes from the

Pembertons' ball that night, thinking that he was far from happy about their present situation. His sister believed that the baronet, Sir Clarence Aubley, was *sur le point* of offering for her, and the major not far behind. The boy didn't doubt Claire's instincts in these matters. She wasn't given to exaggeration.

Jody felt it acutely that his beautiful sister was being forced to marry to secure their future. *He* ought to be working to support them, but Claire— with a stubbornness that could only have come from *grand-maman* Isabelle—refused to allow it. His sister said that the employment opportunities available to fifteen-year-old boys in London were not to be discussed. Jody knew she was right, but still—

He checked his pockets, making sure he had enough coins to hire a hackney, but not so many that the household would suffer greatly if he was robbed. Jody had been careful never to mention anything to Claire about the footpads he occasionally spotted while he waited for her. His sister was not at all missish, but she could still be naive about some things. He slipped a knife into one boot, trusting that the blade would provide security enough.

Claire looked into the mirror, satisfied. There wasn't much she could do about the raven black of her hair— blondes were much more in style this season—but the cascade of ringlets framing her face set off her grey eyes and glowing skin to advantage. She pinched her cheeks and adjusted the *décolletage* of her gown. Nothing too daring—she was an unmarried woman, after all—but this wasn't the gown of a young miss just out of the schoolroom, either. The sky-blue satin became her coloring, and the nipped-in waist showed just enough of her figure. She had been at some pains to convince both her suitors that she was an adult used to some independence in the world and that they needn't worry overmuch about her family situation.

Such as it was.

Claire took a last quick look in the mirror. She knew she was beautiful and didn't care. Beauty had not kept her brother safe on their uncle's estate, nor would beauty alone suffice to gain a marriage to a man closer to her own age. Someone she might even learn to love.

L'amour. "Pah," said Claire, quickly finishing her *toilette* by tucking a small tippet of lace up her left sleeve. It was time to go to the ball.

"Mademoiselle Claire de Lancie," announced the Pembertons' *maître de cérémonie.*

The duchess smiled warmly at Claire. "And where is your dear aunt this evening, Miss de Lancie?" she asked solicitously. Lady Pemberton was an energetic, gregarious woman and her flame-red turban wobbled alarmingly as she spoke. Claire eyed it warily and returned a smile.

"Oh, Your Grace, she had *une nuit blanche,* an absolutely *sleepless* night." Claire had early discovered that a phrase or two of French did wonders for one's reputation in London society. Now she lowered her voice confidentially, as if only she and the duchess were in on the secret of her aunt's illness. "Her headaches get worse and worse this time of year, as you know."

A confidence wasn't quite enough to stop Lady Pemberton's next question. "You're not here *alone* are you, my dear?" she asked in alarm.

Claire felt a few neighboring ears perk up. "Oh, no! *Certainement non!* My brother . . ." Claire gave a laugh and waved vaguely behind her. Fortunately, the dandy next in line chose that moment to move forward and sweep Her

13

Grace a wide bow, taking Lady Pemberton's hand and pressing it to his lips in a smacking kiss. The Duchess bobbed and tittered, and Claire made her escape.

The affair had not yet progressed to an impossible crush, and she looked around carefully, hoping to see Major Trevor. The Duchess of Pemberton was noted for the creativity of her arrangements, and Claire was having difficulty identifying male guests through the maze of palm fronds and Egyptian obelisks set about the room.

Ah, there he was. And heading her way. Claire smiled.

"So, who is she?" drawled the earl in an indifferent tone that didn't fool Lady Pamela.

"I didn't know her earlier, my love," she replied. "What makes you think I do now?"

"Do you not?" questioned the earl.

The figure of the dance parted them for a moment. Glide, step, glide, as Lady Pam moved smoothly around Viscount Richland and back to the earl. He was frowning, and she was hard put not to laugh. Such a strong man—rich, handsome, a wonderful lover—yet he had been felled by one glance from a slim, raven-haired chit.

The marvelously amusing part, thought Pamela, is that he doesn't even know it yet.

"In fact, I do," she admitted, making a *demi-tour*. "Good heavens, is that a sphinx?"

Glide, step, glide. Turn. It was the last figure of the dance and she curtsied to the earl as they came face to face. He bowed, then took her hand firmly, leading her out onto the duchess's terrace.

Claire could hardly breathe, but she kept her smile firmly in place as Major Trevor continued his address.

"My dearest Miss de Lancie, I hope I've not led you to expectations of . . ." The major's voice seemed to be coming from a great distance. He took her left hand in both of his. "I would never wish to cause you any pain."

"But of course not!" Claire forced herself to sound light and cheerful. She brushed a palm frond out of her face and added, "We are friends, are we not? I assure you, sir, I never thought of more."

She could see small beads of sweat forming on Major Trevor's brow. "Oh," he said, clearly relieved. "I am so glad. You see, you are so beautiful, so dashing . . . I knew you must have many suitors far more felicitous than I. But my Agatha . . ."

He glanced behind him, and Claire thought she could pick out the object of the major's affections, a tiny brown-haired wren of a girl. Agatha looked shy and almost lost in an overblown gown embellished with row after row of satin ruching.

"My Agatha," the major repeated. "I can't explain it. The moment we met I felt I couldn't live apart from her a single hour."

Claire was touched by his earnest explanations and, despite the blow to her own plans, she answered him in all sincerity. "I could not be happier for you, sir. If you have been so fortunate as to find true love—"

"Oh, yes, yes!" interjected Major Trevor.

"—then you will find joy indeed. You have my heartfelt congratulations." He kissed her hand, and Claire watched as he made his way back to Agatha, who was now blushing prettily.

Claire sat for a moment and stared blankly at the inscriptions covering a nearby obelisk. Lady Pemberton's attempt at hieroglyphics, she finally decided, and returned her attention to the occupants of the ballroom. Perhaps Baronet Aubley had also found his lady love during the last day and a half. What would she do then? A thin tendril of despair began to wrap itself around her heart.

"Her name is Claire de Lancie," said Lady Pamela, enjoying Edward's startled look. She paused for a moment and let his blue eyes demand more information before she continued. "Her family situation is a bit of a mystery."

"De Lancie." The earl frowned. The name sounded vaguely familiar, but he couldn't place it.

"The de Lancies were minor French nobility at one time, I believe," continued Pam. Her hair shone silver in the moonlight, and she shivered a little in the cool air. "But they've lived in England for the better part of the century."

"I don't believe I've met her father," began the earl.

"Miss de Lancie's parents are both dead." Pam reached up to brush a lock of hair from his forehead. "There seems to be some confusion as to who, exactly, are her sponsors. She speaks often of an Aunt Sophie, but no one has actually seen the woman."

"You are an amazing detective, my dear," said Edward.

Pam gave him a dazzling smile. "I know."

Claire saw him from far across the room. He was a head taller than most of the men, and even at a distance there was no mistaking those chiseled features and the thick, chestnut hair drawn back with a velvet bow. She looked away, worried that—somehow—he would feel her staring at him.

The bosomy matron standing next to her felt no such compunction. "Ah, Lord Tremayne," the woman murmured, with a suggestive sigh. "Always standing a bit . . . taller than the rest." She fanned herself and tittered.

Claire remembered that the shopkeeper had called him

the Earl of Ketrick, and judging from the other nobles now crowding around him he was obviously a respected member of the *haut ton.* She sighed. A handsome man, indeed, but it would never do to catch the attention of someone as powerful as an earl.

Claire found a secluded bench behind an oasis of potted palms and sat down, closing her eyes. Until she saw the earl, Claire had not noticed how exhausted she was. The baronet had yet to arrive, but everything—her search for a husband, the endless frugalities, the lies she was forced to tell every day—suddenly felt pointless. The ballroom, which mere moments ago had seemed filled with laughter and music, ladies in satin and gentlemen in fine cloth coats, now looked bleak.

Major Trevor had found someone to love him. His Agatha had found someone to love her.

Were those *tears* threatening to form in her eyes? Claire cursed herself for being three times a ninny, but after seeing the Earl of Ketrick she had no heart left for the Pembertons' grand ball. She stood, thinking to find her way through the crowd and out to the garden, to find Jody, to go home.

At a touch on her shoulder she turned to see, against all reason, the couple from the draper's shop. The woman. The earl. It was as if her thoughts had conjured him up, and she was momentarily paralyzed with shock. What on earth could this lord and his lady want with her?

"Miss de Lancie!" said the woman. "I thought it must be you. Did I not say so, Edward?"

"Indeed," murmured the earl. He was looking at Claire with strange intensity as his companion continued to chatter.

"I said, that must be Miss de Lancie. Such a gorgeous dress—you know, I'm sure you don't even remember me, so much older and you were just a girl, of course. I'm Pamela Sinclair, my dear," the woman said in introduction, then continued almost without pause. "We met at your Aunt Sophie's place—oh, it must be seven years ago now. How is your dear aunt?"

Aunt Sophie? Claire felt the first glimmering of real fear, and she resisted the urge to turn and run. Who *was* this woman? Claire was quite sure she'd never seen her before this afternoon in the shop. How could she know Aunt Sophie? Aunt Sophie didn't even . . .

The handsome couple was waiting for her to reply, Claire belatedly realized, the woman favoring her with a reassuring smile.

"My aunt is often unwell, I fear."

"What a pity. Oh, but allow me to introduce you to my dearest friend. Miss Claire de Lancie, Edward Tremayne, Earl of Ketrick."

"My lord."

"Miss de Lancie."

"I see the orchestra has returned," said Lady Pamela.

Claire heard the strains of "Love Be Kind," a waltz said to be the current favorite of Sally Jersey, one of the *grandes dames patronesses* of Almacks.

"How perfect. Edward, be a dear. I must speak with Elizabeth Carroll." Lady Pamela turned on her heel and quickly slipped away.

Claire wished she could drop through the floor, but the earl said simply, "Would you do me the honor?" and held out his hand.

He is incredibly handsome, thought Claire, and Jody won't be expecting me yet. Perhaps just this one dance. She smiled up at the earl and allowed him to lead her out onto the floor.

On most occasions the Earl of Ketrick was a charming and

attentive dance partner, but for the first minutes of his waltz with Claire he was quiet, a number of perplexing questions occupying his mind.

Foremost was how Lady Pamela had maneuvered him so efficiently to the side of Claire de Lancie. Why had Pam pretended to know her? And why had she chattered like some ninnyhammer female—that was very unlike Lady Pam—and not given the girl a chance to say much more than a word?

Who was this Aunt Sophie, anyway?

No answers were forthcoming as he swept his partner around the room. The earl soon became aware of the silkiness of Claire's gown under his hand and the warmth of her skin seeping through. She was a marvelously graceful dancer and blessedly tall, so for once he didn't have to spend a waltz staring down at the top of his partner's head.

He should make an attempt at conversation, at least, as Miss de Lancie showed no signs of initiating one herself.

"I am sorry to hear your aunt is so often unwell. You have other relations, I'm sure, to assist you while in town?"

She looked up at him with a pair of clear, unwavering grey eyes. He had the impression that she hesitated a moment, but her answer was calm and matter-of-fact.

"There is no Aunt Sophie," Claire de Lancie said.

After that alarming interview with Lady Pamela, Claire welcomed the respite offered by the waltz with Lord Tremayne. As he showed no signs of wishing conversation, she began to feel calmer and to collect her thoughts. Whoever this earl was—and his hand felt strong and wonderful on her waist—he was no part of her plans, and she doubted she would ever see him again after the dance.

Her thoughts once more in order, Claire had begun casting an occasional glance for the baronet when the Earl of

Ketrick suddenly asked about Aunt Sophie.

At his words, Claire lost the rhythm of the dance and almost stumbled, but then, more acutely aware of the earl's strength than ever before, she came to an abrupt decision. She wasn't a liar by talent or inclination and trying to spin any more of a facer to this man was an unbearable thought. This wasn't the scatterbrained Duchess of Pemberton. This was the obviously astute Lord Edward Tremayne, who didn't look in the least likely to be fobbed off with stories of made-up cousins or Aunt Sophie's megrims.

He was a man, Claire knew, who could ruin her with a single word, and she could only hope the truth would not make it more likely that he would do so.

"There is no Aunt Sophie," she told him.

"No Aunt Sophie?" the earl echoed.

"No. I can't imagine why Lady Sinclair said . . ." Claire hesitated, not wanting to accuse the earl's companion of a falsehood. "I think Lady Sinclair must be mistaken. I don't believe she has ever seen me before today."

To Claire's immense chagrin, the earl didn't seem very surprised.

"Ah. I see," he said. "So who is your sponsor? You must be living with someone."

"There is no one other than my brother Jody. He's fifteen. He usually watches for me in the gardens and when I'm ready to slip away . . ." Claire trailed off.

"You are really living alone? Unprotected?" The earl sounded shocked.

She nodded.

"And you make your way into the amusements of the *ton—?*"

"It's not that difficult, really," Claire told him. "I just . . . show up. I suppose most people assume I'm someone's daughter, or that Aunt Sophie is somewhere about even if they can't remember her surname just then—"

The earl laughed, amused despite himself. "Why?" he asked her. "Why take such a risk?" There was a much longer hesitation at this question, and he watched as a battle of emotions played itself out in her wide, silver-grey eyes.

In for a penny, in for a pound, thought Claire.

"I must find a husband. Soon."

"Is it a lack of funds?"

"No. That is, yes. I have a legacy from my mother, but it is under the control of my . . . uncle."

She seemed unwilling to continue, and Edward was left to wonder if the uncle was as imaginary as the aunt. As they made their way around the ballroom in easy, graceful turns, the earl found his attention straying to the neckline of Claire de Lancie's gown. Her breasts were mounded and held firmly by the fabric of the gown's bodice, and Edward was finding the effect stimulating.

"There are . . . easier paths than marriage for a beautiful woman to make her way," he said finally. A thought had come to mind—

The girl's eyes flashed fire. She stiffened under his touch, and only the firm pressure of his hands kept them moving. "It will cause a scene if we stop in the middle of the floor," Edward told her, again amused.

"*Je ne suis pas une putain!* I am not a whore!" she hissed at him. "How dare you suggest such a thing?"

"My apologies," said the earl. "I was unaware of the importance you attached to conventional behavior."

First an insult, now sarcasm. Claire glared at him, feeling chagrin that one man's strong arms could have made her into such a fool. She had just told a stranger every secret she'd been at pains to hide for the last three months. And now he

21

had the nerve, the gall, to suggest—

"Why does your uncle not help you?" asked the earl. "Does *he* exist?"

"He exists as much as you do," she retorted. "One more loathsome, arrogant, self-important male—"

"I think I get the idea," he interrupted. "So you wish to marry without the protection or knowledge of your relations?"

Claire's anger suddenly deserted her and she felt exhaustion creeping back to take its place. She shook her head wearily in answer to his question.

"Our parents have been dead these nine years and there truly is no one else. Our family is of good name," she added, "and I'm simply looking for an older man, a widower, perhaps, who would be happy with what I can offer."

Edward understood her meaning well enough. An older member of the gentry, his estate secured and heir already in hand, wouldn't need to look much further than a pretty face.

A very pretty face. The final notes of the waltz faded away, and the earl realized that, as his partner had no chaperon, he had nowhere to return her. He looked at Miss de Lancie, his dark eyebrows raised in question.

"I usually claim to have spotted an old friend just gone into cards," she said with a small smile. "Or to need a few minutes in the retiring room."

"Come," said the earl. He led Claire out onto the terrace, and she followed mutely. Was she afraid to say no? he wondered. He didn't dally with young misses. Ever. There were entirely too many ways for such a liaison to go irretrievably wrong. Still, he was reluctant to let this particular young miss disappear.

She was a girl of good name—Pam had confirmed as

much—but had no family to interfere. She was very pleasant to look at.

Edward felt the stirrings of desire. He led Claire to a darkened corner of the terrace until she was backed up against the balustrade, close enough that he could see her pulse jump erratically in the soft hollow of her neck. He reached out and felt the beat of her heart against his fingertip.

She didn't move. Biddable and delicious, thought the earl, forgetting that only minutes earlier she had given him a tongue-lashing for suggesting she might be less than a lady. He was thinking how it would be to bed her, and he liked that she had enough spirit not to quail under his touch or to indulge in girlish protest.

What could she say, after all? Edward doubted that Claire de Lancie wanted to call undue attention to herself in the present company of the *haut ton*. For the moment, at least, she was his to do with as he pleased. His finger trailed down her smooth skin to that very alluring *décolletage*. Desire had turned into an urge strong enough to cause Edward some discomfort. He watched Claire's face carefully, but he could see no answering emotion. She looked . . . detached. Why should he care a fig for the girl's sensibilities? She'd as much as told him she was in the Pemberton home under false pretenses. The earl moved forward and captured her lips beneath his, deepening the kiss as the feel of her body against his erased caution.

Edward did not have the reputation of being a cad, but the luscious figure of Miss de Lancie, combined with the girl's infuriating refusal to respond to his touch, was driving him half mad. She should be melting under his caresses, or at least—thought Edward, his logic a little fuzzy—struggling to fight him off! Indifference was not a response he was familiar with in women.

He kissed her again, keeping his hands firmly around her waist.

Nothing. Edward broke off the kiss to see her looking at him with evident calm, as unruffled as if they had been discussing the weather.

"Are you quite through?" asked Claire. "It won't do, you know. Even an older gentleman will require purity in a bride of my age." She smoothed a runaway tendril of hair. "We should return to the ball."

Are you quite through? The earl bit back the first reply that came to mind. How dare the chit speak to him like that? He was about to remind her of her place and opened his mouth to say—

"Marry *me*," croaked the Earl of Ketrick.

Chapter Two

Edward stepped back abruptly, stunned at the two words that had come out of his mouth. Had he just asked the chit to *marry* him? Miss de Lancie's composure—which had been up to the mark when dealing with his amorous advances—now disintegrated.

"What!" she gasped, and slapped him roundly across the cheek.

This was too much for the earl and he burst into laughter. Claire hitched up her skirts— Edward caught a glimpse of a trim ankle—and ran.

From what Jody could see of it in the dark, the Pembertons kept an especially well-tended garden, mercifully free of brambles. He had found a secluded niche inside the wall at the southwest corner and dozed off briefly while waiting for his sister. It was a perfect hiding spot—Jody had become an expert on this sort of thing—with a row of tall yews between him and the house, and the road just on the other side of the wall. He sat patiently, hearing the murmurs of passersby in the street and the clip-clop of horses' hooves.

Jody rubbed the back of his neck and sighed, feeling thoroughly bored. Whatever thrill he may have found in sneaking around outside the great homes of the *ton* had worn thin. London had proved to be much less exciting than he had hoped, and finding a husband for his sister too much like work. Maybe Cheltdown Manor hadn't been so bad after all. At least he'd had Cousin Harry to talk to, although—well, Harry *was* a bit odd.

He'd forgotten to tell Claire about the young man he had seen on the street earlier that day who had looked like their cousin. But why would Harry Rutherford be in London? It couldn't have been him, thought Jody. Harry would be the *last* person to enjoy town life. Still, it had certainly looked like their cousin, and the other day, at Green Park—

No. It couldn't be. Claire would say he had an overactive imagination, that's all. Besides, when the man saw Jody looking at him, he had turned and walked away.

The minutes crawled by. He was standing up to stretch cramped muscles when he heard the sound of running feet crunching over gravel. Claire? His sister didn't normally run in a ball gown.

"Jody! Jody!"

It was Claire, all right. Jody's eyes were more accustomed to the dark and he intercepted her as she almost collided with him.

"What's wrong?"

"Nothing. Nothing. Let's go."

He wrapped Claire in a sturdy black cloak and helped her climb the half-wall. Leaping over after her, he caught the eye of a passing hackney driver, and within moments they were sheltered and anonymous inside the cab, on the way back to Jermyn Street.

Lady Pamela collapsed on her bed in undignified laughter.

"*Marry* you! You asked her to *marry* you?"

"Why not?" said Edward irritably. "She needs a husband, and I want to get those matchmaking mamas off my back. I haven't been able to attend a single *ton* event this season without being besieged by one milk-and-water miss after another."

"Hmm." Pam smoothed the lilac silk of a pillow sham with one hand and looked at him with absorbed curiosity, as if—thought Edward—he were an unusual zoological specimen.

A worm, perhaps. The earl had the uncomfortable feeling that Lady Pamela hadn't believed a word he said.

He tried again. "She looks strong and healthy, and I'll need an heir eventually. She can stay at Wrensmoor with the children, and I'll spend my time in London. We'd hardly even need to see each other."

For some reason this provoked more howls of laughter from Pam.

He was certainly having no luck with women *this* night, thought Edward sourly. First indifference, now hilarity. He supposed he should be grateful that his mistress—who was currently trying to suppress an attack of giggles—wasn't upset. Any other woman would have descended into paroxysms of jealousy, but Lady Pamela Sinclair possessed a singularly independent mind. Edward assumed that she was as likely to give him his *congé* as vice versa, and at times during the last year he had suspected that they both knew their days together were numbered.

Lady Pamela was passionate, intelligent and kind—all qualities Edward admired—but the fire that flared between lovers had long been missing between them. Perhaps it had been absent from the start. He had occasionally wondered if this was due to some quality lacking in himself—but the earl was not a self-reflective man by nature. He had not chosen to examine the subject more closely.

He looked at Pam now, stretched cat-like on the silk and lace of her bed. She had removed her hairpins, and silky tendrils fell around her face in waves of white and gold. She was as beautiful as any woman he had ever known, yet in his mind he was seeing a woman with raven curls, not blonde. He would not be staying with Lady Pamela that night, the earl realized. Nor, perhaps, any night to come. And he knew that Lady Pam realized it, too.

Jody was looking at his sister in horror.

"You *slapped* him? He asked you to marry him, and you *slapped* him? Why?"

Claire poked at the fire and was rewarded with a few flames springing from the embers. She sat on the bed and combed out her hair, wondering if anything could ever feel as good as her head did after she took out all those hairpins.

She thought, unaccountably, of the earl's touch on her lips.

She had no answer to give her brother. The entire evening had been a disaster. First the desertion of Major Trevor, then Lady Sinclair claiming to know both her and her nonexistent Aunt Sophie, and finally—the Earl of Ketrick. She had no idea why she slapped him. It was not sensible—and certainly not ladylike—and Claire was experiencing a deep uneasiness about the possible repercussions. If he was a spiteful sort of man. . . .

But she felt that Lord Tremayne was not. And he had laughed, after all. Nonetheless, Claire wasn't happy with the night's events. She had come to London to get married, had spent every scrap of money she could find on a decent address and the *accoutrements* needed to make a small splash, and when an eligible man offered for her—an *earl,* for pity's sake—she slapped him and ran.

What had come over her?

"Did you say no?" asked Jody.

Claire looked at her brother, confused.

"Say no?"

"Well, you slapped him, but did you tell him no? That you wouldn't marry him?"

She shook her head. "I didn't say anything, I don't think. I just ran."

"What does he look like? Do you think he's handsome?"

Claire was having difficulty following her brother's train of thought. "What does that matter?" she asked. "With any luck, I'll never see him again."

Jody was watching her intently. "Is he handsome?" he asked again. "How old is he?"

Claire sighed deeply and flopped back on the bed. "I suppose he's a few years older than I am. And, yes," she finished, "he is the handsomest man I've ever seen."

Lady Pamela looked out her bedroom window at the quiet, dark street below, her gaze following Edward as he walked away. She felt a small tug at her heart, more from nostalgia than anything else. There had been some good times between Edward Tremayne and Pamela Sinclair.

She had cared for the Earl of Ketrick as much as she'd cared for any man, but it wasn't the kind of love Edward thirsted for, and she'd always known it. For some men deep passion was not a requirement in a relationship. For Edward Tremayne, whether he was aware of it or not, it was. A banked fire smoldered inside the earl, and when the flames finally burst forth they would consume him.

How she would rejoice to see that blaze. Lady Pamela couldn't really have said why Claire de Lancie had caught Edward's attention, or why she was convinced that the girl held the key to her friend's happiness. Call it woman's intuition, she thought, laughing at herself. Pam didn't have much use for romantic nonsense. But perhaps intuition was unnecessary. Since those few minutes in the draper's shop, she had seen a look in the earl's blue eyes that had never been there before.

The situation clearly required her assistance. Eventually Edward would need to offer again for Miss de Lancie, and Miss de Lancie would need to say yes. Pam gave a contented sigh and pulled the silk duvet over her shoulders, snuggling down into her bed for warmth. She had a number of tasks to undertake on the morrow, and it was time to get some sleep.

Claire was at her desk in the sitting room, perusing the small stack of bills needing to be paid. The bills were manageable so far, but she knew that time was running out. In another month, perhaps two, if she was very careful—

Mr. McLeevy scratched at the door, then entered. "The Baronet Aubley to see you, miss," he said.

Oh, bother, thought Claire, suppressing a laugh when she caught sight of Mr. McLeevy's expression. Apparently Sir Clarence was not a favorite of her butler-*cum*-handyman.

"I've taken the liberty of sending for Mr. Jody, miss," he added. "Perhaps I could delay your visitor for a few minutes until he arrives." Claire nodded. If her brother could behave himself, his presence would be welcome.

Mr. McLeevy departed, but the door burst open again almost immediately as Jody flew into the room.

"Oh, thank goodness he hasn't arrived yet. Claire, you *can't* be thinking of encouraging this coxcomb! How could you stand to talk to him day after day? How could you stand to even *look* at him? Do you remember the waistcoat he wore to Lady Spence's *musicale*? I thought it would blind me, even from out in the street."

"Shh!" said Claire, trying not to laugh. She remembered

that waistcoat. "Sir Clarence will be here any second."

"Oh, Claire, *please*. The Earl of Ketrick offered for you! Don't decide anything until you see him again."

"Jody, I don't think—"

They were interrupted by Mr. McLeevy at the door. "Sir Clarence Aubley to see you, miss," he announced.

The baronet bustled in, his ample girth contained in what was, for him, a relatively staid coat of peacock blue. Claire shot a warning glance at her brother.

"Ah, mah cher mamzelle! You are too, too beautiful today!" He took Claire's hand. "And, Monsieur Jodrel—how good to see you, also."

Hearing his friendly, artless words, Claire was seized by a sudden attack of guilt. Sir Clarence was a kind and amiable soul. He didn't deserve to be laughed at. He deserved . . . someone to love him. Claire tried to push that last unwelcome thought out of her mind.

"I was desolate when I did not see you at the Pembertons' ball last evening," the baronet was saying. "And I was told you had been there earlier! It was most infelicitous! I was hoping for at least one dance."

"Oh," said Claire weakly, "yes. A headache came on suddenly, I fear."

"Oh, mah cher, I am so sorry. You are well today, I hope?"

"I am very well, thank you, sir."

They discussed for a few minutes, the gowns Sir Clarence had seen the night before. He was, as Claire knew, quite interested in ladies' fashions and knowledgeable about the newest styles in both dress and coiffure. The length and narrowness of Lady Ponsonby's sleeves came under scrutiny, as did the color of Lady Pemberton's turban, but eventually the baronet paused to give Claire a meaningful look.

"I had hoped to speak with you about a subject that has

been uppermost in my mind for these several days." Here Sir Clarence paused, glancing at Jody. "Perhaps, if your brother would be so kind to leave us for a few moments . . ."

Claire's heart had plummeted to her slippers. She didn't dare look at Jody.

This is what you came to London for, you little idiot! said the voice in her mind.

Oh, but—

And just what do you plan to do, if you do not marry the baronet? It's too late to take missish over what can't be helped.

I don't—

Do you really want to take Jody back to Uncle's estate? Could marrying this harmless peacock be worse than that?

No, thought Claire. She supposed not. She smiled at Sir Clarence.

"I would prefer that my brother remain, sir," she said. "You may say what you wish to me in front of him."

"Ah, of course, of course." The baronet smiled hesitantly at Jody, then turned his attention back to Claire. "Well, my dear, I am not accomplished in fancy speech, so I hope you will forgive my abruptness. Vooz etts ler trez belle, ler tres—"

Jody choked and started to cough. Claire didn't dare turn away from Sir Clarence to glare at her brother, but fortunately—or unfortunately?—the baronet was unperturbed.

"I have admired you for some time," he continued, "and I would be most honored if you would consent to be my wife."

"Oh, sir—" began Claire.

"I think we should suit very well. I believe you are fond of the country, and you know I make no pretense to being a lord about town. We would make our home at my estate, and of course your brother—"

Claire could see that Jody was about to speak. "I am honored," she said quickly, not trusting what her brother might have in mind to say. "But I must have some time to think on this. It is a great decision, after all."

"Of course, of course." Sir Clarence nodded. He didn't seem terribly put out, thought Claire with relief. If she could have but another day or two, just to think things over, she was sure she could reconcile herself to marriage with the baronet. A few days more, then she would say yes.

Baronet Aubley was a very minor member of London society and of little interest to anyone outside his immediate circle, but he was also talkative. And since weddings were ever a worthy topic of conversation, within a day or two his offer for Claire de Lancie was remarked upon by at least a few of the *ton* gossips. The Duke of Midlands was having a coming-out ball for yet another of his dreary daughters that week, and it was there that Lady Pamela Sinclair heard the news.

"What a horrid squeeze, darling," said Amanda Detweiler, Pam's good friend and confidante in all matters *de coeur*. "The poor duke has two more of the silly creatures in the schoolroom. I suppose he's desperate to marry this one off."

"They're good-natured girls," said Lady Pam.

"Oh, too true," admitted Lady Detweiler, "but I imagine they've had no choice."

She and Pamela were well situated to see through the doorway of the dining salon, and they watched as two footmen added a few meager offerings to the banquet table. The duke was a notorious pinch-purse when it came to meals, although profligate with his wine cellar.

"Do you think we will be fed this time or only watered?" asked Pam.

"I believe it is too soon to tell. My dear, do you remember

that amusing little Yorkshire baronet at the Palmers' rout? The one who spoke atrocious French?"

"Hmm," said Pam. "Oh, yes. Clarence Aubley. He had the most shocking taste in waistcoats, too, as I recall."

"The very one. Caroline says that he has offered for Claire de Lancie. You know, the tall, black-haired beauty, the one with the sickly aunt no one ever sees."

"Aunt Sophie," said Lady Pamela.

"Is that her name? I'd forgotten. Well, Miss de Lancie's given him no answer as yet, I understand, but Sir Clarence seems to have high hopes. He told Caroline she would soon be wishing him happy."

"Indeed," said Lady Pam.

Chapter Three

Jody sat in the kitchen and inhaled deeply. No aroma on earth could match that of Mrs. McLeevy's cinnamon rolls, and his mouth watered as she covered them with swirls of orange glaze.

Mrs. McLeevy looked at him sternly. "Mind you wait a few minutes before you eat half the pan," she warned. " 'Twill make you sick, eating hot bread."

"Mmm," he said.

She shook a finger at him, smiling.

Mrs. McLeevy and her husband, as far as Jody understood it, had come attached to the house on Jermyn Street when his sister rented it for the season, and it had been a serendipitous association from the start. The couple's only child had died in infancy long years before, and Mrs. McLeevy was apt to refer to brother and sister as "our poor orphans." She doted especially on the motherless, fifteen-year-old Jody, and cinnamon rolls, fruit tarts, sweet biscuits and savory meat buns poured forth from the kitchen in profusion for "the young master."

Jody took his first bite of a warm roll and thought unhappily of the conversation he and Claire had engaged in the night before. His sister was going to marry the baronet, and none of Jody's arguments would change her mind. The only bright spot was that he had extracted a promise that she wouldn't tell Sir Clarence of her decision for at least two days. Two days . . . it was a small reprieve.

Mr. McLeevy opened the outside door and entered the kitchen, his eyebrows raised in amused exasperation.

"What're you feeding the boy now, Mrs. McLeevy? One more pan of cinnamon rolls, and we'll be having to roll him down the hall."

Jody laughed. Where Mrs. McLeevy was all roundness and dimples, her husband was wiry and sharp. In Jody's eyes the man could do everything and fix anything, and most days he spent as much time tagging along to help Finn McLeevy as he did sampling Aggie McLeevy's cooking .

"Don't you be complaining to me, Mr. McLeevy. The lad's been stayin' up half the night. He's skin and bones."

"Ach, you're a silly woman. Mr. Jody, I've a letter for you."

"For me?"

"Aye." Mr. McLeevy held it out to him. Jody took the thick vellum envelope and looked curiously at the beautiful script flowing across the front.

Monsieur Jodrel de Lancie
27 Jermyn Street

Claire received letters on occasion from admirers, and flowers, too, but who in London would know that he even existed? Jody tore open the heavy paper. He caught a whiff of perfume so faint that he thought he might have imagined the fragrance, but the message was real enough.

Monsieur de Lancie

My dear friend, Lord Tremayne, Earl of Ketrick, will be riding in Green Park this day at four. I believe he wishes to see your sister again, even though he hesitates to call on her at home.

36

Believe, cher monsieur, *that my sentiments in this matter are most cordial for both your sister and Lord Tremayne.*

It was signed *Lady Pamela Sinclair.*

The McLeevys were watching him with concern.

"No trouble is there, young sir?" asked Finn.

Jody looked up, thoughtful. "No," he said. "There's no trouble at all."

It was a beautiful afternoon, thought Pam. She and the earl were riding in the dappled sunlight of oak and beech, the smells and clamor of the London streets left behind in the fresh breezes of Green Park.

Achilles, Edward's horse, was restive, prancing sideways skittishly and twice threatening to bolt. The earl kept him well in hand, of course, but Pamela liked to think that the stallion was simply reacting to his rider's mood. She didn't wish to see the earl too comfortable.

She had received no reply from Jodrel de Lancie, but she had expected none. She had no way of knowing whether or not he and his sister would be in Green Park, though she had chosen it as closest to their house on Jermyn Street. All would not be lost if they failed to appear, of course. There were always other possibilities, other roads to her goal; this one had simply seemed the most straightforward. She rode serenely at Edward's side, her eyes searching the paths and meadows around her.

Claire was glad Jody had suggested she wear the apple-green muslin. It was her most attractive walking dress, and her spirits needed a lift. Now that her marital options had dwindled to one gentleman—even though that gentleman had offered for her—she was regretting the loss of Major Trevor.

Lady Aubley? She seemed incapable of thinking of herself with that name.

Claire glanced at her brother. Despite their ongoing argument over her marriage, Jody seemed in a cheerful mood today. He was whistling as he walked at her side through a meadow of grass and late daffodils. She loved the parks of London. Some days it was almost possible to forget you were in the middle of a city. The reservoir fountain sparkled in the sunlight, and the sound of splashing water made a pleasant change from the usual din of the streets.

She turned her head as a breeze rustled through the nearby oaks, and caught a glimpse of a man's figure in the shadow of the trees.

Who—?

An iron fist slammed into her right shoulder, throwing Claire to the ground. Utter silence followed, although her ears rang. Then a voice nearby, yelling. Jody's. . . . More voices, farther away. Something warm dripped down her arm. That was all.

Pam knew from Edward's stiffened posture that he had seen the de Lancies. Things couldn't be working out better. She turned towards him, saying, "Edward, look, isn't that—"

She heard something then, a sharp report. Both horses pricked their ears.

The earl shouted and dug his heels into Achilles's sides. The big stallion leaped forward, and Pam's mount, startled, reared. In the few seconds it took her to bring the mare under control, Edward was yards away in the direction of the de Lancies. Lady Pamela galloped after him, her hat fluttering into the dirt. What on earth had happened? She could see the brother, but where was Claire?

Claire had an absolutely awful headache. No. No, it wasn't her head. Her shoulder throbbed; that was why her head hurt. And the park seemed to be terribly noisy today, which only increased the pain. She wished everyone would be quiet.

"Somebody *shot* her!" It was a familiar voice.

Yes, realized Claire. That's right. Somebody shot me.

It was a strange thought.

"Did you see anyone? Did you hear any other shots?" Another voice, deeper and oddly comforting. She strained to hear it again.

"What happened? Oh, good Lord!" It was a woman's voice this time, and Claire—the fuzziness in her head clearing slightly—remembered to whom that voice belonged. Lady Pamela Sinclair. How extraordinary that she would be nearby. Claire tried to open her eyes.

"Lie still," commanded the deep voice. She heard the sound of fabric ripping, and sudden pain shot through her shoulder.

Claire moaned.

"What are you doing? Leave her alone!"

"It's all right. He's just—"

"Ah. This is fortunate," said the comforting baritone.

"What are you talking about? It looks dreadful."

"Yes, but a flesh wound only, not too deep. We must get her home quickly so it can be cleaned. Pam, hold the cloth just here while I get Achilles."

"What—"

Claire decided it was time she became a participant in this conversation. Her head was clearing a bit more, and the pain, which had at first come in disorienting waves, was now clearly

39

centered in her right shoulder. She felt cold and wet from lying in the meadow grass, and, she thought dispiritedly, she had undoubtedly ruined her beautiful apple-green muslin walking dress.

Claire opened her eyes to see Jody looking anxiously down at her. "Help me up," she murmured.

"Lie still." This was Lady Pamela's voice.

"No, I—"

Strong hands slipped beneath her shoulders, setting off a fresh round of pain.

"Hold on, this will hurt," said the earl as he lifted her up.

The pain was exceptional, but she closed her eyes and refused to cry out. When the worst was over, she found herself cradled in Lord Tremayne's arms, staring at a fine white linen shirt spoiled by dark smears.

"You're bleeding," said Claire.

"Mr. de Lancie," said the earl, "perhaps you could assist me. It will be much easier if we can get her onto Achilles for the ride back to Tremayne House."

"I want to go home," said Claire, mumbling into the earl's chest. She was feeling a little woozy, but this lord wasn't going to order her about.

"Of course," said the earl. "As soon as the doctor has seen to your injuries. Mr. de Lancie?"

Claire found herself being placed onto the back of an enormous black horse. Fresh pain lanced through her shoulder and her only memory of the rest of the trip was of strong arms surrounding her and holding her quiet.

"She should recover nicely," said the doctor, "unless there is any impurity of the wound. Now, I could cup her—"

"No!" said Edward and Lady Pamela in unison.

"—but I see you concur that bleeding is unnecessary in these cases."

"It's barbaric nonsense," said the earl. The doctor looked at him over the top of his spectacles, evidently having taken no offense.

"I quite agree, actually. Now, here are some willow-bark powders." He handed Lady Pamela several small glassine packets. "See that she takes one each morning and evening. It seems to control the swelling as well as the pain. I'll show myself out, thank you."

The doctor was at the library door before he turned back to the earl. "And see that she doesn't become overly excited, my lord, if you please."

The rest of that day and all the next passed in a fog of pain. Occasionally Claire would wake up, dizzy and disoriented. Nothing about the room or the bed she slept in was familiar. At other times she would open her eyes to find herself back in Green Park, but the man bending over her wasn't Lord Tremayne. It was . . . It was . . .

She couldn't see his face, but she was terribly afraid. She cried out—

"Claire?"

At the sound of her brother's voice she relaxed and drifted back to sleep.

Later she heard a woman's voice urging her to drink a glass of something bitter and awful. She felt better afterward, for a while.

Claire woke in the middle of the night to find that the haze in her mind had finally cleared. Her right shoulder ached badly, but the sensation was almost welcome, because it let her know that this time she was truly awake. She started to push herself up in the unfamiliar bed and was startled by a voice nearby.

"Miss de Lancie. Don't move."

She turned. In the light of the nightstand candle she could see Lord Tremayne sitting in a chair next to the bed, his long legs stretched out in front of him. Claire remembered now; she was in his house. She had the vague impression that the earl had been sleeping. His jacket was tossed over the back of the chair, and his chestnut hair had tumbled loose from its ribbon.

In the dim light, in the lingering weakness of a day and night spent in bed, the sight of Lord Tremayne stirred something deep within her. Claire sensed, somehow, that her life was about to change.

Once Jody was reassured that Claire was on her way to recovery he became a nuisance underfoot. Lady Pamela finally sent him back to Jermyn Street in the earl's curricle to fetch more clothes for his sister. Not trusting the male understanding of these matters, she had prepared a detailed list of the needed items, and Jody was happy to oblige. The Earl of Ketrick and Lady Pamela Sinclair had risen to almost mythic stature in his mind. He had been baffled and furious in those first chaotic moments after Claire was shot, especially to see a strange man leaping from his horse and bending over his sister. But now Claire had been seen by a real physician, Lady Pamela had smiled at him—she was the most beautiful lady he'd ever seen—and the Earl of Ketrick was taking care of everything. Jody whistled happily, the only cloud on his horizon being the difficulty of explaining the whole affair to the McLeevys.

Claire sat up against her pillows and sipped more of the

bitter tea. The bed was in the middle of the loveliest room she had ever seen. Hung with damask silk in various shades of butter yellow, it was cheerful and warm. She eyed the overstuffed lounging chair facing the fireplace, almost buried in pillows, thinking that it looked a very comfortable place to sit. She was tempted, despite the deep ache in her shoulder, to swing her legs over the side of the bed and walk to the chair. The carpet looked thick enough to swallow her feet.

There was a soft, perfunctory knock on the door, and the earl strode into the room without waiting for a reply. Claire swallowed the protest that instantly sprang to mind. It was his house, after all, and he could walk in anywhere he pleased.

But when the earl saw her, he looked startled. "I beg your pardon. I understood you were still asleep."

"My conversation is not near so intelligent while I am sleeping, my lord."

"I have no doubt."

Lord Tremayne pulled an armchair close to the bed and regarded Claire intently. If he was annoyed by her chiding remark, he did not show it.

"The physician says you may have laudanum for the pain, if you wish."

"I'm tolerably sore, my lord, but I'm not a child. The willow-bark tea will be adequate, thank you."

The earl looked at her curiously, and Claire lowered her eyes. Why was she being snappish with the man? She felt vulnerable in the unfamiliar bed, with Lord Tremayne's presence only a few feet away bringing a blush to her cheeks. It was most improper, of course. She had no business being alone in a room—a bedroom at that—with the Earl of Ketrick. She'd barely known him a day.

"I've not seen my brother yet, Lord Tremayne. If I might speak with him, we could devise a plan for returning to our home. We are both grateful for your assistance, of course, and for Lady Pamela's help as well, but I know you must wish us soon gone."

"You are mistaken," said the earl. "You are both most welcome, and your brother has already returned to Jermyn Street to fetch what things you will need for the next few days."

"What?"

"I assure you, your presence here is no inconvenience."

"Not for *you*, perhaps. But what if I do not *wish* to stay?"

"Miss de Lancie," said the earl patiently, "you are injured. The physician says you are not to be moved." This, at least, was how Edward had chosen to interpret the doctor's parting remark. "It will be most convenient for you to simply remain here."

"Oh!" Claire slumped into the bedpillows, then yelped as the movement jarred her shoulder.

"You see?" said the earl. "And re-injuring yourself will only prolong the healing."

Claire had no energy for argument. She nodded weakly and closed her eyes, thinking Lord Tremayne would leave. Several minutes of silence ensued, but she heard no indication that he had risen from the armchair. Was he still there? A peculiar tension was mounting in the room, and Claire seemed able to hear the beating of her own heart. She couldn't pretend to be asleep a second longer, she would have to open her eyes. . . .

He was still there. This was impossible. Did he intend to sit at her bedside all day? Claire searched for a topic of conversation. Something impersonal.

"Your London dandies must be appallingly careless with their shooting, my lord. It's a wonder more people aren't killed in the parks."

"The parks?" said Lord Tremayne. "Why do you say that?"

"Jody and I have been in town only months, and already it is twice that a stray shot has been fired close by. I am very fond of the parks, my lord, but I begin to wonder if they are safe."

Pam was curled on a sofa in the Tremayne House library, sipping her evening glass of sherry.

"Claire has been shot at *twice?*"

The earl poured himself a brandy. "The first time was two weeks ago. Jody said that he heard the discharge of a pistol nearby. But neither de Lancie seems to view the incidents as a personal threat. Apparently they imagine London to be generally full of exotic dangers to life and limb."

"I've no illusions left about London, my dear, but women do not get shot in Green Park."

"Precisely. Nevertheless, I hesitated to add worry to injury, as it were."

Pam mulled this over, and the earl could see something was bothering her. "Out with it," he said.

"It's the mother."

"Whose mother? You said Miss de Lancie's mother was dead."

"Yes. I hadn't thought to tell you this, but Claire's mother was Estelle Rutherford."

"Rutherford." Edward frowned. The name sounded familiar.

"Sandrick Rutherford's sister."

"Ah." The earl considered this. "Sandrick Rutherford. The uncle."

"I should imagine so. Claire and Jody must have been living with him. It would explain why she went to the trouble of establishing herself in London just to marry a bore like Clarence Aubley. Both the de Lancies should have money, but Claire's only twenty. Rutherford must still control it all."

"Why run now? She would have her portion within the year."

"But not, I would wager, the guardianship of her brother."

The earl met this comment with silence. Finally he said slowly, "She's not in London for herself, then. She's here because of Jody."

"*Exactement, mon cher.* An innocent like Jody. . . . It doesn't bear thinking about, does it?"

"I'll call Rutherford out."

Lady Pamela shook her head and stifled a laugh. Edward Tremayne was legendary in the *ton* for the coolness of his disposition. Yet here was the blasé Earl of Ketrick, about to issue a challenge to a man he'd never met. It was too wonderful. Didn't he realize how thoroughly he was caught?

"And who will protect the de Lancies if you are arrested for dueling?" she asked him.

Edward snorted. "Nobody's going to arrest me, Pam. You know that as well as I do."

"Probably true. But don't kill the uncle, darling. Marry the niece."

His reasons hadn't changed, Edward convinced himself later. Claire de Lancie was young and healthy, and it was time for him to sire an heir. She needed a husband and, despite the slap on the Pembertons' terrace, he didn't believe she wouldn't prefer him to a fat and dreary baronet. Edward wasn't being conceited, merely realistic. He was reasonably young yet—not ten years older than Miss de Lancie—a respected member of the *ton,* and wealthy beyond most women's dreams. Even before Frederick's death when his fortune and prospects were very different, women had flocked around him, so Edward supposed he was well-favored enough in looks.

And he'd had no complaints from any of his lovers, of which there had been more than a few.

It would all work out very nicely. A marriage of convenience, without emotion, in which the grateful bride would be content to stay at his country estate, with the children of course, and his own life could continue much as before. Even better than before, Edward told himself. In London he would be free to pursue the many willing ladies of the *ton*, with no chance of any unfortunate misunderstandings regarding marriage. And during his infrequent visits to Wrensmoor he would have the delectable Claire.

The decanter of brandy was nearly empty. Pam had left several glasses ago, so he poured himself the last of it, sipping slowly and staring into the library fire.

The uncle was a complication. He would have to see about that. Otherwise, all that remained was to speak again with Claire de Lancie. He stood up, swaying slightly. It was after midnight. Too late, perhaps, for this conversation, but Edward was deep enough in his cups not to care.

Someone gently touched her cheek, awakening Claire from a restless sleep. Her eyes flew open, and in the flickering light of the single candle she could see Lord Tremayne once again sitting in the armchair by her bed. It must be the middle of the night. Even if it was his own house, what could he mean, visiting her like this? And he looked . . . different, she thought. Intense. A strange excitement flickered to life inside her, and she fought to maintain calm.

"Miss de Lancie?" The earl's voice was little more than a whisper.

It was too late to feign sleep. With one arm, Claire pushed herself awkwardly into a more upright position, hoping that she was suitably covered by the bedding. Lady Pamela had insisted she borrow one of her peignoirs, and the silk was cut along rather daring lines.

"My lord?" she said reluctantly, meeting his eye and determined not to blush. Her mind was fully alert, but her body insisted on feeling like it wanted to relax and melt back into the bed. It would be so nice just to slip back down, and stretch out beside . . .

Dear me. That was quite enough of *that*. Claire sat up even straighter.

The earl was staring at her, but he did not speak.

"My lord?" she repeated.

"My apologies, Miss de Lancie. But—" Edward hesitated, wishing he'd drunk a little less brandy. He had no memory of what he had been planning to say.

"But?" she prompted, regarding him coolly.

"Under the circumstances . . . You've been in my house this day and night . . ." Edward faltered and came to a stop. He tried again. "Miss de Lancie, I believe we should be married. Your presence in this house without a proper chaperon is highly irregular. And your position in the *ton* is tenuous as it is."

Now she was glaring at him, but he forged ahead. "You've been fortunate and resourceful, of course, but it's only a matter of time before someone discovers that you and your brother are living on your own."

"I suppose you could ensure that they find out, my lord."

It was Edward's turn to glare. "Don't be a little idiot. I would do nothing to harm you, nor would Lady Pamela, but that matters not a whit. The *ton* forgives much by necessity, but they won't forgive being played for fools. And when they discover what you've done, they will cast you out so thoroughly that you could not find a footman to marry."

He hadn't meant to put it quite that strongly, and the stricken look on Claire's face was a stab to his heart. But she must be made to realize that her reputation was at stake.

"What is that to you, Lord Tremayne?" asked Claire. "You saw me for the first time mere days ago, and you could very easily see me for the last time tomorrow. I've offered to leave. Perhaps I should have insisted on it."

What was it to him, indeed? Edward realized that he wasn't really concerned with Claire de Lancie's reputation; he was concerned for her life. He didn't like those two gunshots in Green Park. Neither had Lady Pamela, and Pam's intuition rarely played her wrong. But he still hesitated to tell Claire that he suspected someone might be trying to do her harm.

If they were married—when they were married—he could secure her safety. Edward couldn't have explained why it was important that he be able to protect Claire de Lancie, but there it was. She would simply have to be convinced to accept his offer.

"Miss de Lancie," Edward began again, leaning forward. "I realize I must have surprised you with my precipitate words the other evening. But you still need a husband, and, as it happens, I could use a wife."

"How romantic," she commented dryly.

"I was not aware that romance was on your list of requirements for a husband."

Claire gave a short laugh. "*Touché,* my lord."

"The *ton* will accept the choice of the Earl of Ketrick, and they will soon forget that you were anyone at all before you were my countess. You will have no further need to invent relations or climb over garden walls. And your brother could, of course, live with us for as long as he wished."

Claire took a deep breath. Lord Tremayne had not moved from the chair, but the tension she felt in his presence was overwhelming. She tried to speak matter-of-factly. "My lord, forgive me for being blunt. You have described this proposed marriage as one of convenience for us both. You do, however, wish for an heir?"

The question hung in the air, becoming almost palpable, until Claire wished she could reach out and snatch it back. That strange intensity returned to the earl's expression. He leaned forward and touched a fingertip to her lips. She bit back a small cry, and then another as he rose from the armchair and sat next to her on the bed. He ran a hand over her hair and smiled lazily down at her. Claire couldn't move, her bones seeming to melt under his touch.

He stopped abruptly, and sat back, breathing heavily.

"Yes," he said. "I wish for an heir. For several children, in fact. But I would not trouble you beyond that. Your brother tells me that you prefer the country to London?"

"Yes," Claire whispered.

"Wrensmoor Park would be your home, and our children's. It will be convenient for me to spend a large part of the year in the city."

Convenient, thought Claire. I will be *convenient* for him. Still, she would no longer have to worry about Jody's future. And she supposed it was no worse than what she had expected when she first set out for London.

He is very handsome.

"I will marry you, Lord Tremayne," announced Claire de Lancie.

Chapter Four

The earl was up before seven the next morning, and he composed a note to Lady Pamela while having his breakfast. Although Pam did not wake quite as early as he did, her sources for *ton* gossip were superb whatever the hour, and it wouldn't be long before she learned of his coming marriage to Miss de Lancie. He wanted her to hear it from him.

Were all mistresses so accommodating? Not once in the last several days had Lady Pamela spoken a word of reproach to him, even though they both realized that their association, as it had once existed, would be coming to this quick and unanticipated end. Perhaps he should feel insulted that she was taking it all in such good humor. But Edward knew that Pamela Sinclair was not in the common way, and in fact, the word *mistress* hardly applied. She had been his lover, of course, but she was also a lively and entertaining companion, a beautiful woman on his arm, and a friend.

Lady Pamela had never allowed herself to be used by any man. Their relationship had been as much on her terms as it was on his.

He took another helping of sugar-cured bacon and wondered idly if Claire de Lancie was one of those ladies who generally slept until midday. Not that it would matter, of course, since they would be so rarely in the same household. He began to speculate how long he would stay in the country with his new bride before returning to London. Claire was still young, but he could see no reason to delay starting a nursery. How long, he wondered, would it take before—

He was pursuing this interesting line of thought when Jodrel de Lancie bounced in.

"Oh! I say, sir—I'm sorry, I won't disturb you. Might I have some breakfast? It smells delicious. Claire says I talk too much in the morning, but I can be quiet as a mouse. Scones! Excellent! I didn't think anyone would be about at this hour."

Ah. Another morning person. The earl indicated the chafing dishes full of food on the sideboard. "Help yourself. I assume a fifteen-year-old boy has enough of an appetite to keep my cook happy."

"Oh, marvelous. I mean, I do! I say, sir, have you tried one of Mrs. McLeevy's cinnamon rolls?"

Edward looked at him curiously. "Mrs. McLeevy?"

Jody stopped mounding his plate with fried potatoes. He looked chagrined.

"Oh, my lord, I entirely forgot to tell you. I truly meant to yesterday, but Lady Pamela"—here the boy blushed—"Lady Pamela said not to worry you, that it would be all right."

Jody's headlong rush of words had left the earl at sea. "Lady Pamela said *what* would be all right, exactly?" he asked.

"Well, that the McLeevys could stay. I mean stay here, in your house. With us," he finished, faltering a bit.

"If I might ask," said Edward, "who are the McLeevys? I take it there are more than one of them. Is it two, or an entire brood?"

"Oh, just the two sir, and Mr. McLeevy is ever so handy at fixing things." Jody smiled, his look brightly confident of the earl's understanding. "They were staying with us in Jermyn Street—they came with the house, you see—and when I went back the other day to get Claire's clothes I had to explain what had happened. That Claire had been shot, you know, and they were ever so upset, and—"

Edward held up his hand in defeat. "Very well," he told Jody. "I'll ask Lady Pamela about the matter. In the meanwhile, your sister and I are to be married within the sennight, so I've a few errands to run."

The expression on Jody de Lancie's face following this pronouncement was all that a groom-to-be might have wished.

"Ouch!" said Claire.

"Oh, I'm sorry, miss. Here, just a moment."

Flora tried again to gently ease Claire's day gown over her right shoulder. The girl wasn't a lady's maid—the earl's household had had no need of one before now—but she was trying hard to learn the unfamiliar tasks. Claire was the most beautiful woman in the world as far as Flora was concerned, and her clothes were the prettiest the girl had ever seen. Dressing Miss de Lancie was a clear sight better than her chores in the kitchen, anyways, what with the coal boy trying to sneak kisses and Mrs. Huppins always thinking of one thing more for her to do. Flora reckoned she could be as good a lady's maid as anyone else.

"That's better," said Claire.

"I think you ought be back in bed, miss. I really do. Mrs. Huppins will have me ears boxed if she finds out you was up for breakfast."

Flora indicated the silver platter on Claire's nightstand where a cup of hot chocolate was slowly cooling. "Really, miss, I'm happy t' bring you up whatever else you'd like."

"I'm fine, Flora. I think if I stay in bed one more minute, I'll start screaming."

The girl looked at her, astonished. Oh, heavens, Claire thought. This poor girl spends her whole day hard at work and here I am, complaining about spending a day in bed. Claire determined once again—this was a regular resolution of hers—to be more appreciative of her good fortune in life.

But enough of self-examination. Injured or not, it was time to escape from this bedroom. Claire moved her shoulder tentatively in a small circle and pursed her lips. "Flora, would you have the time to do me a small favor?" she asked.

"Oh, yes, miss, of course." The girl was at Claire's side in a moment, ready to help her back into bed.

"No, I'm quite all right, thank you. But I think Mrs. Huppins will be considerably annoyed if I do not drink her delicious chocolate. Would it be too much trouble to ask you to sit here for a few minutes after and finish it for me?"

Flora wasn't one to question a gift horse, and Claire left the girl happily ensconced in the comfortable armchair, lifting the cup of chocolate carefully, one little finger high in the air.

The earl's London town house was enormous, Claire soon discovered. She was able to find her way down to the first level without much difficulty, but once at the bottom of the stairs, she was lost. This must be the entrance hall, she thought, looking at what seemed to be an acre of gleaming oak parquet. Elegant arrangements of flowers were scattered on various tables and pedestals throughout, and the air was redolent with the fragrance of lily-of-the-valley and rose. It wasn't what Claire might have imagined of a bachelor establishment.

"Can I help you, milady?" A liveried footman had appeared out of a side door. His expression was one of restrained curiosity, and Claire wondered if anyone had informed the earl's staff of the unmarried miss now on their premises.

Well, that was silly. Below-stairs gossip traveled at legendary speed, so of course they knew. Perhaps unmarried misses weren't all that uncommon in Lord Tremayne's household, but she didn't want to think about that. Besides, wasn't Lady Pamela the earl's mistress? How many mistresses did men usually require? Claire couldn't think of anyone to whom she could address that particular question.

The footman was waiting for her reply.

"Oh. Thank you, yes." Claire said. She gave him a sunny smile. "Could you direct me to the breakfast salon?"

"This way, milady." But before Claire had taken two steps, they heard someone striding towards them down the hall.

It was the earl. He directed one look—with raised eyebrows—at the footman, who discretely excused himself. Lord Tremayne then turned his attention to Claire.

"Where do you think you are going?" His tone was abrupt and angry, and Claire was instantly provoked.

"To breakfast, my lord," she replied. "I believe that meal is customary in the morning."

"Breakfast will be brought to your room. Return there at once."

He advanced towards her, and Claire realized that he intended to pick her up and carry her bodily back upstairs. Of all the arrogant, condescending, pigheaded men! She glared at him and backed away.

"I realize my brother and I are only guests in your home, Lord Tremayne," asserted Claire. "Nevertheless, I think that *I* am the person to decide whether I am able to be up and about."

"You have been shot. Perhaps that seems no more than a

romantic adventure to you this morning, but I can assure you it is nothing to—"

Claire interrupted him, furious. "It was no romantic adventure to me, my lord, I can promise you that. I am not so lacking in wits that I would endanger my own health on a whim—"

"What is wrong with your maid, that she allowed—"

"—but you yourself said that I suffered little more than a graze! I am a great believer in fresh air and exercise—"

"Under no circumstances will you take one step outside this house!" roared the earl.

"—and as long as the wound is not bleeding, I see no reason to remain an invalid," finished Claire.

The earl was breathing heavily, trying to bring his temper under control, and for a few moments they stood glaring at each other. "Very well," he said finally. "I will take you in to breakfast. As soon as you are finished, you are to return immediately to your bedroom and spend the remainder of the day there."

"I will most certainly do no such—"

"*Miss* de Lancie," said the earl, "you most certainly will."

Her brother was no help at all.

"Claire! What are you doing out of bed?" was the first thing he said when the earl delivered her to breakfast. She could see from the evidence on his plate that Jody had been indulging in a substantial *petit déjuneur,* and she smiled. With her brother to feed, Lord Tremayne might have to find himself an additional cook.

"Your sister would like to join you for a few minutes," said the earl, fetching a chair and seeing that Claire promptly sat down. "Mr. de Lancie, would you be so kind as to escort her to her room as soon as she has eaten?"

Overbearing, tyrannical—

"Oh, to be sure, Lord Tremayne. I'll see to it." Jody looked up at the older man with something bordering on hero-worship.

Claire sighed. "Traitor," she said to her brother when the earl had left the room.

"Don't be a goose. You were shot!" Jody was loading a plate with bits of food that he knew Claire would like, talking all the while. "I wager other ladies would have taken to their beds for a month. Do you remember when Sarah Jenkins's mother slipped getting down from her horse and got that tiny cut on her ankle? I don't think it even bled and Sarah said that her mother didn't leave her room for weeks! Besides, I'm sure the earl knows all about these things and, well, since you'll be married to him in a few days, you ought to do what he says."

Claire stared at her brother. "In a few *days?* And how do you know about my getting married, anyway?"

Jody set the plate in front of her. "Lord Tremayne told me," he said, grinning smugly.

"Oh, he did, did he?"

"Well, yes." Her brother looked at her with the dawning of alarm. He had great respect for the stubborn streak in Claire's character, and if it came down to a contest of wills between his sister and the earl—well, he wasn't sure the earl would win.

"Oh, Claire, you aren't going to marry the baronet? You can't. Not when Lord Tremayne has offered for you!"

Claire couldn't resist the urge to twit Jody a little, especially after his earlier faithlessness. "Well, I don't know," she said, as if this were something she might need to ponder at length. "I've known the earl only a few days. Sir Clarence owns a nice property—"

"A nice—! Claire, Wrensmoor Park is said to be twenty times the size!"

"—and he dresses with such taste, don't you think?"

Not even a gullible fifteen-year-old would believe that Baronet Aubley's dress was anything but dreadful. Jody threw a bun at her. "Oh, pooh. You *have* agreed to marry Lord Tremayne, haven't you?"

"Nothing airborne in the Earl of Ketrick's breakfast room, please. And yes, I have agreed to marry him."

Jody crowed with glee.

His sister was looking down at her plate in puzzlement. "How odd. These cinnamon rolls are quite the same as Mrs. McLeevy's."

"Darling, this is marvelous news."

Lady Pamela hugged the earl and kissed his cheek as they stood on her front walk, then led him into the house. Edward had called on Pam somewhat earlier than usual but had found her already dressed, pottering in her garden. Her passion for this messy business of digging up mounds of earth to plant one more rose bush or hydrangea amused him, since in all other ways Pamela Sinclair was strictly a city girl.

Her sitting room was comfortably informal and filled with an eclectic assortment of knickknacks. Pam rummaged around in the pockets of her garden apron until Edward, realizing what she was looking for, gave her one of his handkerchiefs. She brushed the dirt from her hands and rang for tea.

They had always been honest with each other.

"I won't be back, Pam," he said.

She nodded. "I know."

"I mean, I will be back to town. Without Claire. But . . ." He hesitated. "I don't know why it should matter. Perhaps it's because she knows you and has seen us together."

"Edward, my dear, I like Miss de Lancie. I wouldn't have you."

She was entirely sincere, and Edward knew it. The tea arrived, and they sat in silence for a few moments as Lady Pamela poured.

"Do you think it would be wrong—would it offend you—should I take another mistress?"

Pam raised her eyebrows. "What a shocking question," she said, looking unperturbed.

"You are in London much of the year. We will no doubt encounter each other quite often, and people have not been unaware of our association. I would never wish to cause you pain."

Much as she respected the earl, Lady Pamela found it difficult not to laugh. Men. Such idiots, sometimes, and so full of themselves. She sipped her tea and wondered, too, if she could ever explain a woman's heart to a creature as thoroughly male as Lord Edward Tremayne. For Claire's sake—

"Edward," she said, looking at him seriously, "if you are thinking of taking another mistress, *I* am not the person whose feelings you should consider."

He hesitated for a moment. "You mean Miss de Lancie? But I have made the nature of our marriage and my requirements completely clear to her. She is a practical woman."

"Hmm," said Lady Pam, appearing unconvinced. "Even a practical woman might not want the *ton* tabbies batting tales of your mistress in her face."

"She will be spending her time at Wrensmoor Park. My activities in London will be of no concern to her."

"Indeed."

And it was left at that. Edward thought that Pamela was being rather hard. He would be spending most of the year in London, so of course he would take a mistress. What else was

59

he to do? He had never been such a profligate as to consort with prostitutes. And he saw scant reason to consider the feelings of Miss de Lancie, who had, by her own admission, come to town for the single purpose of marrying the first eligible gentleman who offered.

Edward left Lady Pamela soon afterward, with a quick kiss on the forehead. Although it was probably the last time he would see her for some weeks, neither of them commented on the matter. Pam kicked off her shoes and settled in with another cup of tea, brooding over the endlessly changing faces of love. Would men and women ever agree on the subject?

Jody, true to his word, insisted on accompanying Claire back to her bedchamber after breakfast. There they spent a few minutes in earnest discussion over the note Claire was writing to Sir Clarence. Jody agreed to see to its dispatch, and he left his sister reclining comfortably in bed. She stayed there no more than moments, however, listening to the sound of his footsteps fading away down the hall, before venturing in search of the library. She assumed that Tremayne House, like all the great homes of the *ton*, had such a room. If she was going to be locked inside all day, at least she could find a few books to read.

It took some time—the footmen seemed to be avoiding her, and she made several wrong turns—but in the end her journey proved worth the effort. She had never seen so many volumes together in one place, and the air smelled wonderfully of leather. The sun streamed in through windows stretching the full height of the room and Claire saw several large, comfortable armchairs beckoning someone to curl up in them. She sighed happily and began to investigate what the earl might have in the way of ancient Roman or Greek histories.

Quite a bit, as it turned out. Claire selected a likely-looking edition of Herodotus, sat down in the biggest, most comfortable-looking armchair of the lot, opened the volume, and promptly fell asleep.

Edward returned home from Lady Pamela's and went immediately to his study, sending for his man-of-affairs.

"I am being married within the week," he told Justin Mac-Kenzie without preamble. Not a twitch from the imperturbable Scot. "Arrangements will need to be made for a special license."

"Yes, my lord."

"I will have instructions for the lawyers concerning the settlements to be made on my wife. By—say—tomorrow morning. Have Fitzwilliams ready with the necessary papers."

"Yes, my lord. It might be helpful if I could make the name of the lady known to Mr. Fitzwilliams."

"What? Oh, yes. Claire. Claire de Lancie." Edward made a note to find out if Miss de Lancie had a second Christian name.

"Very good, my lord."

"Oh, and, MacKenzie—"

"My lord?"

"I need to find the current lodgings of one Sandrick Rutherford, gentleman. He may not be living in London, but I should think he's somewhere close by. Make inquiries through the usual channels and hire the runners if you need."

"As you wish, my lord."

Justin MacKenzie left, and the earl turned back to his desk, where a number of other papers required his attention.

It wasn't until Flora brought lunch up to Miss de Lancie

that anyone noticed Claire wasn't in her bedchamber. The girl, terrified that Lord Tremayne would ask for Claire before Flora could find her mistress, ran belowstairs. She knew that her best chance of finding Jody was in the kitchen.

"Oh, Mr. Jody! She's gone!"

Jody was helping himself to a large slice of Mrs. Huppins's cheese tart. He looked up at Flo and smiled. She was a thumpingly pretty girl, he thought. "Who's gone?"

"What's all this yammer?" demanded Mrs. Huppins with a swipe at Flora's backside. "Mr. Jody indeed. Don't be interruptin' Mr. de Lancie when he's havin' his lunch."

"It's Miss de Lancie! She's not in her room!"

"Ach, you silly girl, you couldn't find a pig in the henhouse. She's probably just sleepin' quiet in her bed."

"No, I looked careful! The bed hasn't been touched since 'twas made up earlier!"

Mrs. Huppins snorted in disgust. With a beautiful room like that t' sleep in, she thought. And now folks with work to do were havin' to traipse all over creation looking for the precious miss. Why couldn't the quality stay put like they were supposed to?

Jody tried to reassure Flora that his sister couldn't have gone far. He sat and thought for a moment while he ate another slice of cheese tart and one of Mrs. Huppins's sticky buns. The pastries couldn't compare to Mrs. McLeevy's cinnamon rolls, but Jody was a diplomat and partook liberally of both women's cooking. He had heard hints of kitchen squabbling during the past day or two, and he knew that Mrs. Huppins and Mrs. McLeevy were still negotiating territory.

Where might his sister have gone? Jody and Claire were both very fond of horses. When they had lived on their uncle's estate, Claire had a favorite mare that she rode every day possible. It was something she had missed in London and he wondered whether she could have taken one of the earl's lot? Jody thought that Lord Tremayne's stablehands would have instructions not to let a young lady out on her own, but he was also aware of his sister's powers of persuasion.

Well, it was a place to start, and Jody was as anxious as Flora to find his sister before the earl noticed she was missing. "Come on," he told the girl, grabbing one last sticky bun. "Let's check her chambers again and then try the stables. I've been wanting to see those, anyway."

Jody followed Flora up the stairway and through connecting hallways toward the back of the house. It was probably unfortunate that the earl chose to exit his study just as Jody and Flora were hurrying by, and equally unfortunate that neither of the two could manage a convincing lie.

"Jodrel? Flora?"

They stopped sharp, Flora, with a gasp, ducking behind Jody and holding on to one of his arms for dear life. Her heart was pounding so hard she thought it would burst. The earl was as kind an employer as Flo had ever known, but still. . . . She could be discharged, Flora realized with dismay. She'd lost her young miss.

"What seems to be the problem? And where are the two of you going in such a rush?"

Jody spoke up. "Oh, sir. Hello. Um, Flo was just taking me to visit the stables. You know, to see . . . to see the horses."

The earl's expression was disbelieving. "Flora was taking you to the stables? To see the horses?"

"Yes, my lord. I hear your stables in town are particularly fine." Jody tried to smile confidently at the earl, but this was too much for Flora, who now worried that Lord Tremayne might think that she and Jody—well, that she was no better than she ought to be.

She started to cry. "Oh, sir, please," said Flora. "I didn't know to be looking in on her any earlier!"

"It isn't Flora's fault," interjected Jody with some heat. He didn't want the earl to be angry with his sister, but he couldn't let the young maid take the blame. "Claire gets fidgety. She just doesn't take very well to—"

"She seemed so tired, I didn't think she would leave her room!" wailed Flo.

"Enough." The earl took out a handkerchief and handed it to the girl. "Flora, I'm sure there must be tasks awaiting you somewhere. I'll attend to Miss de Lancie."

Flora cast him a frightened look, blew her nose once, loudly, and fled.

The earl turned to Jody. "I take it your sister is nowhere to be found?"

"No, sir. That is, yes, sir."

"And she has been nowhere to be found since—?"

"Breakfast, sir. I did take her back to her room, like you said, but I guess she must have gone somewhere after that. I thought the stables might—Well, Claire loves to ride and she hasn't had much chance lately."

The earl closed his eyes and sighed in exasperation.

In the end it was Lord Tremayne himself who discovered Claire, still asleep, in the library. Herodotus was on the floor next to the armchair—he looked, curious, at the book's title—and much of her hair had escaped its pins, falling over her shoulders in a mass of black satin waves.

He lowered himself into the armchair facing Claire's, and for several minutes simply sat there watching her. She was quite the loveliest woman he had ever—Edward stopped himself and looked away. The earl had always thought of Lady Pamela as the loveliest woman of his acquaintance. But he found himself staring again at the girl curled in the armchair, her slippers kicked off and her toes peeping out from under her day dress. The thin muslin of the bodice was close fitting, revealing curves that left the earl feeling a bit warm. Edward thought about some of the young misses of his acquaintance, the lines of their figures little different than those of a boy. He found himself imagining what it would be like to have Claire de Lancie in his bed. No—to have his countess in his bed. His weeks spent at Wrensmoor would certainly be different from those in the past.

The earl had avoided marriage for years. He'd seen little point to it, other than the begetting of an heir. Why should he now be contemplating his wedding day with something that felt suspiciously like anticipation?

Claire woke to feel strong arms around her. With each breath came a comforting male scent that she had already learned to associate with Lord Tremayne. He was carrying her up a staircase, Claire realized, and she was acutely aware of his hands cradling her in a way that felt terribly intimate. As if those hands knew everything there was to know about the other parts of her body as well. She felt his breath warm against her hair.

"Mmm." It all felt so good. She curled her arms around the earl's neck and snuggled deeper into his embrace. She heard his short, sharp intake of breath, but his footsteps persisted in their strong, steady tread. Claire was about to drift back into sleep when she felt herself being dumped unceremoniously onto a bed.

Her eyes flew open. "My lord!" she exclaimed, momentarily unable to say anything more. Her dress—dear heavens, the skirt was almost up to her knees. She hurriedly pushed it over her ankles and glared at the earl.

He regarded her stonily. "Our wedding will be three days hence," said Lord Tremayne, his voice taut and cold. "After the wedding we will travel to Wrensmoor Park."

"Three days—"

"Until then, your home is Tremayne House. I have arranged for Madame Gaultier to attend you here, and you may choose whatever gowns and other items you will need for a trousseau."

"But in only three—"

"Madame Gaultier will have everything you require ready in time." The earl's tone allowed no room for disagreement.

How dare he be so presumptuous?

"My lord," said Claire, her eyes flashing with annoyance, "I do not know this Madame Gaultier, but I have every suspicion she is too dear for my purse."

"It is my intention to pay for the trousseau of my countess," said Lord Tremayne. "You may order as you wish, and the bills will be sent to me."

"I will speak with my own *modiste*," hissed Claire, knowing she had no such creature to consult. Her London gowns had been her mother's, which Claire had carefully adapted with fresh lace and ribbon to be *à la mode moderne*. She tried to stand. The earl sat on the bed, blocking her attempt to rise.

"Miss de Lancie," he said, enunciating each word with icy clarity, "let me make myself very clear."

"Oh, by all means, my lord," said Claire, "you may make yourself clear at length. I've no choice but to listen."

"We will be married Friday at noon. For the next three days you will not set foot outside this house. You may visit the library or the sitting room or any other room you wish as long as you are accompanied by Mr. de Lancie or myself. Otherwise, you will remain in your bedchamber to rest."

"So I am your prisoner!" exclaimed Claire bitterly.

"No, Miss de Lancie," denied Lord Tremayne, "but you *are* my responsibility."

Chapter Five

Claire did not see the earl for the better part of two days. Madame Gaultier arrived as promised, and though Claire suspected she had no more French blood than did Flora, proved to be a *modiste* of remarkable taste and speed. Two gowns would be completed and sent to Tremayne House by Thursday morning, with several others to be delivered to Wrensmoor Park shortly after their arrival. Claire's choice for the wedding was a simple walking gown with a flounce of silver gauze over a white satin underskirt and a short train. The bodice was fitted, with a square neckline, and embroidered with seed pearls.

Jody had taken one look at it and pronounced it fit for an angel, and in her heart Claire was also pleased. If Lord Tremayne would persist in treating her like his own private charity case—some poor thing he was willing to marry only because she would provide him an heir—then Claire was determined she would be a very well-dressed charity case. No one was going to look at her and think that the Earl of Ketrick had married beneath him in style.

Madame Gaultier had been insistent on the subject of nightdresses. Claire protested that she had plenty of *habillements* and wraps for the bedroom, but the *modiste* had simply said that she would select the necessary articles for mademoiselle and have them sent directly to Wrensmoor.

68

There would be a number of smaller items sent in as well—slippers, shawls, underthings in ribbon and lace—but mademoiselle was not to concern herself with those, either. The woman was more stubborn than *she* was, Claire decided, and she gave up all attempts at protest.

Justin MacKenzie had served the Earl of Ketrick for close to five years and had proved himself to be a reliable and efficient man-of-affairs. Lord Tremayne had not doubted that he would eventually locate Sandrick Rutherford, but even the earl was surprised that it took MacKenzie less than forty-eight hours.

Sandrick Rutherford currently resides at Cheltdown Manor in the borough of Lewisham, read the note delivered to Edward as he sat down to Thursday's breakfast. *I have been unable as yet to discover whether he also keeps a place in town, but Mr. Rutherford spends a great proportion of his time in country. You will find him there at present. JM*

Reaching Lewisham borough before afternoon would be no great effort for Achilles, and Edward was saddled up and off within the hour.

Claire watched from her window as the earl rode off eastwards, towards Belgrave Square. She wondered what had caused him to leave Tremayne House in such a tearing hurry. She wondered if Lady Pamela Sinclair's home lay anywhere in that direction.

Later in the day Claire endured a final, exhausting session with Madame Gaultier, after which she and Jody sought refuge in the library. They had just finished a game of piquet when the door swung open and they heard an elderly female voice.

"Oh, a pox on your fussing, Boggs. I'm quite capable of introducing myself."

A diminutive lady bustled in, followed by the earl's butler. Claire thought she seemed rather oddly dressed, only discovering later that the gown was in the first stare of fashion for the 1750s. The lady was using a cane, thumping it loudly on the floor with each step.

"And I suppose this is the brainless little chit that my idiot nephew has decided to marry?"

Thump, thump went the cane, followed by a stammered reply from Boggs that Claire didn't catch. Her brother was staring at the butler in amazement, having never before seen the man look anything but imperturbable. Why, his face was actually red.

Jody had started to stand as the lady—Lord Tremayne's aunt?—advanced into the room, but she waved him irritably back down. Claire found herself the subject of close scrutiny by a pair of piercing blue eyes. She gasped as the woman grabbed her chin.

"Come on gel, open up and show us your teeth. I can see what Edward wants from you—that boy was always led around by what's in his breeches. If you'll be breeding every year, you'll need to be healthy."

Fortunately for Claire's composure, the butler did not hear this, as Boggs had already fled the room. But Jody heard, and her brother was on his feet immediately.

"Leave my sister alone!"

"Jody—"

"And who the devil are you?" asked the lady, brandishing the cane in Jody's direction. "The chit's brother, you say? *I* didn't hear about any brother."

That was enough. Claire had not spent several months among the tabbies of London society without learning to control her temper, and she was loath to show rudeness to a person who, however odd, was apparently a member of Lord Tremayne's family. Nevertheless, it was time to remove both her brother and herself from the field of battle.

She stood. "Your pardon, ma'am. I shall hope to make your acquaintance when Lord Tremayne returns, but in the meantime, my brother and I are needed elsewhere."

"Oh, don't cut up snappish with me, gel," said the aunt, pounding her cane on the floor for emphasis. "I'm Lady Gastonby." *Thump.* "You are a little nobody—" *Thump.* "—and this is the Earl of Ketrick you're marrying, not some viscount's third son."

"Good afternoon to you, ma'am," said Claire, dropping a quick curtsey. She and Jody managed to leave the room without breaking into a run.

The earl was ushered into the library at Cheltdown Manor to wait for Sandrick Rutherford. The room looked comfortable and well-tended, with thick carpets on the gleaming wood floor, and a fire crackling in the hearth. From what he had seen as he and Achilles made their way through the grounds of the estate, Edward had deduced that Lord Rutherford's finances were in good order. He wondered if this would prove to be a problem or an advantage in the discussion to come.

As expected, within moments he heard the sound of quick steps approaching the library door. Sandrick Rutherford had never met Lord Tremayne, but he was the Earl of Ketrick, after all. The man would hardly have the nerve to keep him waiting long.

"My lord," said Rutherford, entering the room and extending his hand to Edward.

"Lord Rutherford," said the earl.

"Please, please, be seated. I have sent for brandy, and I am, of course, at your service." Sandrick Rutherford was a thin, almost emaciated man with lank blond hair and poor color. He's had the pox for years, decided Edward, thinking he would be glad to leave Cheltdown Manor as quickly as possible. The thought of Claire living with this dissipated wreck made his skin crawl. And as for Jody—

The man's smile was forced, and Edward knew he was nervously wondering what business Lord Tremayne might have with a minor lord of rather doubtful reputation. The earl smiled at him blandly and sat down. He leaned back in the chair and stretched out his legs as if he had all the time in the world to come to the purpose of his visit. He saw his host flinch.

"Forgive me, Lord Tremayne," began Rutherford, "but I am, regretfully, unaware of how I might be of assistance to you."

A weak-minded toady. It was just as well, thought the earl. He didn't have time for arguments today.

"You are, I believe, the uncle and guardian of Claire and Jodrel de Lancie?" he said, deciding to come straight to the point. He was rewarded by a look of consternation on Rutherford's face.

"Ah. Ah, yes. My niece and nephew are not currently making their home with me, but—"

The earl continued as if Rutherford hadn't spoken. "Miss de Lancie and I are to be married tomorrow."

The look on the man's face told Edward everything he needed to know. Rutherford was horrified, furious—and scared out of his wits. He's been using Claire's money, thought the earl. Probably Jody's, too. Good.

"You can't! I mean, my lord, this is an honor, of course, but my niece is underage, she cannot marry without my permission. Claire is young, not in the least mature, you know. It will be years, *years* before she—"

The earl interrupted him again, his voice cold and harsh. "Your permission? You haven't seen your niece or nephew in months and, in fact, you have no idea where they are. They could be rotting in the gutters of London for all you've searched for them." This last was conjecture on Edward's part, but it obviously hit home. Rutherford stared at him, unable to reply. You've been making free with the de Lancie inheritance, haven't you? thought Edward. And if Claire and Jody aren't about to require any part of it, so much the better.

And wouldn't things be even easier for Sandrick Rutherford if Claire and Jody were dead? Edward felt a chill run down his spine as he considered that the de Lancies' uncle might, at this point, have very little to lose.

"My lord, this is infamous!" Rutherford was on his feet, waving his arms in agitation.

"I think not." The earl brushed an imaginary piece of lint off his coat.

"You obviously know where my niece is. I demand that you return her at once! I will have you arrested for . . . for—"

"Shut up."

Rutherford's mouth closed with a snap.

"Let me explain what you are going to do, and I suggest you listen carefully, because I have neither the time nor the patience to repeat myself."

Rutherford sat down hard in a chair.

The earl opened the leather portfolio he had carried with him and extracted a sheaf of papers. "I very much doubt that anyone will question my right to marry Claire de Lancie. Nevertheless, as her guardian, you will sign papers giving your permission. As soon as we are married, of course, your involvement with Miss de Lancie will be at an end."

Rutherford was breathing heavily, infuriated but not daring to speak.

"You will also sign papers turning over the guardianship of Jodrel de Lancie to me, effective this day."

"My lord, I will do no such thing!"

The earl stood. "This becomes tiresome. You will do exactly that. In return"—Rutherford went abruptly silent—"you may retain Miss de Lancie's fortune, or what you've left of it. I will, of course, require Jodrel de Lancie's full portion to be put into my keeping."

"Ah, well, my lord," began Lord Rutherford, licking his lips. "Perhaps, with some adjustment, we could reach a manageable arrangement."

"No. The arrangement is as I have outlined. Otherwise," said the earl, standing directly over Rutherford's chair, "I will extract Miss de Lancie's legacy—every last ha'penny—from what is left of your miserable hide."

Rutherford looked up at the earl with impotent loathing. "I see," he muttered, examining the papers Edward had put in front of him. He hesitated, then began quickly scrawling his signature on the various sheets.

"Good. And one last thing, Rutherford," said Edward. "My fiancée has recently been shot at twice in the parks of London. I do not like it. Should any further attempt be made to harm her or her brother, I will be back to question you about it personally." The earl gathered the papers, turned on his heel, and walked out.

Edward was mounted on Achilles, ready and thankful to leave Cheltdown, when he heard someone calling his name.

"Lord Tremayne!"

The earl turned around. Sandrick Rutherford stood at the tops of the steps, a pensive look in his sunken, watery eyes.

"You may have no reason to believe me," said the man, for

once looking directly at Edward, "but I did not shoot at my niece. I have done many things the *ton* delights to accuse me of, my lord, but I would not attempt to murder my own kin." He turned and walked back into the house.

Edward stared after him for a moment, then gave heel to Achilles.

Claire sat on her bed, watching the door. Where was Lord Tremayne? Perhaps he was taking his pleasure with Lady Pamela—the night before his wedding, no less!—while she sat captive in her room, afraid to leave for fear of running into his dreadful aunt. Jody was probably safely ensconced in the kitchen. She doubted that even Lady Gastonby was capable of intimidating Mrs. Huppins, but Claire would be easy prey at the dinner table.

"Send the brainless little chit away," she imagined the woman saying to Boggs. "I won't dine with the likes of her!"

Maybe she could ring for Flora and have the girl bring her supper on a tray. But the thought of backing down from a threat didn't appeal to Claire. She had stood up to her uncle, and if she was to have any kind of marriage at all, she would certainly need to stand up to her husband as well. Perhaps she could practice with the aunt.

Claire gathered her challis wrap around her shoulders and took a last look in the mirror. She had dressed carefully, in the belief that she would surely be dining with the earl on the night before their wedding, Lady Gastonby or no. The gown was one of Madame Gaultier's new creations, a rose sarsenet with lace cap sleeves, and the close-fitted bodice which Madame seemed much in favor of, clung to her form like a second skin. The dress showed more *décolletage* than was her tendency, but Claire believed that Lord Tremayne could survive the shock of seeing a fair amount of her bosom.

Her black curls were piled high on her head, threaded through with a delicate gold chain. She wore no other jewelry and this, Claire knew, would be her one major defect in dress. She did not have the bracelets and rings, the necklaces, stomachers, and brooches, to make much of an impression as a countess. He'll have to be content with my silver-grey eyes, thought Claire, laughing to herself. Romantic nonsense!

Edward leaped down from Achilles and handed the reins to the waiting stableboy. He should be just in time for dinner. After being away from the house on one piece of business or another for the best part of the week, he was in-explicably eager to see Claire again. She was remarkably pretty, he reminded himself, so—of course—any male would look forward to seeing her. If a man had to marry, at least his wife could be decorative, and Claire de Lancie was that.

Boggs was waiting for him on the top step of the entryway, his expression one of long-suffering martyrdom.

Edward grinned at him. "What is it, Boggs? Don't tell me Mrs. Huppins has sacked the last three parlormaids again."

"Lady Gastonby arrived at noon, my lord." The butler's tone suggested that this occurrence was a disaster on par with Tremayne House burning to the ground.

Edward groaned. "Blast and damn! I *told* her—"

"She has introduced herself to Miss de Lancie."

The earl's reaction to this piece of news was unrepeatable.

Claire took another spoonful of Mrs. Huppins's roast carrot soup and wondered if time itself was contriving to torment her. The mantel clock seemed unusually slow, and for the past half of an hour she had heard its every single tick. She mentally cursed both Edward Tremayne and her own brother

76

for leaving her to eat dinner alone with this rude, interfering, insulting old—

"Aunt Penelope, how delightful to see you." The earl strode in and, to Claire's surprise, stopped to give her a quick kiss on the cheek. Claire blushed and hoped no one noticed. "My love," Edward said to Claire, "please forgive my tardy arrival."

My love? And had Lord Tremayne just *winked* at her? Claire could see Lady Gastonby opening her mouth to speak, only to be interrupted by the earl.

"Dear Aunt Penelope doesn't stand on ceremony, you know, but I'm sure you would like to be formally introduced. Lady Gastonby, this is Mademoiselle Claire de Lancie. We are to be married tomorrow."

Edward paused to take a breath, which was all the encouragement his aunt needed. "And without as much as a by-your-leave to your family!" denounced Lady Gastonby. Claire cringed as she saw the woman reach for her cane. "I declare, Edward, something is wrong! The de Lancies—who are they? Where are the chit's parents? I know of no—"

"Aunt Penelope," said Edward, taking the seat at Claire's side, "I'm sure you could not have heard me correctly just now. Miss de Lancie is my *fiancée*. By tomorrow afternoon she will be the Countess of Ketrick."

"Pish-posh," said Lady Gastonby. "What does that signify? Any whore can play the countess, and this bosomy little miss of yours—"

Claire rose and turned to leave, but the earl caught her hand in his and would not let go.

"That is quite enough," he informed Lady Gastonby. "Your ill temper grows tiresome. I will escort Miss de Lancie to her room, and you, Aunt, may use this opportunity to decide whether or not you choose to remain under my roof."

To Claire's amazement, Lady Gastonby didn't seem the least discomfited. "Oh, very well," she told the earl. "She's tolerably pretty, I suppose. Good teeth." She waved her hand vaguely in their direction and went back to her soup. The earl tucked Claire's hand under his arm and ushered her out of the room.

"I'm sorry," he said as soon as the door had closed behind them. Claire had not yet found her tongue, and the earl stopped to take both her hands in his. "Unfortunately, Lady Gastonby never married, and so she had no husband to—to smooth the rough edges, I suppose. Her relations have always affected to be amused by her blunt speech and I suppose we must have encouraged her. It was a mistake, I can see now."

"Whoever's fault it may be, my lord," said Claire, "I will not be treated in such a manner, even though she is your aunt." She was trembling with anger. Her family might not compare in importance to that of the earl of Ketrick, but it was no excuse for incivility.

"Miss de Lancie."

She looked up at the earl's almost gentle tone and her heart slammed into the wall of her chest. His jacket seemed to be molded to his broad shoulders. And she could see the muscles of his legs through the smooth fabric of his trousers. She would be marrying this man tomorrow. The incredibly handsome and virile man standing right in front of her. Claire took a deep breath. "Ah, yes?" she managed.

"Please do not trouble yourself over my aunt. She will treat you with courtesy, as will the rest of my family." He smiled, and Claire's hand on his arm tightened involuntarily. The earl's smile transfigured his face. He looked suddenly younger and . . . approachable.

They had reached the bottom of the staircase. "Your

family, my lord?" she asked, forcing herself to speak lightly. "Do you have brothers or sisters?"

"Only a brother, Frederick. He died several years ago."

Claire could hear the pain in his voice. "I'm sorry," she murmured.

At the door to her bedroom Lord Tremayne took her hand out of the crook of his elbow and raised it slowly to his lips. Time stopped as he leaned down and touched his lips gently to hers. She shivered, and then her hands went around his neck. The earl's shoulder muscles tensed under the fine cloth of his coat as his hands went to her waist, and she was crushed against him in a deepening kiss. She thought she heard him moan softly.

She could have stood there forever. But he released her abruptly and stepped back.

"You must still be hungry," he said. "Let me send Flora down to fetch your dinner."

"Hungry? Yes . . . um, that is, no," stammered Claire. "I'm not sure."

"Well, I am," said Lord Tremayne. "Hungry, I mean. Let me send for something for both of us and we will have supper together in your room."

"Oh, my lord, but—"

"Don't worry," he said, giving her a roguish grin. "I won't tell my aunt."

And so they dined together in front of the fire in Claire's bedchamber. Flora served them, clucking at Lord Tremayne as if she were Claire's chaperon and not mere days out of the scullery.

"My young miss needs her rest," she muttered under her breath. "And married tomorrow t'ain't the same as married today, to my way of thinkin'."

Claire smiled down at her plate and hoped Lord Tremayne hadn't heard.

"Flora," said the earl as they finished eating, "thank you. You may go."

The girl looked so scandalized that Claire was tempted to laugh. "It's all right, Flora," she tried to reassure her. "Lord Tremayne and I just have a few matters to discuss before the wedding tomorrow."

"Oh, but, miss—"

"Flora," said Lord Tremayne firmly, "your concern for Miss de Lancie is appreciated. I will take good care of her, you may be sure. Now go."

And so Flora went, muttering under her breath the whole while.

When the bedroom door had finally closed behind her, the earl abruptly stood and began to pace the length of the room. Claire kept her attention focused on the fire and hoped that he couldn't tell how nervous she was. Every time she was alone with Lord Tremayne, a tension seemed to appear from nowhere and grow until she felt like a rope pulled to its breaking point. Would it always be like this? How could she be married to someone who created such disquiet within her?

Of course, Claire reminded herself, he wasn't planning that they would spend much time together. Perhaps that would be best, after all.

The earl was now standing directly in front of her, and, she realized, holding a small rectangular box.

"The Countess of Ketrick's jewels will be yours, of course. There are a number of things—I don't remember every item, I'm afraid. They've been with the lawyers for safekeeping for quite some time."

"Oh," said Claire, faintly. She hadn't thought of that, but of course there would be jewelry. Why would Lord Tremayne even bother to mention it? She would have little reason to wear a countess's jewels, dining alone at Wrensmoor Park.

"You could pick out something for our wedding if you wish—I could send for them immediately, even tonight—but . . ." The earl hesitated. "This is my wedding gift to you. I would be honored if you would wear these tomorrow."

A wedding gift? Dear heavens, she hadn't even thought of a wedding gift!

"Oh, Lord Tremayne," Claire said, with a sinking heart, "I'd not thought to . . . to get you anything, and—"

"We are to be married tomorrow," said the earl. "Could you not call me by my Christian name?"

"Yes, of course, but . . ."

"I shall begin to think you dislike my gift," he said. "Do you not wish to open it?" He handed her a slim case of burgundy leather.

She fumbled with the clasp and then—"Oh, my lord," breathed Claire, "they are beautiful."

"They are beautiful, *Edward*," said the earl.

She was looking at a necklace of square-cut diamonds, alternating with emeralds, and set in gold. A pair of matching diamond earrings completed the set, and, in their elegance and exquisite workmanship, they were beyond anything Claire had seen on even the noblest ladies of the *ton*.

All this, for Claire Juliette de Lancie? The charity miss he was to leave immured at his country estate? She couldn't make any sense of it, but she chose to ignore the tiny prickles of doubt. The earl took the necklace from its satin-lined box and carefully fastened it around her neck. The stones were cool against her skin, but when his fingers touched her it seemed to burn.

"They become you well," he said. Then, touching her gently, he asked, "Does your shoulder trouble you? I can see only a small part of the wound. It seems to be healing well."

"Oh," said Claire, "there is very little pain anymore. But, my lord—" she said, "—Edward. I have nothing to give you in return." Still bewildered by the extravagance of the gift, she felt Lord Tremayne pick up the necklace, the tips of his fingers brushing her collarbone. Slowly he lowered it back to her neck. The prickles of doubt gave way to alarm as Claire felt his hands move lower, his fingertips lingering on her skin.

"Nothing to give? Oh, but I think you do," said the earl, his voice rough. Claire looked up at him, and even in her naivete and lack of experience she could not mistake the look in his eyes. He leaned over and picked her up out of the chair as if she weighed no more than a feather pillow.

"My lord, I—"

"Edward," he said. He carried her to the bed and sat down on it, cradling her in his lap.

"My—Edward, please—"

His kiss stopped her protest. He leaned back, gently toppling them into the mounds of bedding. His lips on hers became urgent, demanding, and she wondered what she had been planning to say. Please, stop? Please do not bed me until we are married?

Theirs was no match of mutual love and respect, Claire reminded herself. It was a marriage arranged for practical reasons, for the both of us. If her sole purpose as the Countess of Ketrick was to provide Lord Tremayne with an heir, what did it matter if they began the transaction today rather than tomorrow? Had she forgotten something? Was some piece of logic missing? But the earl was caressing her breasts through the thin fabric of her bodice, and her thoughts scattered under the onslaught of new feelings.

"Claire," murmured the earl, nuzzling her neck, his hands moving insistently over her. He began to unfasten the tiny pearl buttons of her bodice.

Insistent. Claire felt she was melting into the pillows. The earl's breath was hot in her ear and his fingers were setting her skin on fire. The "marital duties" that she had often heard whispered about seemed more pleasant than she had been led to believe, and she suspected she might enjoy the experience of lovemaking.

But—insistent? Tomorrow the Earl of Ketrick would own her, body and soul, and he could insist. Not today.

"No," said Claire, scrambling out of Lord Tremayne's grasp.

At that moment, *no* was not a word Lord Tremayne wanted to hear. "A pox on virgins," he muttered and grabbing for her, he tossed Claire back onto the bed. "Don't try to play the prim little miss with me. You wanted a husband? You have one."

"This has nothing to do with . . . virgins, my lord," exclaimed Claire, trying to sit up even as the earl pushed her back onto the bedcovers. "It is a matter of courtesy."

"Courtesy? Courtesy is exactly what I want from you," he said, with a grin that made her shiver.

His hands were strong and warm, his body so close to her, she could hardly think. "I do not like your definition of the word, my lord."

"*Edward,*" said Lord Tremayne, seemingly oblivious to her protest. "You are delicious, Mademoiselle de Lancie." His lips were tracing a line down her neck to the farthest extent of her *décolletage.*

"No," she said again, her voice flat. "Stop this." Claire knew that he might be beyond reason or simply not care what she wanted, or what she said; nevertheless, she felt calm. If he chose to force her, she could not prevent him, but she would not willingly give in.

Lord Tremayne stilled, then rose from the bed. He strode to the fireplace, and stood there for several minutes, breathing heavily.

"Your pardon, Miss de Lancie," he finally said, still not looking in her direction. "We will continue this . . . argument . . . after our wedding. But from tomorrow, mademoiselle, it is an argument that I will win."

Chapter Six

Lady Pamela Sinclair pulled back the velvet carriage drape with one elegantly gloved hand. She hadn't attended the wedding, of course. Most improper for a former mistress. But she couldn't resist seeking a glimpse of Edward Tremayne and his new bride as they left St. Alban's. She felt some responsibility for the event, after all.

It would be a small, quiet wedding; attended by Claire's brother, naturally, and—alas—Lady Gastonby. According to Amanda Detweiler, the earl's dreadful aunt had shown up on the doorstep of Tremayne House yesterday afternoon, and Boggs had nearly refused her admittance. The butler and the dragon! How Pam wished she could have seen *that* encounter.

Even with Lady Gastonby present, she imagined that Edward's wedding would be far pleasanter than his brother's. Pam still remembered her dismay all those years ago at the ostentation of the ceremony and the sight of Frederick Tremayne giving his hand to Melissa. The sainted Melissa Bourne-Sumner, daughter of . . . oh, what did it matter? Some ancient family with an equally ancient heritage of debt.

Lady Pamela's memory could recreate Frederick's wedding in detail, and even some of the events leading up to it. The temper tantrums she had heard! Nothing was ever right for Melissa—not the wedding dress, not the veil, not the flowers. Even the spectacular jeweled collar Frederick had given her, a Tremayne family heirloom, was the subject of bitter complaint.

"Dreadful, old-fashioned thing," the silly girl had cried, refusing to wear it. Frederick had just shrugged.

She could still see Melissa—tiny and delicate, the image of innocence—in a dress of blinding white silk, walking up the long aisle at St. Alban's. Frederick waiting before the altar with his careless, easy grin, and Edward—

Naive, eighteen-year-old Edward, the perfect younger brother and adoring brother-in-law. Melissa had twisted both men around her finger.

In Edward the cool Tremayne exterior hid a heart that cared and could be hurt; in the older brother, on the other hand, it hid nothing much at all. Frederick—the eleventh earl, by the time of his wedding—had been the perfect social creature, delighting in his beautiful young wife and the balls and soirees, the routs and musical evenings that made up the most of their lives. Any part of him not taken up with parties was devoted to horses or to making absurd wagers with his rowdy friends.

Pam's mouth crooked in an unbidden smile, as she remembered times past. Frederick Tremayne was one of the least complicated men Lady Pamela Sinclair had ever met and, in truth, she had not liked him the less for it.

Movement on the steps of St. Alban's—She peered out the carriage window and saw Lady Gastonby and Jodrel de Lancie, and then the earl, Claire on his arm.

She looks beautiful, thought Pam. Her expert eye took in the details of Claire's dress—the full skirt with its understated train, the nicely fitted bodice with what looked to be embroidered seed pearls—all very elegant, very first stare. Her hair was pulled up, and soft raven curls cascaded from atop her head. Something glittered around Miss de Lancie's neck, and Pam thought back to the night of the Pembertons' ball. Had the girl worn jewelry on that occasion? Lady Pamela didn't think so, and was satisfied to think that Edward had likely given Claire the necklace.

The distance was too great for her to be sure of Claire's expression, but she had known the Earl of Ketrick far longer. *He has the appearance,* thought Pam, greatly amused, *of a man who's just been hit by a runaway hayrack.*

Lady Pamela let the drape fall back into place and tapped on the carriage roof. It was time to move on.

The new Countess of Ketrick sat up straight and smiled, endeavoring to hide her weariness. Sheer terror had carried her through the ceremony, but now that she was no longer worried that Sandrick Rutherford would pop up in the middle of St. Alban's and force her back to Cheltdown Manor, her exhaustion was reasserting itself.

Claire had scarcely had the time to think about her uncle until this morning, but as she entered the church she had suddenly wondered—

What if he found out?

What if he was *here?*

By the time she heard the words "If any man can show just cause why these two may not lawfully be joined together," Claire had thought herself close to fainting. But then she felt the earl's eyes on her, his hand strong under her elbow, and the moment passed.

Another wave of fatigue washed over her, and she turned towards the carriage window, stifling a yawn. When Lord Tremayne had left her bedroom the night before, Claire hadn't even tried to lie down to sleep. She had changed into a nightdress and then—with a warm shawl draped over her shoulders—sat in a daze at her window. It had rained earlier in the evening, and the pavement shone with puddled water. For once, the city air smelled fresh. Claire had followed the shadows that crawled across the street below with the rising of the moon until it seemed like an hour or more passed. She had no notion of how long she had sat there, half drowsing, but suddenly the quiet was interrupted by footsteps on the staircase and then the slamming of the front door. She watched the earl—Edward—as he left Tremayne House and strode down the street, disappearing into the London mist.

It was well after midnight, and Claire was sure he was going to Lady Pamela. Her heart thudded, and tears swam in her eyes, but she remained motionless at the window and ordered herself not to be a fool. Edward Tremayne had promised her nothing—*nothing*—in the way of sentiment or fidelity in their marriage. Theirs was to be a marriage of convenience, and he was behaving in exactly the way he had always assured her he would. That was all.

Besides, despite everything, she liked Edward's mistress. Claire left the window and went to her bed. Eventually, she slept.

The Earl of Ketrick looked at his bride, sitting serenely confident on the well-upholstered cushions of his finest traveling carriage. Edward had not slept at all the night before, but Claire seemed as fresh as ever. He was inclined to resent it.

Lord Tremayne had not gone to see Lady Pamela. He *had* considered a visit, in fact, but—imagining the poor reception he'd receive from his former mistress—had decided to walk over to White's instead. In the early morning hours the club was at its most crowded and convivial, and he soon found several of Frederick's old friends. Viscount Chedley, the Alnwick brothers, and Lord Cecil Drere—they clapped Edward on the back and told him that he was a sorry sight—they hadn't seen him in ages, and what was this about a wedding? Impossible! Too dreary! Every last one of the men was well into his cups and Edward had a yeoman's work to catch up.

The headache he currently entertained as a result was not improving his mood.

The group had spent the earlier part of the evening at Gaston's—an overpriced bordello catering to younger members of the *ton*—and Edward was treated to a full description of their exertions.

"Old Pardy's raised her fees again, but I say it was worth it," said Teddy Alnwick, a handsome, curly-haired man who was, at least for the moment, the soberest of the lot. Noises of agreement erupted from the other men. "The flexibility that girl had! It was incredible, old man, just incredible."

"Sht-stamina. That's the ticket," slurred Lord Cecil.

"Indeed," said Lord Tremayne, taking a gulp of brandy. Gaston's was not one of his usual haunts, but Teddy had a gift for vivid description, and a visit to the establishment was beginning to exert some appeal. The group launched into a discussion of the relative degrees of pleasure afforded by certain positions, when Alnwick had a sudden thought.

"I say, old man," he asked Edward, "you wouldn't be on the lookout for a new mistress, would you?"

His question was greeted with laughter and cries of "Indeed, yes!" and "Capital idea!" from the others.

"Why would I need a new mistress?" Edward felt irritated, remembering that one thing he had always disliked about Frederick's friends was their lack of discretion. Lady Pamela—or any other woman he might choose to consort with—was nobody's affair but his own.

"Man's got to have a mishtress." This was the contribution of Cecil, who belched and slipped down in his chair. Edward looked at him warily. He had firsthand experience that, out of all the intoxicated men sitting there, Lord Drere was by far the most likely to cast up his accounts.

"Well," said Teddy Alnwick, edging slightly away from Cecil, "Lady Pam was at the Bucklands's rout last night—you usually attend those sorts of affairs with her, you know, and I thought—"

"*What* did you think?" growled the earl, glaring at the hapless Teddy.

"Ah, well—you know. She's so independent. 'Twas surprising enough when the lady . . ." He trailed off.

"My dear Alnwick, Lady Sinclair's activities do not concern you one way or the other," drawled Viscount Chedley. Edward looked at him in surprise. The viscount's amatory abilities were little short of legendary, but he was generally even more closemouthed than the earl.

"*All* ladies' activities concern me," protested Teddy.

" 'Shtrue," added Cecil.

The viscount looked at Edward and shrugged as if to say, "What am I to do with the puppies?"

Teddy Alnwick now rose unsteadily to his feet. "What is love?" he declaimed loudly, to a burst of guffaws from the neighboring table.

"What is it, Teddy?" someone cried.

"Love," said Teddy, "is the end of a man's life." There was more laughter as he collapsed into the nearest chair.

The earl frowned at Teddy and cleared his throat. "I may, in fact, be interested in finding a new mistress sometime in the next month or two," he conceded. The Viscount raised his eyebrows, Alnwick looked pleased, and even Lord Drere sat up a bit straighter.

"Ah, well, that's quite a different matter," said Viscount Chedley. He stood and gave Edward a flourish and bow. "You've been out of the market for some time. Allow us to assist you."

The earl's carriage was the most comfortable coach she had ever ridden in, thought Claire, and so it was too bad she couldn't enjoy their journey more. She had made a few brief attempts to engage Lord Tremayne—Edward—in conversation, but he answered in monosyllables, and eventually she gave up. But every time Claire glanced his way he was—well, staring at her. She didn't know quite what to make of it.

The previous evening she had been able to interpret his expressions perfectly. He had wanted to bed her, and rather urgently, if Claire's limited experience was any judge. But this was different. His look did not seem to be one of dislike, but evinced an odd intensity, as if she represented some problem for him. Claire wasn't sure what that could be. Perhaps he was regretting the precipitous manner of their courtship—if it could be called such a thing—and marriage.

She turned again to face the window and to the dappled sun shining through the beech and oak trees at the side of the road. As she watched, the carriage passed through a tiny hamlet—no more than a few cottages clustered around the turn-off to an easterly road—and she saw . . .

The hair stood up on the back of her neck as Claire recognized the scenery. The cottages. The turn-off. The road to the eastern half of Lewisham borough and the home of her uncle, Sandrick Rutherford.

Claire turned away from the window and resisted the impulse to dive onto the floor of the carriage. She'd known Lewisham was in the direction of Kent; she should have realized they would pass this way. Don't be such a ninny! Claire told herself. You're married now. Your uncle no longer has any power over your life.

But even the thought of the man sent a chill down her spine. She tried to think back over her first conversation with the earl at the Pembertons's ball. How much had she told him about her family? She knew she had been careful not to mention the Rutherford name, but had she said anything to Lord Tremayne about an uncle? She rather suspected that she had.

Sandrick Rutherford was her guardian, and she had not yet twenty-one years. Surely she should have sought his permission to marry? And what about her inheritance? It wasn't a great deal of money—enough for a small cottage somewhere in the country, perhaps—but she had no means of getting it out of Lord Rutherford's hands before she turned twenty-one. And even then, as an unmarried female, her wishes were unlikely to prevail against those of her uncle and his lawyers.

But now she *was* married, and her inheritance, wherever it might be, belonged under the control of the Earl of Ketrick. How on earth was she going to get it to him?

Lord Tremayne was looking at her curiously, and Claire realized that she had been wringing her lace handkerchief into a twisted knot.

"It is a beautiful day, my lord," she said, giving him a cheery smile and trying to relax. She would have a splitting headache if this kept up.

"*Edward,*" said Lord Tremayne. "Indeed it is. Are you comfortable, lady wife?"

"Oh, yes, my—Edward."

"Good. It seemed you might be feeling somewhat tense."

"Oh, no . . . Edward."

"You are sure? There is an inn just a mile or two from—"

"Oh, no! I mean, I am quite well, Edward. Truly."

To Claire's relief, the earl seemed willing to leave it at

that, and she returned to her worries about Sandrick Rutherford. The most perplexing aspect of the entire situation was the question of her uncle's reputation. Claire had no one with whom she could discuss the matter, of course. But as she understood it, from hints and whispers, the problem was not so much his preference for men—eccentricities of that sort might be tolerated—as his preference for young boys. There had been some old scandal, mostly hushed up, and her uncle had stayed away from London society for years in consequence. Even his subsequent marriage and the birth of a son—her innocuous, doughy cousin, Harry—had been insufficient to restore his standing in the *ton*.

When Claire's sights had risen no higher than an elderly baronet, the issue of her mother's maiden name had seemed unimportant. Who would bother to find out? Who would care? But an earl, and one with a name as old and honored as Tremayne, and now *she* was his countess—oh, why hadn't she considered all this earlier? The Earl of Ketrick allied with Sandrick Rutherford's niece—Edward would be furious with her for not informing him. Claire's stomach clenched as these thoughts whirled around and around in her mind.

Still, the rocking of the carriage was hypnotic. It was a marvelously well-sprung vehicle, or a very smooth road, or . . . The accumulated fatigue of days of stress finally overpowered Claire, and her head drooped against the side cushions. She no longer had any idea of what road they were on or how long they had been traveling. How far away was Wrensmoor? Would they need to stop for the night? She should ask Lord Tremayne. . . . Claire was asleep.

Edward looked out the carriage window at the verdant hills of Kent rolling by. The hops fields were in full bloom, and oast mills popped up now and then on the horizon. His headache was abominable and he wished once again that he'd had his wits more about him the previous night. He looked at Claire, asleep against the cushions, her hands still knotted together in her lap. His wife . . . 'Twas a disconcerting thought, that he had a wife, a person for whom he was wholly responsible. He was responsible for his servants, of course, and all the tenants at Wrensmoor Park. But the care of servants and tenants required, as a rule, only money, and Edward had more than enough of that commodity.

Responsible. Edward found his thoughts returning once again to Green Park and gunshots. Sandrick Rutherford had seemed the logical suspect, but after Edward's visit to Cheltdown Manor he was no longer sure. Who else might have wanted to harm one of the de Lancies? Someone with a grudge? A distant relation hoping to claim an inheritance?

No, Rutherford was still the obvious choice, but Edward found himself unwilling to leave Claire's safety to probabilities. He had left explicit instructions for Justin MacKenzie, and if there was any way to discover who had fired at Claire— or Jody—in Green Park, MacKenzie was the man to find it.

His glance strayed back to Claire. As she had walked down the aisle towards him at St. Alban's, she had looked more beautiful than ever: The carefully arranged curls of glossy black hair framing her face, the jewels he had given her around her neck and the gown, suggesting the curves of the body underneath even as it covered them. That same very female body now rested on the carriage seat across from him, and Edward found his headache receding slightly as he gave scrutiny to Claire . . . Tremayne. His wife.

Having a wife was different from having a mistress, he decided. Mistresses needed to be wooed and cosseted, plied with gifts and attention . . . Well, not Lady Pamela, of course, but she was the exception. The earl had enjoyed the favors of several women before Pam, and each of them had demanded that he prove his devotion in ever new and costly ways.

But now—a wife. You could do as you pleased with a wife, could you not? Everything, or nothing at all. The earl considered how he might wish to arrange their days at Wrensmoor, and how long he would stay before returning to London. Perhaps he would tire of his new wife quickly. He gazed out the window, thinking again of the various liaisons he had enjoyed over the years. Tiring of a woman? It was something to be sought after, not delayed. For, if one did not tire of her, if one remained smitten . . .

He would not be like Frederick, thought Edward. He would not love his wife.

He should, therefore—and why hadn't he thought of this sooner?—bed Claire as often as possible for the next few weeks. She would soon be breeding, and he could resume his life with a new mistress in town. It was the perfect arrangement.

He glanced at Claire again. Although she had changed into a traveling gown after the wedding, she was still wearing his necklace. The gems flashed, shifting and catching the light with the rise and fall of her breathing. He became acutely aware of the luscious roundness of her breasts, encased in smooth silk. He wondered if she was uncomfortable, sleeping upright like that in a carriage.

Almost before he realized what he was doing, Edward had moved to sit beside his wife. Being taller than she, he now had an enticing view of her *décolletage*, and his fingertips traced the contours of her breasts above the taut fabric. Claire stirred, and Edward could smell the fragrance of roses in her hair. He inhaled deeply. He noticed that one of the pins holding her curls in place was loose, and he pulled it out. A ringlet of black satin hair tumbled almost to her waist. He pulled out a second pin, and a third.

"Hmm?" A sleepy murmur came from his wife, and without thinking Edward bent down to kiss her softly. Claire's arms crept around his neck, and she returned his kiss with fervor. Edward was lost. He knew that lovemaking in a moving carriage was a tricky business, but if Claire was willing, he was in no mood to resist. They were in an awkward position, however, so he eased her down onto the cushions and began to unfasten the buttons to his trousers.

His headache had completely disappeared.

"My lord!"

His wife, who mere moments ago had been kissing him eagerly, was blushing furiously and struggling to sit up. Belatedly Edward realized that only now was she truly awake.

"Let me up!" She squirmed frantically underneath him, and the feel of her body moving against his did nothing to restore his self-control.

"We're married now, if you recall," he told her, whispering hoarsely into her ear. "You no longer need withhold yourself from me." The earl was very aroused, and he had no experience of being refused by a woman.

"Oh!" exclaimed Claire, and she pushed against his chest with both hands.

He fell, hard, onto the floor of the carriage, and was thankful for the soft carpet. If the little minx thought that he would stop now—! The blood surged through his veins, and he reached up for his wife. Down she came in a cascade of silk skirts and raven hair.

"Lord Tremayne!"

"My name is *Edward,*" growled the earl, rolling over to pin her beneath him. He kissed her hungrily and his hands moved first over her breasts, then to the back of her gown. Claire was struggling against him, and he couldn't manage the row of tiny pearl buttons with one hand. Edward thought to tear off the dress; he had done this before, but only when the lady in question was as eager as he to see her garment removed. He reached up to grasp the fabric of the gown's bodice—

Claire shuddered in pain.

—and he rolled away from her, appalled at what he had done. Her shoulder—good heavens, how could he have forgotten it? A small spot of blood now stained the lace of her right sleeve. Claire's eyes were squeezed tightly shut, but he could see tears wetting her lashes.

"Claire, oh, my dear, I am sorry."

She tried to sit up on the floor of the carriage. He reached to help her, but she waved him away.

"Let me see your shoulder," he said.

Claire looked at him numbly but said nothing, and he took that for acquiescence. Moving to sit beside her, he gently eased the fabric of her right sleeve away from the injured site. Claire remained silent, but he could feel her flinch, and he cursed himself under his breath. Most of the injury was well healed, but a small area had broken open again, and it oozed blood. He took a handkerchief from his pocket and pressed it gently against her skin.

Claire said something that the earl did not catch.

"Shh," he answered, and kissed the top of her head.

"No, my lord," she said in a stronger voice. "Let me speak. I will not withhold myself from you, even in a carriage. That was not my intention. But in the future you will give me some notice of your designs. Surely you knew you were wedding a maid and not a whore ready for dossing at the toss of a skirt."

Edward felt even further stricken. Never again, he vowed, would his wife suffer any hurt at his hands. He helped her back onto the carriage seat, and she leaned against the cushions with a sigh. Several minutes passed in silence, the carriage rolling smoothly through the Kentish countryside, and then Claire burst into tears. Edward gathered her into his arms, and she remained there for the next hour and a half, until they reached the Greyboars Inn, where they were to have supper.

"Are we near to Wrensmoor?" asked Claire, warming herself in front of the inn's massive fireplace. It was a cozy room, and the smells wafting from the kitchen boded well for their coming meal. The earl had brought her a glass of wine, and she sipped it slowly.

"It is a morning's journey only," replied her husband.

Claire knew he was watching her carefully. Perhaps he was waiting to see if she would swoon from his rough usage in the carriage. But he need not have worried. The Earl of Ketrick was still the handsomest and most virile man she had ever met, and it was the unexpectedness of his advances, not the advances themselves, that had led to her protest. If he had but given her a chance to awaken fully and collect her wits, well, she would have given him everything he asked for, and freely.

Perhaps she should tell him so, thought Claire—or, perhaps not. Where his wife was concerned, a man might prefer a shy maid to a wanton. Claire was not entirely naive concerning the . . . activities . . . between a husband and wife in the bedchamber, but she was unclear about certain aspects of the male point of view. No doubt the situation was different with a mistress, but would a husband expect his wife to enjoy lovemaking? Or would he be horrified to find her . . . enthusiastic? Claire had no idea.

It would probably be best, she decided, not to appear overly eager. The well-bred ladies of her acquaintance had often described marital relations as an unpleasant duty, and that might very well be what the earl would expect of her—

simply that she would do her duty. Claire took another sip of wine and was surprised to find the glass empty. She was feeling warm and pleasantly relaxed, and she smiled up at the earl as he brought her more wine.

"Do you always stay the night at this inn?"

"If I am traveling alone, on Achilles, I can reach the estate by mid-afternoon. But we had a late start, and in company—"

Edward broke off, and Claire was left to wonder what company he might mean. Was he used to staying at the Greyboars Inn with Pamela Sinclair? Did the innkeeper and his wife wonder about the new lady at his side? He had referred to her as his countess, but perhaps he had done the same with his mistresses. Claire took a deep breath, feeling herself tremble.

"I will have your supper brought up to the room," said the earl, looking at her with concern.

"I am quite fine here, thank you."

"Do not argue with your husband, my love," said Lord Tremayne, and without further ado, he took her arm and led her upstairs.

The supper was simple and delicious; a small roasted hen and side dishes of potatoes Anna and a cold soup. Edward had ordered another bottle of wine, and Claire was finding that her husband was a comfortable person with whom to converse.

"No, 'twas only Frederick and myself," he was saying, in response to her last question. "Our mother died when we were children, and my father when I was fifteen and Frederick—" Edward hesitated for a moment. "Frederick was nineteen when he became earl."

So her husband had no one else in his immediate family. Claire knew what it was like to lose one's parents at an early age, but at least she had Jody.

"My brother is looking forward to seeing Wrensmoor Park," she told Edward. "He has great hopes for your stables there." Jody had informed her, with all the high-minded maturity of his fifteen years, that he would not come to the earl's country estate until Claire was settled in for some weeks with her new husband. Her normally amiable brother was inflexible on this point, telling Claire he would come to Wrensmoor "when I feel up to the travel."

"Jody is welcome to stay at Wrensmoor as often and as long as he wishes, but we should, perhaps, be discussing his education as well. Does he wish to attend Eton?"

My goodness. In the flurry of wedding preparations Claire had entirely forgotten the opportunities that might be opening for Jody.

"I will ask him, my lord," said Claire, giving Edward a wide smile. She had noticed this evening that each time she smiled at her husband, something odd happened—some subtle shift in his posture, she thought, almost as if he flinched. She didn't know why he should flinch, or why she should enjoy seeing it, but she did, and so she had been smiling at the earl more and more often.

" 'I will ask him, *Edward*,' " instructed Edward.

By the end of supper Claire had consumed several glasses of wine. The earl suspected that the quantity was considerably more than she was accustomed to, and although he wasn't convinced that his wife was flirting with him, she *was* smiling rather often. It was having a pronounced effect on his composure. His idea from the beginning had been to share the room—and the bed—with Claire. They were married, after all, even if the innkeeper's wife seemed disinclined to believe it, and his bride was his to take whenever he wished.

After his less-than-gentlemanly behavior in the carriage, however, Edward decided that their wedding night should be postponed until they reached Wrensmoor.

But now . . . now he wasn't sure what to think. The room was, of course, the best at Greyboars Inn. Claire was smiling and conversing with him in good humor. The fire was blazing, the chamber was warm, the bed looked comfortable and—with any luck—not prone to squeaks.

She was his, and he could bed her whenever he wished.

"My lord . . . Edward. There seems to be a bit of a tangle. Could you assist me?" Claire was sitting in front of the fire removing pins from her hair. She indicated the hairbrush next to her, and Edward began to pull it through her hair.

"Ouch," said Claire.

"Sorry," said Edward.

"Here, give it back to me. Have you never brushed a woman's hair before?" His wife was laughing.

He watched as she combed out the end of each ringlet, and then advanced upwards through the mass of glossy black curls. When she reached the top and nearly the whole had been tamed, he took the hairbrush back. Hair crackled and shone in the firelight, and he brushed the length of it, over and over. He then ran his fingers through it, marveling at the silky feel.

"You'll just tangle it all up again," Claire protested.

"No I won't," said Edward, and he lifted a handful of the satiny mass to his face, inhaling the fragrance of roses. He tugged on it, very gently.

"My lord?"

"Come here." The earl pulled her onto his lap. He kissed the nape of her neck and whispered into her ear, "I am giving you fair warning this time. I am going to help you out of this gown."

"Hmm." Claire said nothing else, and Edward began, slowly, to unfasten each tiny button at the back of her dress. There appeared to be hundreds of them, and he fumbled often, distracted by the sight of the thin chemise and her smooth skin underneath. His left hand strayed from its task, and he cupped the swell of one breast. Claire was trembling, and his urgency and need grew. When, after what seemed like an hour, he had unbuttoned her to the waist, he eased the dress from her shoulders. Claire stood and let the gown fall to the floor, her curves beneath her chemise outlined by the firelight. He reached for her—

Then he saw the blood on the strap of her undergarment. His breath caught hard in his chest. He had known it would be there, expected it, but even so it was a shock. He looked up at his wife, wondering if she was in any pain.

Claire was biting her lip and watching him, her silver-grey eyes those of an untouched miss, nervous yet trusting. Her hair fell around her shoulders, long and black and satiny. The chemise did nothing to obscure the lines of her body, thought Edward—the hand-span waist, her long, slender legs, her voluptuous breasts. He could hardly take his eyes from her.

Then, for a moment, the image of Melissa, tiny and red-haired, came to his mind. He saw her delicate face with its dusting of freckles, her slim, almost boyish figure and saw, too, the sea of blood that had ended her life.

The earl lifted his wife into his arms and carried her to the bed. He lay down next to her and held her until her breathing was deep and regular and he was sure she was no longer awake. She had not spoken, and for a long time Edward did not sleep.

Chapter Seven

"H'yah!"

Claire heard the earl shouting, and the carriage slowed to a halt. Her husband—who had been riding ahead—now brought Achilles to the window of the coach, the stallion offering her a friendly nicker. She craned her neck to see Edward's face, and although it was partially obscured by the bright sunlight at his back, she could tell he was avoiding her gaze.

"We've only another mile or so before the turnoff for Wrensmoor," he said, glancing down at her for a brief moment.

Claire nodded. He looks marvelous on horseback, was her unbidden thought. The earl's shirt was open at the collar, and his sleeves were rolled up, exposing the brawn and sinew of his forearms. She watched the play of muscles under the skin as he kept Achilles under control and she felt a shiver that went all the way down to her toes.

The earl gave heel to Achilles, and the carriage began to move once more. Claire's gaze followed horse and rider—the two most powerful creatures within the current confines of her world—as they rode ahead. She took one of the small, velvet cushions scattered around the inside of the carriage and threw it after them as hard as she could. The cushion careened off the road with a small shower of pebbles and landed in a patch of lily-of-the-valley. Nobody noticed, of course.

He was so handsome and she was so furious with him.

Achilles needs to be ridden, her husband had told her that morning as they were preparing to leave Greyboars Inn. Well, that might be true, but Claire doubted it was the real reason she was stuck in this carriage, all *alone*. Even the beauty of the Kentish scenery was not enough to improve her present state of mind.

She had woken that morning confused and disoriented, and it had taken her several moments to recall exactly why she was in an unfamiliar bedroom. Sunlight glinted off the mirror standing opposite the bed, and as she saw her reflection, she realized that the Earl of Ketrick was sitting beside her, pulling on a pair of riding boots.

For a moment, Claire had stared at him, startled at the idea of being alone with a man—who was dressing—on a bed. She had the memory of being held as she drifted off to sleep, but nothing more. Surely she would remember if—if—

"There's no hurry," Edward had said, and Claire looked up at him, bewildered. No hurry? For what?

"Your pardon?"

He had slipped into a loose riding jacket and pulled his hair back into its usual mare's-tail. "I will have a maid sent up to assist you in dressing," said Edward. "When you are ready, of course." He turned towards the door.

"Where are you going?" Was this the way a man and wife treated each other in the morning? she wondered. Like strangers?

"Breakfast," said the earl, and he opened the door and walked out before Claire had a chance to say anything else.

Infuriating male! Claire threw her legs over the edge of the bed and stood up. If he thought he was going to leave her in this place all by herself with some non-existent maid to help her do up her gown and not so much as a by-your-leave . . .

Claire saw herself more clearly in the mirror and realized she was wearing only a thin chemise. She sat down on the bed and thought hard. She remembered her husband brushing her hair the evening before and kissing the back of her neck. He must have helped her off with her gown, too—she couldn't have managed all the buttons herself. And then he had apparently shared the bed with her all night . . .

The nerve of the man! Did he not want her? Wasn't she pretty enough for him? She was his wife!

The idea that the Earl of Ketrick had wed her for the sole purpose of begetting a child, and couldn't even be bothered to—to—bed her, had at first confused Claire, then stirred her anger. She had something that Lord Tremayne claimed to need, and she had been entirely willing to keep her side of the bargain. She was not his charity case! If her husband thought he was going to get away with this—

Those indignant thoughts had kept her company all morning, first at the breakfast table—the earl was finished and gone by the time she arrived—and now in the coach. Alone. Underneath the indignation, although she might try to deny it to herself, lay the seed of self-doubt. Claire had never been conceited about her appearance; she'd done nothing to earn it, after all. But she had seen desire in the earl's eyes on several occasions and assumed he was attracted to her. In fact, she realized, she had counted on it. If her husband coveted her, then perhaps she would have some measure of equality in their relationship. Not the kind of equality she truly wanted—but it was a beginning.

Claire thought back now to what she had seen of her reflection in the inn's bedroom mirror. The thin chemise had clung to her body in a way no gown ever could, and she was trying not to come to the obvious conclusion: that when Lord

Tremayne saw her *en déshabillé* he had lost interest. Perhaps he preferred a more petite woman, or a blonde one. Or one whose bosom was not as . . .

Pah. This was getting her nowhere. She could do nothing about her height, her hair color, or the size of her breasts. She looked out the carriage window at the countryside they were passing. The scenery near Maidstone was remarkably pretty, she decided. Closer to London the road was so dry and traveled that every leaf and blade of grass for miles around had been covered in a layer of dust. But here it was dewy and green. A series of rolling hills retreated to the horizon, interrupted by hedgerows and an occasional larger copse of trees. The fields looked well tended and fertile, with a good crop of—well, what was it? Claire stuck her head out the window to get a better look, catching a sort of queer, bitter smell, not unpleasant, but—

"Miss de Lancie!" yelled the earl, almost in her ear. Startled, she looked around to see him immediately behind her, riding to the side of the coach.

"*Who?*" asked Claire, thinking to twit him.

"Do not stick your head out of the carriage!" he yelled. This was a dictum familiar to generations of children of the English gentry, and the effect was to make Claire feel like a child. She stuck out her tongue at the earl and promptly retreated to the interior of the coach, well satisfied by the response she saw on his face. She was *not* his charity case, and she was *not* a child. Tonight, vowed Claire, tonight she would prove it. She would make him forget any doubts he ever had about marrying her.

The lane leading through Wrensmoor Park to the house was wide and shady, with a line of English oaks at each side. It seemed an hour since they had turned off the main road and passed through a pair of enormously tall iron gates into the estate grounds. Claire was eager to see the house, but every time the carriage crested one hill, yet another hill appeared in front of them.

There was a commotion in the tall grasses under the oaks, and she smiled as a family of deer led by a magnificent buck leaped across the road behind the carriage. Turning forward again, she gasped.

Before her stood a stone castle, built on an island in the middle of a wide blue river. Turrets and crenelated ramparts of a warm sandstone rose from the wide sward of green, and tall casement windows sparkled in the sun.

It was the most beautiful setting for a house—for a castle, Claire amended—that she had ever seen. Was this Wrensmoor? Wrensmoor Park, where she was to live? Her breath caught in her throat. How could Lord Tremayne ever be willing to leave this place?

The lane they traveled sloped gently down towards a causeway leading to the island. Claire could see sheep grazing on the opposite bank of the river and a few puffs of smoke rising from somewhere inside the walls of the outer bailey. Fruit trees dotted the fields on this side of the river, with more espaliered against the lower ramparts of the castle.

"Do you like it?"

The carriage had stopped without Claire's being aware of it, and her husband was looking down at her through the window, amusement on his face.

She stared up at him. "How can you bear to live anywhere else?" was all she could manage to say.

The earl frowned. "It's a big place," he said finally. "It gets lonely."

Claire said nothing. It was an uncomfortable remark, and her husband seemed to realize it. He abruptly dismounted and tied Achilles to the spring bar of the carriage.

"I'll ride with you the rest of the way," he said, climbing into the coach. His broad shoulders and long legs seemed to take up more space this time than they had before, and she felt almost light-headed with the impact of his physical presence, as if he was using up all the air and leaving her none to breathe. Remembering her earlier resolution to prove to the earl that his wife was a grown woman, Claire felt chagrined. It would be all she could do to remain calm when she was in the same room with him, let alone the same bed. She wasn't going to prove anything to this man.

The earl had not slept well for what seemed like weeks. Last night was the worst of all, with his new wife asleep in his arms, her round bottom nestled warm against his loins. Claire was an active, wriggly sleeper, and each movement had caused fresh torture. Edward was currently feeling rather grumpy about it.

The sight of Wrensmoor and Claire's stunned reaction to it had done nothing to lighten his mood. How could he bear to live anywhere else? she had asked. How, indeed. Memories from childhood flooded back each time he rode over the crest of that last hill and saw the river and its castle below. Wrensmoor had been everything a young boy, or a young man, could desire, and Edward had spent most of his life there thinking exactly that.

That he had everything he could want and he would never leave.

Gravel crunched under the wheels of the coach, and he knew they had reached the causeway. There was a draw-bridge in the middle, which his wife eyed dubiously.

"It hasn't been raised for nearly a century," he reassured her. "I think the fifth earl fancied himself a medieval knight, but my father had it solidly nailed together."

Claire smiled at him, and his heart missed a beat, which made him even grumpier. He seemed unable to control his reactions to his wife, and Edward considered that this was only because of the unnatural restraint he had imposed upon himself. All this fuss over a chit that he should have bedded nights ago. It was plain foolishness, and Edward was determined that the events in the bedroom at the Greyboars Inn would not be repeated. His wife's primary role—her *only* role—was to be bedded by him and to bear his children. He was suddenly confident that once he had possessed her body he could get her out of his mind.

The carriage passed through the outer walls and the stables of Wrensmoor and into the ward of the castle. Another swath of emerald green greeted them, with Wrensmoor Hall at its far end. In front of the hall an enormous fountain sprayed into the air, and Edward saw Claire looking at it curiously.

"Dolphins *and* mermaids?" she commented.

"The fifth earl again," said Edward with a smile.

"Ah."

The carriage continued around to the wide steps of the entryway. Boggs had arrived earlier to supervise final preparations, and Edward saw his butler at the head of a group of servants lined up to greet him and his new countess. He probably should have warned Claire, thought the earl. She would be unprepared for a household of this size. It took nearly a hundred men and women to maintain Wrensmoor Hall and the surrounding castle keep. They weren't all present right now, of course. Nevertheless—

But Claire surprised him. As he handed her out of the carriage, she gave Boggs a quick smile and moved from the butler smoothly along the waiting row of servants, addressing more than one of them—those she knew from Tremayne House—by name.

"It's Constance, is it not?" she asked one plump, rosy-cheeked parlormaid.

"Oh, yes, milady," whispered the girl, blushing furiously. Edward could tell that his wife had won a devoted subject.

"And you are—?" This was addressed, with a blinding smile, to a young footman, who now stared at Claire with the eyes of an adoring puppy. Edward frowned. Being jealous of a skinny youth with spots was beneath the dignity of the earl of Ketrick, and ridiculous to boot. It wasn't as if he loved his wife.

Claire had reached the top of the steps, and Edward followed in her wake, as warmly welcomed by the staff as she was but feeling disgruntled and oddly out of place. His wife had just greeted his servants as if they were her own. They *were* her own now, but still— Edward realized that he had been contemplating a period of some months during which he would need to remain at Wrensmoor, while Claire adjusted to her role in the running of the estate. Months! Fie on that, thought the earl, I have no time to coddle a young miss. How dare she expect me to stay so long? I will have her breeding and be back in London in the arms of a new mistress in no time.

Claire opened the doors leading onto the balcony of her bedroom suite and stepped outside. The view was of the river and its grassy banks below, with wooded hills in the distance. A few deer grazed almost directly beneath her windows, and she had seen several covey of quail. Wouldn't Jody be in alt! The park was lovely beyond description.

Sheer delight was the only way she could describe her own reaction to the earl's home. *Your* home now, too, she reminded herself, feeling a rush of disbelief that she was now the mistress of Wrensmoor Hall. Her chambers would benefit from a woman's touch, it was true, but if the current furnishings were plain, they, like everything else at the hall, were also spotlessly clean and showed the clear marks of loving attention. A huge stone fireplace occupied much of one wall, and the four-posted bed was draped with white silk. Most of the floor was covered in a thick, figured carpet, although clean rush matting was laid in front of the hearth and the balcony doors.

The ceiling was high, with oak beams carved in a pretty trellis of ivy, and a number of heavy tapestries hung on the walls. Best of all were the several large windows, which made the room sunny and warm.

I will be happy here, she thought suddenly.

At the moment, however, she was simply exhausted. Two days in a coach, no matter how well-sprung it might be, were enough to wear out even the healthiest of young women, and Claire was feeling aches and pains in areas of her body that had never complained before.

"Milady?"

The young girl she had spoken to earlier scratched at the half-open door and entered the room.

"Yes, Constance?" said Claire.

"The master said as how's you're to have a bath when you wants and Mrs. McLeevy says you needs t'eat so, um, your pardon, milady, I'm just wondering which you'll be wantin' first."

Mrs. McLeevy was here at Wrensmoor? That was odd, thought Claire, but perhaps this was Lord Tremayne's way of settling the ongoing fireworks in the London kitchen. Mrs. Huppins had proclaimed herself well able to take care of all the cooking required at Tremayne House, thank you very much, and two days ago the normally amiable Mrs. McLeevy had become so aggravated as to declare that she believed *her* cinnamon rolls to be superior to Mrs. Huppins's sticky buns.

It was kind of the earl to keep the couple on, and Claire made a mental note to thank him.

She sat down on the edge of the bed, feeling the stiffness in her shoulders. Her traveling gown had been clean this morning, but it was now covered in road dust, and the thought of warm water and fresh clothing was remarkably appealing.

"I think," she told Constance, "that I would like a bath."

Bliss, thought Claire, as she sank chin-deep into the copper tub and watched her hair fan out on the water's surface. The tub had been set up in front of the fireplace, and a screen now shielded her from draughts, not that this beautiful room seemed to have any. A fire blazed merrily, and Claire inhaled the fragrance of scented soaps and lavender water.

She chuckled softly to herself. There had been a brief *contretemps* earlier, when Flora had arrived with the rest of the luggage and encountered young Constance assisting her mistress out of her traveling gown. Everything was set right now. Flora was to be Claire's lady's maid, and Constance—when her other duties permitted—was to be Flo's "apprentice." Lord Tremayne had offered several days ago to let her hire a more qualified woman, but Claire said no. She had some experience of lady's maids and knew they could be as snooty and overbearing as the *grandes dames* they served. Claire judged that cheerful inexperience was far preferable.

She had not seen her husband since he escorted her up to the door of her rooms. Edward hadn't even entered the bedchamber, telling her only to ring for whatever assistance she might require. Claire wondered where he was.

The earl stared at one of the tapestries on the far bedroom wall. Another just like it hung in his wife's chamber, although he had not thought to mention that the pair covered the doors to a short connecting passageway. Probably Constance had pointed this out to her by now. Surely Claire would anticipate that her rooms would be linked with his.

Had she locked the door on her end of the passage? It was normally left unlocked, this being easier for the maids, and no one having used the countess's rooms for years. Edward stared harder at the tapestry and told himself to just walk through the door. It was time to establish that his rights included his presence in Claire's bedchamber at any time he wished. She could not lock him out! How dare she even consider it?

He had planned their day carefully. His wife would rest for the remainder of the afternoon while he spent an hour or so with his steward and another hour inspecting the stables. They would have a private supper this evening in his rooms, and he would then present to her the schedule he had chosen for their weeks together at Wrensmoor. Claire was welcome to use the daylight hours as she chose, but she was to be in her bedroom and available to him during specified evenings, and at night. Oh, and early mornings, Edward added to himself. He must remember to mention the mornings.

Once he was satisfied that the principles and procedures of their married life were clear to his wife, he would bed her. This delay—he was convinced—was essential to starting their relationship on the proper footing. Forgetting his earlier notion of "unnatural restraint," he now felt that it was fortunate that events had not progressed further at Greyboars Inn. Much more prudent to limit and define expectations from the very beginning.

These arrangements were the result of considerable thought on Edward's part. He did not wish to hurt Claire, and if they began their married life willy-nilly, as others he had known had, the possibilities for misunderstanding would be many. On the other hand, if matters were spelled out directly, then Claire would know what she could presume from him, and as importantly, what she should not presume. He would show her the consideration due the Countess of Ketrick at all times. His wife need not fear the public, painful scenes he had witnessed on countless occasions in the salons and ballrooms of the *ton*. Her name would not appear in the betting book at White's.

But she would stay here, at Wrensmoor, and he would not.

The earl wondered what his wife was doing. The walls of the castle were so thick that one could hear nothing between rooms. Perhaps she needed something that Constance could not provide, or was tired and faint from their journey. Wrensmoor was new to Claire, and she might hesitate to ask—

Edward was striding through the passageway between their suites before he was conscious of making the decision to do so. The door was unlocked and swung smoothly back on its hinges as he pushed the tapestry aside and entered his wife's bedroom.

"Flora?"

He stopped short. Claire's voice came from behind a screen standing in front of the fireplace. Edward could hear faint sounds of splashing, and from that, and the smell of lavender water, he knew his wife was taking a bath. The thought of her unclothed and in the copper bathing tub was having a definite effect on his . . . equilibrium.

"Flora? Constance? Could you bring me another towel?"

114

Edward located the requested item. He hesitated for a moment, thinking that he should probably warn Claire, and then stepped behind the screen.

"Oh." His wife, who was standing up in the bathtub, one towel wrapped around her hair, regarded him with evident calm. She hadn't made even a squeak of surprise, although a gentle blush now crept up her cheeks. "I beg your pardon, my lord, I did not hear you enter." She took the proffered towel from him and quickly began to dry off. Small rivulets of water coursed down the swell of her breasts and onto the flat plane of her abdomen.

"This . . . this is quite a beautiful room," Claire was saying, her voice betraying a trace of nervousness. "Warm and sunny. I should be very comfortable here, my lord."

"*Edward,*" muttered the earl.

"Your pardon?" She looked at him in confusion.

"We are married. I believe it is customary to call one's husband by his Christian name." The earl, who was staring at Claire's body, was having some difficulty enunciating his words. Her skin was glowing from the warmth of the bath water, and her curves were delicious beyond any expectation. There was a plan. He knew he had made a plan for the day. The steward, Achilles, the principles and procedures of their marriage—

"I beg your pardon, you are quite correct. Especially in present circumstances!" She laughed softly and smiled at him, her blush deepening.

It was the smile that did it, Edward swore later. Not the curve of her hip, not the tendrils of silky hair clinging damply to her neck, not even the droplets of water trickling between her breasts. It was her smile. He was immediately and ravenously aroused and past any hope of self-control. Edward pulled Claire from the tub. He carried her, naked and still

115

dripping, to the bed and lowered her to the white lace coverlet.

"My lord—Edward!"

The earl grinned in satisfaction, seeing his wife's composure finally start to crack in earnest. She scrambled under the sheets and stared up at him, wide-eyed. He stripped off his jacket, thinking—There will be no more cool looks from *this* young chit.

The cravat followed his jacket to the floor and Edward sat on the edge of the bed to remove his boots. He looked around to see his wife holding the bedding up to her chin and watching him with nervous but frank fascination. Edward unbuttoned his shirt and tore it off; the bedding rose a little higher, but her eyes didn't leave him. He stood to unbutton his trousers—

"Oh!" Claire blushed a fiery red and buried her face in the sheets. The earl grabbed the covers and threw them aside, thinking that if he did not make love to his wife now, right now—

There was a scratching at the door.

"Milady? Are you ready to dress?" They heard Flora's voice, faintly, from the doorway. The door creaked open.

"No! Milady is *not* ready to dress!" roared the earl. "Leave us!"

The door closed, followed by a burst of giggles and then the sound of retreating footsteps. Edward lowered himself onto the bed and took several deep breaths, wondering how he would ever manage the restraint needed for an untouched maid. The pressure building in his loins was nigh ungovernable, even now. If he touched her, kissed her, stroked her breasts—

Claire tentatively reached over to him and pulled the velvet ribbon holding back his hair.

Edward groaned and covered her body with his.

Claire awoke from a dreamless sleep feeling rested and at ease. Something seemed odd, however . . . Good heavens, there was a *man* in her bed. She sat up, heart pounding, and realized that she herself was completely unclothed.

It's your husband, you goose, came a little voice, and Claire blushed as memory flooded back. Oh, yes. Her husband. Edward Tremayne was lying next to her, on his back with his eyes shut, apparently undisturbed by her abrupt movement. He must really be asleep, thought Claire. At the moment, that was probably for the best. She needed time to think about what had just happened between them.

She had felt some pain. Edward had been trying to warn her, Claire thought, although his words were rushed and hoarse. She had gotten the impression he was trying to restrain himself, to proceed slowly, but in the end the effort was unsuccessful. He had been upon her like a force of nature, unstoppable and fierce. Even with the resulting soreness, however, Claire was undismayed. A small smile came to her lips. She could tell even now that the physical aspect of the marital relationship was one that—eventually—she would greatly relish.

Her husband shifted in his sleep, and the bedding slipped further. He was magnificent, Claire thought, with a shiver. She admired the broad, smooth expanse of his chest, and the muscles of his arms looked like those of a day labourer, not those of a gentleman. She wondered what happened now. How often did one . . . engage in this sort of activity? Would her husband wish to bed her every night? Would he come to her bed, or she to his? If he came to her bed, would he leave . . . afterwards?

Being a country girl, Claire had comprehended in a general way the mechanics of marital relations, but she realized now that they carried many complications. The whispering and hints of the ladies of the *ton* had not prepared her for the way she felt when she was in the arms of Lord Edward Tremayne, for the powerful force of physical intimacy. This could not exist separate from the rest of their lives together, she thought to herself. One could not keep this in a box and expect that nothing else would change.

But her husband must know this already, thought Claire. He has bedded many women, he would know how they were to proceed. She slipped back down under the bedding and, nestling against Edward, fell back to sleep.

Not too much later, Edward awoke from a dream of Claire to find her nestling against him, soft and warm, her hair entangling her arms and his. She wiggled, and he groaned. His need for her was as urgent as before, and he cursed himself as a thoughtless cad, to even consider bedding her twice today. He hadn't been gentle the first time, and she must be bruised and aching. If she would only lie still—

"My lord?" came a whisper, a sound that went right to the earl's—"Edward?"

She twisted to face him and her breasts brushed his chest. He crushed her against him, and they kissed and caressed and kissed more until all rational thought left him and he drew his wife beneath him and made love to her once more.

Chapter Eight

"She's gorgeous," said Claire. She looked at the grey mare with admiration. The glossy coat, elegant conformation, and proud set of the head all bespoke an animal of noble and expensive ancestry. She held out a lump of sugar and chuckled at the soft feel of the mare's lips nibbling it from her palm.

"Jody said you loved to ride but didn't have the opportunity in London," explained Edward. "I thought it was time you had your own mount."

"Thank you. Oh, thank you," Claire replied. Touched by the earl's thoughtfulness, she reached up to curl her arms around his neck and kiss him. He pulled her against him, and his hands cradled her bottom as his lips came down hard against hers. They remained entwined, swaying slightly, until the sound of Mr. McLeevy's advancing footsteps brought their embrace to a halt. Claire noted with satisfaction that her husband's breathing was ragged. She gave him a saucy look through lowered eyelids and was rewarded when he grabbed for her. She danced out of his reach.

"So impatient, my lord," said Claire demurely. "Is tonight not soon enough for you?"

"Wretched minx."

"Eh, she's a beauty a'right," said Finn McLeevy, who was on his way to supervise repairs on the stable door. "For a horse. What ye be naming her?"

Claire hadn't thought about it yet. She pursed her lips and considered, running a hand along the mare's silky mane.

"Vixen," suggested the earl, with a gleam in his eye that Claire hoped Mr. McLeevy didn't notice. The look was making her feel warm and very unsettled.

"Athene," said Claire. "Achilles and Athene make a pair, don't you think?"

"Aye," said Mr. McLeevy, who was aware of Claire's fascination for all things Greek. "Let's just be hoping she'll have half the wit of her namesake." He continued on his way and Claire smiled after him. Finn McLeevy had many talents as a handyman and had proved his value already at Wrensmoor, but he was no lover of horses. "Daft, stupid animals," he called them, "always eatin' just what be makin' 'em sick."

The earl was looking at her accusingly. "But Athene was a goddess," he said. "Achilles was only a mortal man."

"Exactly," said Claire with an impish grin. Edward grabbed for her again and, on a whim, she took off running down the stable aisle. Her husband gave chase, and she ducked through a side door, only to discover she was at a dead end. Edward caught up with his wife next to a freshly cleaned stall and with one swift motion, picked her up and threw her into the pile of straw. Claire whooped and, scrambling to her knees, started to throw handfuls of straw at her pursuer.

"You're filthy!" declared Edward. "The Countess of Ketrick is never filthy!"

"Mortal! Mere mortal!"

Edward countered her assaults with his own, and they collapsed in laughter, wrestling in the straw. In a few minutes Claire, winded by the attempt to fend off her much stronger assailant, conceded defeat. She flopped onto her back and started picking bits of straw out of her *décolletage*.

Edward pulled her onto his lap and began to help, his fingertips brushing over the smooth mounds of her breasts.

She murmured encouragement into his ear.

"It's going to be terribly itchy later," he told her.

"I suppose I'll need to take another bath," said Claire. "So will you."

"Mmm."

Eventually their playful embraces grew so heated that Edward knew he would soon be unable to stop. He didn't mind being caught with a woman in the stables. He *had* once been caught with a woman in the stables, come to think of it. The gypsy's widow, he recalled, close to thirty and he a randy lad of seventeen—but oh, she had been a very willing widow, indeed. He smiled at the memory.

Nevertheless, he reminded himself, he didn't want his new countess to be an object of fun to the castle population. It would be best to confine their lovemaking to the bedchamber. He gave Claire a last, lingering kiss, and reluctantly pulled her to her feet. They both made themselves as presentable as possible for the short walk back to the hall.

"Were these your brother's rooms when he was the earl?" asked Claire. She sipped a glass of excellent Bordeaux and warmed her feet in front of the fire. She and her husband were both freshly bathed and wrapped in robes of thick velvet. A matching pair of robes . . . Claire idly wondered if she was the first woman to wear hers.

Supper had been served in Edward's rooms. They were similar to Claire's, although to her eye rather sparsely furnished. The earl was apparently not a man to require elaborate or luxurious surroundings, but what he did have was of the finest quality. The fireplace was a huge stone rondavel in one corner, set with pillars at each side and the Ketrick arms carved along the top. Claire's eyes kept straying in the direction of the earl's bed, which was much larger than her own. Although not a four-poster, it boasted a massive carved headboard at one end and an almost equally massive footboard at the other. Despite its size, the bed looked cozy with its layers of blankets and a swansdown duvet.

"Frederick?" replied Edward. "Yes. Yes, these were his rooms. Melissa had yours."

"Melissa was your sister-in-law?"

"Hmm. Yes."

Claire knew that Frederick's countess was also dead. She wondered at her husband's reaction, since the mention of Melissa had left him subdued. What kind of relationship had Edward had with his brother's wife?

His reply had been curt, but now Edward added in a lighter tone, "Their portraits are in the long gallery, if you would like to see them. It's just through the banqueting hall—"

"Oh, please." Claire was eager to learn everything she could about her new husband and other than his brief mentions of his older brother and Frederick's countess, she knew almost nothing of his family.

An arched door led to the banqueting hall, and from there they padded quietly through the chapel and into the long gallery.

"What an unusual floor," commented Claire, looking at the narrow planks of almost black wood.

"Double-dovetailed ebony," said Edward, "believed by some to impart a medieval ambience to the room."

"The fifth earl, I take it?"

"Precisely."

The long gallery ran along the west side of the castle, with family portraits hung on the inner wall. As they walked along, Edward pointed out the better-known members of the Tremayne family, plus a few of the more eccentric ones.

"This is Philip Tremayne, the second earl's firstborn son, who went on crusade with Edward the first. It is said that he renounced the title to remain with the king."

"Did he never return? The king did."

"According to the word of his younger brother, Philip was killed in battle at Haifa," said Edward. "But a rumor persists in the family that Philip *did* return some years after the king, only to find that his brother had married Philip's own wife and sent his children—including his first son, who by rights should have become earl—into exile in the north."

"Oh, dear."

"Indeed. Some confusion remains as to which nephew actually became the next earl. At any rate, supposedly upon finding his wife at his brother's side and his children exiled, Philip went mad and threw himself into the river from the top of the donjon."

"Ah," said Claire, surmising what came next. "And his ghost—?"

"Walks the parapets every midsummer's eve, crying out for his lost children and faithless lady."

Claire shivered despite herself at the gloomy legend. She felt her husband's strong hand at her back and they continued to view the rest of the portraits, including the fifth earl, outfitted, of course, in full Arthurian armor.

"My father and mother," said Edward, as they neared the final paintings. "And this is Frederick. And Melissa."

Claire's gaze was drawn to this last. Even with the license taken in portraiture, it was clear that Frederick's countess was an unusually petite woman. Melissa's perfect oval face was ringleted with red-gold hair, her eyes wide and guileless, a sprinkling of freckles completing the effect of piquance and innocence. She's but a child, though Claire, with shock. Even the gown Melissa wore, a white muslin sprigged with tiny pink rosebuds, seemed chosen to accentuate the countess's extreme youth. One almost wanted to scoot her right back into the schoolroom, thought Claire, who felt less charmed by the picture than, perhaps, she ought to have been.

The neighboring portrait, on the other hand, brought Claire a smile. Frederick was a slighter version of her husband, just as handsome but with no hint of the gravity she often saw in Edward's face. His expression seemed to be saying, "Splendid! Now what shall we do next?" and Claire's impression was of a man who approached life *con brio*. She felt, for the first time, a keen sense of loss for this brother she had never met.

"She was the joy of his life," said the earl, looking at Melissa.

The tone of his voice, a mixture of nostalgia and regret, made Claire uneasy. She didn't mind competing with Lady Pamela for Edward's affections; a live mistress was an adversary she could understand. But this tiny child-countess? An innocent martyr of . . . of what? She wondered suddenly how Melissa and Frederick had died, yet hesitated to ask her husband.

Instead, she admired the portraits of his mother and father, and was rewarded with several stories of youthful indiscretion. On their way back to his rooms, Edward pointed out a few remaining flecks of black paint on the portrait of a sixteenth-century countess, on whom—her husband claimed—he and Frederick had once painted a thick moustache.

"She does look quite disagreeable," said Claire, looking at the proud, frowning face.

"Yes," said her husband, "we rather thought she deserved

the moustache. Frederick claimed she probably possessed one anyway, and that we were simply improving the likeness. But it took two months and three supposed experts on oil paintings to repair the damage, and my brother and I were restricted to the castle for the entire time."

Claire laughed. "You poor things. Confined to a mere castle!" She reached up and brushed a lock of chestnut hair back from her husband's brow, searching his face for the mischievous boy that he must once have been.

" 'Twould have been more pleasurable being confined with you," Edward said, and bent to kiss her. For a moment only their lips touched. Then Edward caught her arms and backed her against the gallery wall. His hands moved over her with almost frantic haste, opening her robe, and they kissed and caressed each other until Claire's legs could no longer hold her and she was in danger of sliding to the floor. The earl picked her up and carried her back to his bedroom and his bed.

"I can't bear this," she heard him whisper as he tore off his own robe and lowered his body onto hers. The remark puzzled and disturbed her, but only for a moment, as the rhythm of Edward's lovemaking caught her up and carried her away.

"Mmm," Claire said, somewhat later. She rolled over onto her side to look at her husband. "I believe I now comprehend what all the fuss is about."

"The . . . fuss?" said her husband drowsily, his eyes half closed.

"Yes. About . . . you know . . . making love. I could never understand—"

"The fuss?" Edward interrupted. His eyes were now open.

"Yes. Aren't you paying attention? All the stew men get

into over . . . well, being bedded. You know."

"Hmm."

"It's really rather nice," she said tentatively.

"Nice?" Edward had now rolled up onto an elbow.

"Yes, nice. Very much so. I can see why men so often wish to do this. I'm confused, however, about some of the stories I have heard from some ladies."

Edward was looking at her with fascination. "Pray enlighten me," he said.

"The younger women—well, I suppose some of them are just frightened." Claire frowned suddenly, thinking of a conversation she had once had with Melanie Potsworth. Pain like a red-hot poker, indeed!

"The older ladies say it is a duty to be endured. But, Edward," added Claire, her face alight with sudden comprehension, "perhaps their husbands were not . . . were not . . . *doing* it quite correctly. I heard Lady Fremont say that *her* husband wished to—"

"Ah," said the earl, his voice sounding strangled, "there's no need to—"

"But it sounded rather odd. Do people really—"

"I can't imagine what Jessie Fremont was thinking, talking like that in front of an unmarried girl."

"Oh, she didn't know I was listening, but all the ladies talk about it."

"Good Lord," groaned the earl.

"And I heard Lady Peters say that during—"

His kiss silenced her, and there was an end to conversation between them for some time.

The next day Edward suggested that it was time to saddle Achilles and Athene and ride down to the river for a lunch *al fresco.*

The idea delighted Claire. "But the river is right there," she said, pointing out the window of the breakfast parlor.

"Ah, yes, but we will go to a *different* place on the river. A secret place, much frequented by small boys in trouble at the castle."

"These boys seem to have spent a considerable amount of time in wayward pursuits," remarked Claire.

"But at least they managed to get out into the good country air once in a while," said Edward.

"Indeed," replied his wife.

The estate itself, as Claire knew, stretched on for miles. She and Edward had long since lost sight of Wrensmoor Hall as they rode, sometimes along the valley, sometimes leaving the river to climb over a series of wooded hills. Near the castle the riverbanks were broad and grassy and dotted with sheep. As they traveled farther, the meadow lands sloped into wooded hills, and the river itself narrowed and twisted.

Athene was a joy, her gait smooth and effortless, and Claire felt that she was almost flying over the ground. It had been so long since she had ridden last. . . .

She sighed, remembering when that was, and the one worry that she had yet to face. She had almost pushed Lord Sandrick Rutherford from her mind these last few days, but she knew he would keep popping up until she decided to tell Edward the truth about her family. He had been remarkably uncurious about her uncle, but one day he would surely ask.

He will be furious to find himself allied to a man of such dubious reputation, thought Claire. He will think—he will know—that I was hiding it from him.

But Wrensmoor had proved lovely beyond dreams, and her introduction to married life unexpectedly . . . satisfying. Somehow, the time had never seemed right. The earl was at her side now, on Achilles, and she felt the small, warm flutter that troubled her each time she looked at him. Romantic nonsense! she chided herself. Yet the earl was so handsome, and his arms were so strong around her when they made love.

"Frederick and I used to race to that tree," Edward said, pointing to a majestic oak standing alone at the top of the next hill. "Whoever won got the best seat for lunch."

The best seat? Claire wasn't sure what this signified, but she was grateful for the distraction from her current thoughts.

"*Ça va!* Challenge accepted," she said, and twitched the reins. That was all it took; Athene took off at full gallop.

"Claire—no, wait! *Damn!*" Edward gave heel to Achilles and raced after her. He knew, as she did not, that the terrain of this particular slope was treacherous—rocky and with a narrow ravine that was hidden until you were almost on top of it. He'd received half the bruises and scrapes of his childhood during the sprints up to that oak tree, and as for Frederick—

Claire's bonnet and hairpins flew off in a shower as she and Athene thundered up the hill. Oh, freedom! This had always been the major attraction of riding for her, especially at Cheltdown. On horseback she and Jody had pretended they were alone in the world, gloriously free from the stifling atmosphere of the manor, their uncle's threats, and Cousin Harry's general strangeness.

Oh, do let's not drag poor Harry into this, she told herself. She looked up to see the oak beckoning like a sentinel of victory, and then back, to see Edward hard at her heels. Another twitch on the reins, and—

Athene gathered herself, muscles bunching, and soared into the air.

Good grief, what—? Claire saw the gash in the earth flash by almost under her heels, and with a thud they were down. She reined in Athene, worried that the mare might have been hurt, and was about to dismount as Achilles thundered to a stop.

"Of all the idiotic, witless—what on earth do you think you're doing?" Edward barked at her, jumping down from the stallion.

"I'm sorry, my lord, a moment please," said Claire, too concerned about Athene to heed the fury in her husband's voice. She knelt and ran her hands gently along the mare's legs, feeling carefully for any swelling or evidence of a broken bone. Athene was breathing hard, but Claire decided the animal was otherwise uninjured. She looked up to see her husband giving her the devil's own glare.

"What?" she said, suddenly aware of his anger.

"You are a sorry little fool! What in hell possessed you to—"

"I will not permit you to curse at me, Lord Tremayne!" Her anger flared as quickly as his. "I admit I should not have taken Athene so quickly up an unfamiliar hill, but—"

"Reckless, irresponsible—"

"But I am an experienced horsewoman, and Athene was more than up to the task of—"

They were eye to eye now, arms gesturing and voices raised.

"Sheer lunacy! I should not allow you to ride again!"

"*Allow* me!" Claire's indignation now knew no bounds. "My lord, Athene has suffered no injury, and—"

"*I don't give a tinker's damn about the horse!*" roared the earl, silencing them both. He sat down in the grass and put his head in his hands.

In the sudden quiet Claire heard the soft blowing of

Athene and her own labored breathing, along with Edward's. She knelt at her husband's side. "Edward?"

"Just don't—don't go out alone," he said. "I will not permit you to ride alone."

"Yes, my lord," said Claire. She sensed her husband's disquiet and recognized that this stricture was only good sense, even if she might prefer it expressed in a less high-handed manner. 'Twas foolishness to ride unknown ground as she had, much as she hated to admit it. Edward had been right.

Her husband's temper was a volatile one, thought Claire, and he proved it again now, grabbing her and tugging her into his lap.

"Is this the 'best seat' you were referring to, my lord?" she said, laughing. She squirmed away, knowing that resistance would inflame him further, wanting to see desire instead of anger in his eyes. She tried to stand, but he caught a handful of skirt and tumbled her into the grass. He was astride her in a moment, his fingers working nimbly at the hooks and fastenings of her riding costume. She reached up to unbutton his shirt and he groaned as she caressed him in return.

"Claire" was all he said then, and they made love in the green grass, under the blue sky, the horses grazing in peace and indifference nearby.

The "best seat" proved to be a perch in the tree. Claire sat on a broad branch of the oak, her back against its trunk, and watched as Edward—sitting comfortably astride the same branch, seemingly oblivious to being ten feet off the ground—opened the picnic basket.

"Tree-climbing and wine don't mix," he commented, pouring her a glass of lemonade.

Claire wasn't inclined to disagree. "I take it you and Frederick spent a fair number of hours in this oak," she said, hoping to draw out another childhood story. "Did you often dine this well?"

Edward smoothed a table linen onto the bark between them. "The cook was usually good for a pastry or two," he said, extracting an assortment of cold meats and cheeses from the basket. "We thought we were getting away with something, coming here, but I think the staff was just as happy to have us out from underfoot."

"What about your parents?"

"They were very little at Wrensmoor, actually," said Edward. "Mother spent most of the year taking the waters at Bath, and my father . . ." He hesitated. "My father was happiest with the entertainments of London."

"You and Frederick were alone, then?"

"As were you and Jody," Edward pointed out.

"Yes, but not by choice." She had loosened her boots, and one of them picked that moment to fall off. She watched it tumble to the ground and thought of her own childhood, which had been incontrovertibly happy until her eleventh year.

"How did your parents die?" he asked.

It was Claire's turn to hesitate. She had wanted to hear about Edward's family, not talk of her own. A discussion of her parents would inevitably lead to her uncle. Still, he had asked—

"They said it was diphtheria."

The earl nodded, familiar with this scourge.

"They sent Jody and me away when Angeline first took sick—"

"Angeline?"

"Our sister. She was a year old."

"Dear Lord," said Edward. His eyes were gentle as he watched her.

"The disease progressed quickly with Angeline. She was dead inside the sennight. But then both my parents became ill."

Edward leaned forward and took both her hands in his, though for once she scarcely noticed the warmth of his touch. She felt numb, which was the way she always felt when she thought about those terrible first weeks at her uncle's house. She and Jody had waited—waited for the letters to arrive, waited to return, to mourn a baby sister with their beloved parents, waited to go home. . . .

Numb, deadened to all feeling. She was long past caring, anyway—it was all too long ago to make any difference. Claire didn't realize she was crying until Edward shifted his position and took her in his arms. They both leaned against the comforting solidity of the oak, and she sobbed until her eyes were red and burning and she had made a sodden lump of the earl's handkerchief. He stroked her hair and murmured soft comforts into her ear as she wept for the tiny, beautiful Angie, for her mother and father, and for Jody, orphaned at the age of six.

Finally she cried for the eleven-year-old Claire. The child who—thrown into an unfamiliar household, responsible for her terrified little brother—had never been given the opportunity to grieve. In all the years since her parents' deaths, there had never been anyone to help shoulder the burden. Never anyone whose help she could rely on—until now. Eventually the sobs quieted, and—as Edward held her—Claire fell asleep.

They took a different route back to the castle, their progress silent and slow, Claire experiencing a mixture of relief and chagrin. Relief that the earl's broad shoulders were there for her to cry on, and chagrin—well, because it felt so good. It was a relief to relinquish the cares of being in charge, of always being strong. She *could* be as strong as any man, but it was no longer a requirement, and her heart felt more at ease than it had in years.

Don't be a silly miss, she berated herself. He'll be in London most of the time, and then what will you do? Cry into the butler's cravat?

No, she would worry about that later. When her husband was gone.

They came to a small creek with a stone cross standing on its opposite bank. The horses splashed across, and Edward dismounted, beckoning Claire to follow. She walked to the cross and read the words carved into the grey stone. *Frederick John Tremayne*. There was no other inscription.

She looked at Edward curiously, but his face betrayed nothing. "Your brother is buried here?"

"Oh. No." Edward shook his head as if to clear it. "Frederick broke his neck in a fall from a horse. This is where we found him. I imagine he was trying to jump the creek."

Claire tried to keep the puzzlement from her face, but the earl must have guessed what she was thinking.

"It's just a creek, I know—not much of an obstacle," Edward said. "But it was a cloudy night, and he was riding fast . . . and recklessly. Frederick didn't know any other way to ride."

"I'm sorry," said Claire, knowing that there were no words to erase the pain. "It must have been terrible for you."

Edward nodded. "My brother would have liked you," he said, and Claire felt the swift dart of a bittersweet joy. "I wish you could have known him."

They walked on for a while, leading the horses. The sun was warm on her back, and Claire removed her boots and tied them to the pommel of the mare's saddle. The turf here was soft and thick, and her toes were delighted to be given their own small freedoms.

Her husband had fallen silent. She had assumed that married couples had a great deal to talk about, but until now she and Edward had shared nought more than a bed. Claire blushed, recalling their last few nights. How would she ever get to know her husband if they never spoke to one another? She'd had a glimpse of his past today, 'twas true; still, she knew so little. Claire gathered her determination. Since he had been willing to show her Frederick's memorial, perhaps her husband would not be offended if she asked something more about his brother.

"Did Frederick and Melissa prefer town?" asked his wife. Edward had stopped to pick brambles out of Achilles' mane and heard only the last few words of her question.

"Hmm? London?"

"Did your brother spend most of his time in town? Or at Wrensmoor?" Claire smiled up at him, her cheeks rosy from their walk. Her riding costume followed the curves of her body so closely that his mind saw straight through to the smooth skin underneath. Edward felt the painful tightening in his groin that had been his constant companion during the last few days.

"Ah. Yes."

Claire raised an elegant eyebrow at his answer. "You are wool-gathering, my lord," she said, and the wench grinned at him as if she knew exactly how he was afflicted. It wasn't fair, he thought, that she possessed a body like that.

"My brother did well by the estate and his tenants," he said, working to recover his composure. "But Frederick was easily bored, and he could never endure being alone. He and Melissa would arrive at the castle, intending to stay for months, and a week later leave again for London."

His discomfort now increased at the sight of Claire's feet, her toes appearing and disappearing into the grass with each step. Feet could be remarkably sensual, Edward realized. But the meadow was really too exposed for a tryst—

"He didn't like Wrensmoor?" His wife sounded disbelieving.

What were they talking about? Oh, yes. Frederick.

"He liked it very well, I think, but there were many more people in London. On occasion, it seemed as if Frederick had invited them all here, but even then it was never enough."

Claire had acquired an enticing smudge of dirt across the top of one foot. He longed to tumble her into the grass and wipe it clean, then continue up the curve of her calf to—

Edward sighed deeply. His wife would begin to think him unable to let a single hour go by without bedding her. It was not too far from the truth, and he forced his attention back to the conversation.

"By the time he married Melissa, I was at Oxford," he told Claire, determined not to look at her toes, "but I spent part of each vacation at the castle."

"And the rest of the time in London?"

"Yes . . ." said Edward.

They walked on in silence for a while, until the turrets of the great hall came into view.

"I think Wrensmoor is the most beautiful place I've ever seen," said Claire, her sincerity clear.

"Yes . . ." said Edward, hesitantly once again. "I believe so, as well."

"My lord—" began Claire, then stopped.

Her husband smiled down at her. " 'Edward,' " he corrected.

Claiming a moment of forgetfulness, Claire did not ask the question uppermost in her mind.

How long would the earl stay at Wrensmoor, this time?

Chapter Nine

"Edward?"

"Hmm?" He draped an arm over his wife, feeling relaxed and sated. It had never been like this before, he realized, a bit amused by the irony of his situation. Oh, there had been pleasure before, and plenty of it. But never this feeling of . . . contentment. Perhaps he could put off his return to London for a few more weeks.

"Edward?"

"Hmm?" It wouldn't be right to leave his young bride by herself in this huge castle so soon after their marriage. Being the *chatelaine* of an estate such as Wrensmoor was a major undertaking. It would take quite some time for her to become familiar with the supervision of the household. Months, perhaps. He reached out with one hand, eyes still closed, and ran his fingers through a silky length of her hair. In his mind, he saw the raven mass of curls framing Claire's face as she had lain on top of him only a few satisfying minutes ago.

"My lord, does a man require more than a single mistress, or is one generally enough?"

Edward's eyes opened. He wasn't sure he had heard his wife correctly.

"Lady Pamela is your mistress, is she not? I would not say so in company, of course—I rather like her. But—"

The earl was sitting up now. He frowned at his wife.

"What on earth can you be about, asking such a thing? Mistresses are not a fit subject for discussion between man and wife, I assure you." He started to burrow back under the covers.

"Oh, I've no wish to discuss mistresses in general. Only yours."

Edward lay back, sighing, and stared up at the silk canopy of his wife's bed. He was about to tell Claire that even *his* mistress was none of her affair, but he decided against it. It *was* her affair, of course, just not one he especially wanted to talk about. Many of the *ton* wives openly tolerated their husband's paramours, but he had never envisioned Claire—

She was looking down at him, her expression curious. "So—do you generally have just the one? Or is there someone besides Lady Pamela? What if—"

Edward groaned. "Just one," he told her.

"But not at Wrensmoor, am I right? One in London, but when you are here—"

"Just one, Claire," he repeated firmly. "And only in London."

"Oh." His wife pondered this in silence for a few minutes, and the earl decided it was the right time to renew his acquaintance with her breasts. He reached over to fondle one of the luscious mounds—

"Edward?"

The earl pulled his hand back and grunted in exasperation. "Yes, Claire?"

"How soon will you be returning to London and . . . Lady Pamela?"

This question stopped Edward cold for a moment. The answer was complicated. He would be returning to London, yes, but not to Lady Pamela. Claire had no way of knowing that, of course, and he hadn't planned to discuss the matter with her. But, why not? We do not have a *romantic* marriage, he reminded himself. She knew all along what to expect from me.

He decided to give Claire a truthful—but brief—explanation. "I will be returning to London shortly," he said. "Perhaps in . . . a month or so."

"And if I am not yet *enciente?*"

He stared at her. "Pardon?"

"Well, I'm not sure how long it should take. Do you know? If one's chances increase with the number of times—"

"Claire," said the earl, "we shall not discuss this. If you are not increasing by the time I leave . . . then there will be other times."

"Do you miss Lady Pamela?" asked Claire. Her silver-grey eyes glittered in the firelight.

"No. Well, yes," said the earl. He found it difficult to tell even a small lie to his wife, who was regarding him with a grave, intent expression. "But Lady Sinclair is no longer my . . . my mistress."

"What!" Claire exclaimed, sitting bolt upright. "Why not?"

Had Edward been paying sufficient attention, he would have realized the look on his wife's face was one of not only surprise, but fear. At that moment, however, his notice was focused on Claire's impertinence. How dare she question him!

"My lady," he said, sitting up and giving her his most commanding look, "it is really not your concern, whoever my mistress may or may not be. It will never be an issue at Wrensmoor, which is where you reside."

"But Lady Pam—"

"Lady Pamela and I have agreed to end our association," said the earl, hoping that his stern tone made it clear this conversation was not to continue. His wife was quiet, and he congratulated himself on his masterful handling of the situation. Perhaps now he could—

"Edward?"

"Enough!" roared the earl, more loudly than he intended. He slammed his feet down onto the carpet and stood. Well, she could get hysterical if she liked, but it was high time that his wife remembered the rules of this marriage. Rules that *she* had agreed upon from the beginning—Edward threw on his robe and stalked to the fireplace, giving the coals a vicious poke with the andiron. Sparks flew up, and he stomped one out on the rush matting.

Perhaps it was not too soon to return to London after all. He had no wish to indulge a clinging wife who became a watering pot every time he failed to answer every question—

It took a minute before he realized that the room was quiet except for the crackling of the fire. No heart-rending sobs were coming from the bed. He turned around to see his wife still sitting up, regarding him evenly.

"Are you quite through?" Claire asked. "You are my husband. Your life is of interest to me."

"A mistress is of—"

She interrupted him. "Your mistress is a major part of your life, is she not? I see no reason why I should not be kept informed."

She picked up a chased-silver hairbrush from the bedside table and began brushing out her hair. Edward watched, hypnotized by the rhythmic strokes and the glossy black curls shining in the firelight. His wife had worn one of Madame Gaultier's more exotic creations that evening, and the silk hid almost nothing from his view.

This woman is to provide you with an heir, Edward thought to himself. She will have your children. You have given her everything else she could possibly need.

This is not a marriage of sentiment. This is not a marriage of love.

"Claire," said the earl, returning to the bedside. She looked up at him, her gaze clear.

"I—" Edward stopped, then began again. "I will be returning to London sooner or later, and yes, I will be . . . selecting a new mistress."

"Who—"

The earl put a finger to her lips. "I have no one in mind as yet. I will tell you her name when . . . when I have decided, if you still wish it."

"Very well," said Claire, her expression unreadable. "I do wish it."

"I don't see why. We agreed your home would be Wrensmoor, did we not? Soon there will be children—" The earl faltered, wondering at the hollowness he suddenly felt inside. His children, at Wrensmoor—without him.

"Yes, we agreed. It is very well, my lord, thank you." Claire gave her hair a few more strokes and set the hairbrush aside. "Do you wish to come to bed now?"

"No. . . . That is, yes. I will sleep in my own rooms tonight." He left.

That night, for the first time in over a year, Edward dreamed of his brother's death. The dream, as always, was pitilessly exact in its accounting, and once again Edward felt the panic and anxiety; the fear that had ended in his discovery of Frederick's body lying motionless at the creek's edge.

He had relived the night of his brother's death so often in his dreams that the events were imprinted permanently in his mind. He had heard a knock at his bedchamber door, then more knocking as he came clawing upwards from an uneasy sleep. Moonlight flooded the room with an eerie luminescence, and he could hear shouting in the corridor, the harsh sound of male voices.

"Edward! Hallo, old man, wake up!"

That's Drere, thought Edward. Why is he knocking on my door? The man's usually too drunk to sit up by this time of night.

"Edward!"

Teddy Alnwick? Thoroughly mystified by now—what could Frederick's friends possibly want with him?—Edward swung his legs over the side of the bed.

Only five men stood at his door, but at the time it seemed like twenty gibbering dandies poured into his bedroom, all talking at once, and exclaiming something about Frederick. Although Edward could hear the words well enough, he could not decipher their meaning.

"Lucifer!" he thought he heard someone say.

Lucifer? Frederick's stallion?

He tried to tell them that he could not understand what they were saying, but no sound came from his mouth, and the air itself seemed to slow him down, no matter how he hurried to dress. He couldn't find his shirt, and his boots slipped through his fingers when he tried to pull them on. What were the fools bawling about now? The commotion increased as he tightened his grip on the leather, his knuckles white with the effort.

It was a bet, they told him, panting, as he ran. Frederick's been such a dismal bore lately, we were only trying to cheer him up. Your brother swore he knew the terrain like the back of his own hand—

Edward, the devil's knees, man, slow down!

They raced to the stables, where a groom was trying to calm Frederick's stallion, who was lathered and blowing and riderless, the reins hanging and trampled into tatters. Cecil is going to get himself killed if he doesn't stand back, Edward had thought without emotion. Lucifer reared, hooves flailing.

It was hours before he found Frederick, the body dimly seen in the light of earliest dawn and cradled in the dewy grass, with his head at an . . . unnatural angle. Edward dismounted and ran to where his brother lay, falling to his knees with a guttural cry.

A full-tilt ride through the night, ending abruptly, the "where" of his brother's death defined with brutal precision on the turf.

Fury surged through his veins. Hadn't there been sorrow enough? Was there nothing better Frederick's idiot friends could think of for an evening's wager?

Edward reached out to gently smooth back the hair from his brother's forehead, absurdly worried that he would do further injury to his neck. He took Frederick's hands, to kiss them—

Something glittered in his brother's left hand.

It was a woman's gold locket and chain, finely wrought. He stared at it for untold minutes, certain he had never seen it before, unable to look away. Inside was a lock of hair and an inscription—

The stream caught the morning's first light as the sun rose over the side of the hill. With a convulsive movement Edward threw the locket far away from the broken body lying there in the cool grass. He heard a small splash and imagined the figured gold sinking under the water, never to be found, never to be seen again. Never—

It was at this point that Edward always woke up, heart pounding and his nightshirt drenched with sweat. In his dream, he could never manage to read the words of the locket's inscription or make out the color of the strands of hair. In waking, of course, he remembered them too well.

"My lady?"

Claire looked up from a steaming cup of tea. She had risen early, as usual, trusting she would find the earl in his customary place at the breakfast table. They ate in the east solarium, which was her favorite room in the castle. Even on rainy days it offered a marvelous view of the river, and this morning Claire's attention had been focused on a family of geese as they made squawking forays to the water's edge.

She gave the butler an apologetic smile.

"I beg your pardon, Boggs, I'm afraid I've been woolgathering again. What is it you wish?"

"My lady, the earl . . . requests your presence in his study." He cleared his throat.

Why, the unflappable Boggs looks nervous, thought Claire in surprise. Oh heavens, please don't tell me Lady Gastonby is here! I am truly not ready for Lady Gastonby.

She was mentally phrasing a tactful question—do we have visitors today, Boggs?—when he cleared his throat again and began a second halting address. "Lord Tremayne has ordered . . . has instructed me to request that you attend him as soon as possible."

Claire wasn't fooled by Boggs's attempts at polite wording. Ordered, indeed. If her husband's need to talk to her was so urgent, why wasn't he at breakfast?

Well, it wasn't the poor butler's fault, and Claire hoped she had managed to hide her annoyance. "Thank you, Boggs," she told him in a confident, cheerful voice, "I will be there directly." She sat back to enjoy a second cup of coffee.

It was a long walk to the earl's study, past the music room and the library, through the great hall, and into the west wing.

If she didn't pay attention, she could make a wrong turn and end up at yet another staircase leading to a destination she could only guess at. Wrensmoor Castle was huge, and the floor plan had not been laid out by someone with a logical turn of mind.

Was her husband angry? wondered Claire, thinking about the earl's hasty exit from her rooms the previous night. Would he be announcing his return to London?

She paused in the great hall to get her bearings. Huge bunches of flowers, glorious in their color and fragrance, were scattered throughout, and she marveled, as always, at the number of blooms the estate hothouses managed to produce.

How could the earl bear to spend all his days in London when he had this?

Claire thought back to the evening before. She had not understood why her husband objected so strongly to her questions concerning mistresses, although at least she had managed to establish that—for him, anyway—there would be only one of them. Perhaps men did not usually discuss such things with their wives, but, as Edward had pointed out to her several times, they did not have a usual marriage.

Still, it was difficult to believe he no longer desired her. She allowed herself a small smile. Edward may have left her bed rather precipitously last night, but they had made love once—no, twice—that day already. And hadn't he been fondling her breasts yet again, all the while telling her that his mistress was none of her concern? Men! So absorbed in their dignity, and so obvious at the same time. The gossips claimed that a man tired quickly of even the most beautiful woman, but it didn't seem reasonable that Edward could have so abruptly lost interest.

But perhaps, she thought—the idea like ice water dripping

over her heart—with a need so acute, any woman would do.

Oh, glory, she was lost again. Claire stepped back from the staircase she had almost stumbled into and looked around her. Ah, yes, the tapestry with the odd-shaped . . . stag. And that rather fine bust of Homer. The earl's study was just down this hall over here.

"Edward?"

The earl did not greet her—or even glance up—and Claire was immediately irritated. "My lord, I have better things to do than stare at the top of your head."

"Sit down," said her husband. "It's time we discussed a few matters of finance." He motioned to a chair opposite his, and—for lack of a better option—Claire sat, feeling like a child summoned before her father.

Finance? Good heavens, was he going to lecture her on household economies? She hadn't spent a ha'penny since coming to Wrensmoor, although—oh, dear, was he talking about Madame Gaultier? Claire was sure the bills from the *modiste* were staggering, and she could have told him it would be too much, but he had insisted—

"My lord, no doubt you have received the first reckonings from Madame Gaultier," she said, trying not to sound defensive. "I tried to explain the problem to you at the time, but you were away from Tremayne House most of those two days, and—"

The earl was looking at her curiously. "Madame Gaultier? You say she is here?"

"No, my lord, the bills. The bills for the gowns and the—well, everything else. I knew they would be enormous, but—"

The earl leaned back in his chair, and put his hands behind his neck. Dear heavens, he is handsome, came Claire's unbidden thought. She was endlessly fascinated by the strong planes of Edward's face, the piercing blue of his eyes. His sleeves had been rolled up to avoid the ink pot, and she tracked the shifting muscles and tendons of his arms, remembering their strength around her waist.

"We seem to be at cross purposes," said Edward. "I believe Madame Gaultier was paid before we left London. Justin MacKenzie would know the exact amount, but it does not signify. I am speaking about marriage settlements."

"Oh." Claire drew in a breath, momentarily too stunned to speak. Settlements? This was even worse!

"My lord—"

Her husband frowned at her. " *'Edward,'* " he said. "You are my wife. My name is Edward."

"Yes, Edward, but—"

"I have proposed the following amounts to be settled on you absolutely. Fitzwilliams agrees that they should be adequate, but if you wish to consult your own lawyers—" He paused, and handed her several sheets of paper.

Claire stared at them, unable to read a single figure.

"As I have said, this money is yours alone. Obviously, an additional amount will be provided for you and your brother in my will. Now as for your quarterly allowance—"

Her husband continued to speak, but Claire didn't hear a word. Her eyes had managed to focus on the top sheet, the numbers written out in Justin MacKenzie's impeccable hand. The figure indicated was too large to be immediately comprehended. Her husband said it was hers?

"But, Edward, I had not thought—"

The earl interrupted her. "If you feel the settlements inadequate, I am perfectly willing to consider an adjustment."

"Oh, no!" Inadequate? How could he even—?

"When you are satisfied, I will have Fitzwilliams draw up the final papers."

Claire chewed absently on her lower lip, unaware that Edward found this small habit of hers tolerably erotic. The entire issue of dower money and settlements was worrisome, and she was puzzled that her husband had not mentioned contacting her uncle. And he had spoken so curtly, as if he was angry with her.

"Very well, my lord," she said slowly.

The earl groaned. "Very well, my Lord Edward Ashley Tremayne, twelfth Earl of Ketrick," he said with a theatrical sigh. Claire chuckled.

Claire didn't realize that Edward was even more anxious than she was to be rid of the entire subject of finances. He knew his wife's character better now than he had the week before their marriage, and he had a healthy respect for her sense of independence. By law, Claire was owed her portion of the family's estate, and he'd had no right whatsoever to allow her uncle to retain one penny of it.

Assuming a penny of the money was left, of course, which he doubted. Edward swallowed a disgusted snort, remembering how Sandrick Rutherford had reacted to the announcement of his niece's forthcoming marriage. An immature miss, Claire's uncle had called her. The duplicitous fool.

A fool, yes, but one who'd had control over the de Lancie money. Patience would never be one of Edward's virtues, and his bargain with Rutherford had seemed, at the time, to be the quickest route to a solution. Claire lost nothing by it; the *apport absolu* he had fixed on his wife was fifty times the legacy from her parents. Nevertheless, the earl could not convince himself that she would approve this peremptory handling of her affairs. If she found out. . . .

She was chewing her lower lip again. The earl, deciding

that there were a number of more pleasant ways to spend the day with his wife than talking about marriage settlements, stood and moved to the side of her chair. She looked up at him, her eyes almost silver in the morning light, and he bent to kiss her.

"My lord," she murmured against his lips.

Edward took her hand and, looking about for the nearest place for two people to sit together, pulled her over to the window seat next to his desk. Castle walls being thick, it was an exceptionally deep window seat, decorated with a number of comfortable cushions and a velvet curtain that could be drawn to shut out the draught.

"I bet this was the perfect place for boys to play hide and seek," Claire said. "Were all these cushions always here? You could almost make a pile with them and disappear underneath."

"You are exactly right. But there was one problem." Edward had spoken without thinking, and now he hesitated. His relationship with his father wasn't something he had planned to discuss.

"Hmm?" said his wife, looking out the window. It was partially open, and as they were two stories above the water, Edward grabbed her waist and pulled her back.

"What problem?" she asked.

"Well, if my father caught me, there was the end to it."

"Why? I should think he'd have been charmed by the thought of a small boy hiding in his study and forced to be quiet."

Edward had no easy reply to that, so instead of answering her, he leaned back against the side wall and drew her against him. She snuggled into his lap, and they sat listening to the faint sound of geese squabbling below.

He wanted to nuzzle her hair, but there were a number of

pins holding it in place, so he began to remove them. The loosened curls fell in a slow cascade of raven black, and she shook her head a little, sighing in pleasure.

"Oh, I'm sorry to say it, but that feels so good," said Claire. "I'm not sure why women agree to inflict such misery on their poor scalps."

"Because," said Edward, who had pulled a handful of hair aside to kiss her neck, "it looks so wonderful tumbling down."

"Mmm," she said, and smiled up at him. "Did your mother complain about hairpins, too?"

Edward took a deep breath. Such an innocuous question, really, and it was embarrassing that he had told her so little about his parents. Still—

"I hardly knew my mother," he told Claire. "She spent very little time at Wrensmoor after I was born—I don't suppose she was here for more than a month or two a year. She died when I was seven."

"Oh Edward, I'm sorry," Claire began.

"Shh," he told her, putting a finger to her lips. "It's all right. I felt it, of course, but Frederick and my father suffered much more. In a way, I don't think my father ever recovered from her death. Strange, really—they spent so little time together when she was alive."

"Perhaps if the love is deep enough, proximity is not required."

Edward nodded. "Perhaps."

Why had he told her so much? His childhood had been idyllic in its own way—a castle, a river, the cook sneaking him treats, the groomsmen allowing him run of the stables—but his mother had never been a part of it. And his father—

More than a decade after his death, the old earl's attitude toward his younger son could still cause pain. Frederick had been the golden-haired boy, happy, charming, thoughtless Frederick. Perhaps it would have been better if Edward hadn't adored his older brother as well. His father clearly considered his second son a disappointment by comparison, and for years Edward had agreed with him.

The river murmured, the geese quieted, and they drowsed in the warm sun, although—with Claire nestling close—the earl could not truly sleep. Tremayne House has no window seats, Edward was thinking, and he made a mental note to summon the carpenters when he returned to London.

Claire won't be coming to town, reminded a niggling inner voice. Would you put in a window seat for your new mistress?

"Edward?"

"Hmm?"

"Do you know yet when you will return to town?" his wife asked, a bit muzzily, as if she had been reading his thoughts in her sleep.

"No . . ." he said. "I have no plans as yet." Speaking the words, he realized they were the truth. He had no thoughts as yet of leaving Wrensmoor. It must be the first time in years he hadn't itched to return to London from the day he arrived in the country.

That's hardly a mystery, he reminded himself. Not with Claire here, and no need to wait weeks before he could take a woman into his bed. He wondered how he had managed in the past, when it seemed that he could no longer endure even half a day without bedding his wife. If the past week was an indication of the current strength of his . . . requirements, once in London he would need to find a mistress very quickly indeed.

Claire twisted in his lap and grinned at him mischievously. "My lord," she said, "it occurs to me that hide-and-seek is for children. Might I ask how you employed this window seat as a young man?"

"I believe it was vacant, madame wife," he replied. "I bedded most of *my* young ladies in the hayloft."

She giggled, and Edward could resist no longer. He began to caress her, and they shared a long, heated kiss until Claire broke away, panting for breath.

"Oh, Edward, do you think—"

He pushed her down into the cushions, consumed by the intensity of his need. She tried to squirm away, and he realized she was fretting that someone might walk into the study. He reached over for the curtain and pulled it closed with a quick jerk. Claire was still struggling to get up.

"But, my lord, anyone could hear—"

"I don't care," he said, unbuttoning his trousers. He ran a hand along the smooth length of her calves, and she sank back down into the cushions.

"Claire," he said over and over as they made love. "Claire."

Chapter Ten

"Come to bed, my love."

These words were repeated each night as Edward lay back in a mound of pillows, smiling his lazy, toe-curling smile and watching Claire brush out her hair in front of the glass. The words thrilled her, but at the same time they made her uneasy. "The incident in the window seat," as Claire had come to think of it, marked the beginning of weeks of contentment and passion between her and her husband. Even so, she was not really his "love" at all.

The mild English midsummer had arrived, and warm sun washed over the Kentish hills. She and Edward rode every day in the cool of the morning, roaming wide with Achilles and Athene. Claire learned a lot about the countryside from her husband. It was clear that he delighted in his estate and took his responsibilities to the people living there seriously. Wrensmoor Park was a far larger place than Claire ever could have imagined. She gathered up names and bits of local history and was heartened—but not really surprised—to learn that the earl was held in considerable respect by his tenants. The land was rich and husbanded well. The hops fields that she had smelled from the carriage that first day were expected to yield a good crop that year, and Edward checked on their progress every few days.

"Jimmy!" he would call out, as they rode up to the oast

house. "Come on out, ye scurvy dog!" It was apparently an old joke between the two men. Jimmy Wyndhall would emerge with a fistful of hops vine, and the two men would confer over whatever one conferred over with hops.

Once Claire took a few of the queer little pine-cone shaped flowers and crushed them between her fingers. "Bitter," she said, inhaling the pungent aroma.

The foreman's face was badly scarred, the mark of a sword cut running from forehead to chin. He gave Claire one of his crooked smiles. "Aye, milady. Bitter it is, bitter it should be."

"I take it this is an advantage for the brewing of ale?"

"Aye, milady, right necessary. The Englishman wants 'is beer," said Jimmy with a satisfied grin, "and 'tis our job to give 'im the bitter hops for it."

The amiable, albeit ferocious-looking, Jimmy Wyndhall was a favorite of Claire's, but she also took particular delight in the children of the estate. Apparently her husband was known for his own interest in the children, and Claire wondered at this, since he seemed to have spent little time at Wrensmoor during the past few years. The young ones crowded around the earl at every cottage where he stopped, and he knew virtually all of them by name. She cherished the memory of one late-afternoon visit, when Edward, babe in arms and another child riding on his broad shoulders, had been led by an insistent nine-year-old to see the tree fort "what we builded all by ourselfs." Her husband had expressed his admiration for the youngsters' construction skills and promised to allow them to attach the Ketrick coat of arms to the tree.

"For," as he told the child, "I am thy liege lord, and thee must be ever on the lookout from this noble tree for those who would ere plunder our castle."

This speech produced paroxysms of delight in its hearers, and Claire suspected other tree forts would soon be scattered throughout the estate.

Husband and wife often spent evenings together in the library. They had quickly discovered a shared love of ancient history, and Edward was astonished to find that Claire's ability to read classical languages was nearly equivalent to his own. It became a game for one of them to pick out an obscure passage and read it aloud in Greek or Latin. The listener was then required, on penalty of a kiss—Edward's idea—to both translate the excerpt and identify its author.

The earl succeeded at this diversion rather less often than Claire believed he ought to.

" 'Dariou kai Parysatidos gignontai duo,' " she read one evening. " 'Presbyteros men Artaxerxes, veoteros de Kyrus.' "

Her husband frowned in a parody of concentration. He shook his head. "I don't seem to recall that particular passage," he said.

"Ha!" said Claire, and she flounced over to sit on his lap. "Deceitful knave, I have caught you *la main dans le sac.*"

"Red-handed?" He grinned at her and tried to take his kiss, but she batted him away.

"Indeed, and well you should be ashamed. For that, my dear sir, is the first line of Xenophon's *Anabasis*—'Darius and Parysatis had two sons born to them—' "

"My memory seems to have failed me—"

"—and therefore, a line which you know perfectly well, as does every other schoolboy in England."

"Hmm," replied Edward, unrepentant. His caresses grew warmer, and Xenophon dropped from Claire's hand to the floor. She had a lace fichu tucked into the neckline of her gown; Edward's removing it was the work of a moment, and he tugged at the fabric of her bodice until he had exposed almost the whole of her bosom.

"You will tear my gown, and Madame Gaultier will be terribly upset," Claire told him.

"I will buy you any number of gowns," he growled, "but this one is coming off."

His fingers were entwined in her hair. Pulling her head back, Edward pressed a searing line of kisses from the angle of her jawbone to her breasts, and she felt that strange, demanding excitement build, the heat that seeped into her bones and made her light-headed. She could deny him nothing.

"Edward," she breathed, and was rewarded with an impassioned groan. The next minutes were breathless with turning and twisting about until eventually—Claire giggling helplessly—they fell off the armchair and onto the floor in a tangle of half-removed clothing. Once safely on the thick carpeting, the rest of the exercise was more easily accomplished.

From similar occasions the servants had learned that the library was off-limits in the evening. Although this embarrassed Claire—who was quite correct in thinking that she and Edward were the topic of amused speculation belowstairs—she had also grown accustomed to the repeated evidence of her husband's desire.

It was, as Claire reminded herself often, not everything she wanted from her marriage, but it was a start.

They spent each night together, in her bed or in his, sometimes not sleeping until the dawn. There was no further talk of the earl's return to London, and Claire had begun to hope—to dream—that her marriage might take a more companionable turn.

There have been no further incidents of gunshots in
Green Park . . .

Edward read through Justin MacKenzie's most recent
communication, frowning. His man-of-affairs had been unable to discover who had fired at the de Lancies, and the in-
vestigation seemed to have reached a dead end.

*There have been numerous reports of suspicious persons
"lurking about" in the wooded areas, but this is a perennial
complaint . . .*

The earl put the letter down on his desk and rubbed his forehead. Perhaps the incident had been nothing, after all. Some
fool boy, handling a firearm he didn't understand, or a drunk—
Or perhaps not. Edward couldn't shake the nagging
feeling that something beyond a mere accident had occurred.
And Pam had thought so, too. Sharpening another nib, he
wrote MacKenzie a quick reply with further instructions. He
had hoped for a clear resolution to the matter, but as it was,
he was loath to allow Claire to return to London—
Claire? In London?
Edward allowed himself a small, rueful chuckle. When
had he started to think about his wife accompanying him to
town? He would need to be more careful with his . . . imagination in the future.

One day the earl cried free of a meeting with his steward
and gave Claire a tour of the more remote areas of
Wrensmoor Hall. She was amazed by the number of odd little
rooms he showed her, tucked away into various corners of the
castle. Late in the afternoon he took her down a back stair-

case to the armory, and Claire was both fascinated and slightly appalled by the variety of weapons stored there.

"Good heavens," she breathed, hoping the place was kept locked.

"They're of no practical importance now," Edward pointed out. "Battle-axes, maces and other weapons. Only a grown man could wield most of them. Believe me, Frederick and I tried."

Claire ran her fingers over the jeweled hilt of a broadsword. "Would they have used something like this in a real battle?" she asked, thinking it must weigh more than a stone and a half.

"I think not." Edward took the sword down from its iron bracket and held it *en guard,* seeming to barely notice the weight. She saw his shoulder muscles bunch under the fabric of his coat, and for a moment, time spun backward. In Edward's stance Claire saw ancient years when the lords of Wrensmoor were expected not only to provide for their people but also to fight for them. She turned away, short of breath and overwhelmed once again by the sheer physical presence of her husband. He seemed to take up the whole of the room, and a melancholy question came to Claire's mind. In the life of such a powerful man, was there any place for her?

Mon cher frère . . .

Jody slit open the letter from his sister and took another bite of sugared ham. Breakfasts at Tremayne House were his idea of heaven, and he told Mrs. Huppins as much every other day. She'd taken to baking a dozen fried-apple tarts in the mid-morning, and Jody usually discovered a small errand he could do for her around that time. The tarts were nearly as good as Mrs. McLeevy's cinnamon rolls, though he had not admitted this to anyone, fearful that word might reach the kitchen at Wrensmoor.

He chewed appreciatively as he scanned the pages of Claire's neat handwriting, trying to read between the lines. Jody understood, in general terms, the nature of the arrangement his sister had made with Lord Tremayne, and he thought—well, it was stupid. Foolish and unworkable, and he had told her as much. He adored Claire, and the Earl of Ketrick was as close to a hero as Jody had known in his fifteen years of existence. He wanted them to be happy together.

Athene is normally sweet-spirited, but she has a plucky streak, especially when it comes to Achilles. Each time he tries to move ahead, Athene will nose forward. The earl is adamantly opposed to racing, I suppose because of Frederick's death, so he pulls back on Achilles, who becomes quite annoyed. Athene will drop back, then do it again. I think she is actually teasing the poor stallion.

Despite his worry, Jody smiled. If the earl and his sister would stop being so stubborn about everything, then he could finally visit Wrensmoor and explore a whole new stable of horses. Perhaps Lord Tremayne would buy him his own mount. Well, it was too presumptuous to think *that,* but surely there would be a nice horse for him to ride. And the river sounded like fun, thought Jody, envisioning the possibilities presented by castle walls and windows looking directly out over water.

He continued reading, hoping to find more on the vellum pages than Claire's cheerful description of the countryside and the rooms of Wrensmoor Hall—although the armory did sound intriguing. But what was all this fuss over tapestries? Musty old things. What Jody was really looking for was news about his sister and Lord Tremayne. Perhaps it was too much to ask that they fall madly in love, but *something* must be happening. Jody, unreconciled to his sister's marriage of convenience, searched each of Claire's letters for evidence that she had not thrown her life away on a man who would never love her.

Surely you can tear yourself away from London by now, his sister had written. *Mrs. McLeevy is sorely put out that we cannot manage to consume more than a pan of cinnamon rolls each day.*

Besides, the library here is even finer than that of Tremayne House, and, oh, my dear brother, I can hardly wait for you to see the castle stables.

It's not me you should be waiting for, thought Jody. Obviously it would be a little longer before he could visit Wrensmoor, and he wrote his sister to tell her so.

Chapter Eleven

"I saw that one move."

"It did not move."

"It most certainly did! I think your eyes are becoming weak with age, my lord. As the younger player, let me assure you that the stick—that one, right there—moved."

"Women are quite prone to letting their imaginations run away with them, I believe."

"And men can't even see what is in front of their own eyes."

"It did not move."

"Did too!"

"Did not!"

"Oh, very well. It's my turn, anyway."

Edward and Claire sat on her bedroom carpet and played jackstraws in front of a crackling fire. Her father had taught her the game, she knew, although she could no longer remember playing it with him. Claire reached forward and deftly flipped a stick out of the middle of the pile. She smirked up at her husband. "You are losing, my lord."

"I never lose."

The earl picked up a stick with his fingers and Claire sat mesmerized as he used it to trace the line of her jaw from her ear to her chin. His touch was so gentle, she could barely feel the tip of the jackstraw as it glided from her chin, down the side of her neck, toward—

"My lord," said Claire, "I don't believe this is part of the game."

Edward smiled lazily at her as the stick grazed lightly across her skin, lower and lower.

Claire reached out and grabbed the jackstraw. She popped it down the front of her bodice and grinned at him.

"There. It's mine now."

"I don't believe so," said Lord Tremayne.

I wonder if other couples end each game of jackstraws with lovemaking, thought Claire some time later. She stretched contentedly and peeked over at her husband, thinking he looked rather vulnerable lying half-naked on the carpet. Edward was ticklish, she had already discovered, and she inched closer, planning her attack.

Closer, closer.

"I'd reconsider," said the earl without opening his eyes.

Claire waited, saying nothing. Suddenly his arm shot out, and she pounced—

They grappled on the floor until Edward pinned her underneath him. His lips came down on hers, hard and possessive, and after a short while Claire could no longer remember who was more ticklish, or who won at jackstraws, or anything else except the way she felt when she was bedded by the Earl of Ketrick.

As the weeks went by in a castle in the middle of a river, circled by the grassy hills of Kent, affection grew between the earl and his new countess. Claire wouldn't call it love. They were satisfied with each other's company and the sharing of mutual interests and intelligent conversation. Edward bedded her with a hunger that continued to take her breath away.

But the earl did not love her, she was convinced, even

though he remained amiable and kind. Perhaps it was the tone of his voice, invariably cool until the moment he began to think of taking her to bed. Or the endearments he used: "my lady wife" had a beautiful, formal sound, but it was something one used in company, not—as Edward often did—in the privacy of their own rooms.

Perhaps the problem was the lovemaking itself, although it always thrilled her. *Edward* thrilled her. But the gentleness of their first nights together, when he was worried about the young miss beneath him, and even the lusty good spirits of the next few weeks, had slowly given way to something different. A harsh, even desperate, note had crept into their physical intimacy, almost as if he bedded her despite himself, as if he was driven to it against his true will.

No, he does not love me, thought Claire. But then, he never said he would. She no longer asked Edward about his return to town, but she was sure he planned to depart soon. There was an empty feeling attached to that thought, and Claire vowed to fight it. I will be happy here without him, she told herself. Quite happy. Because I am a sensible person, and because I have no other choice.

Melissa walked down the aisle towards him, her wedding gown a deep crimson. Frederick was nowhere to be found, and Edward realized that he himself was the groom. He looked around at the unfamiliar church. This was surely not St. Albans. And where were his parents? Where was Claire? The wedding must wait, it wasn't time—

"Dearest Edward," said Melissa in her breathy, childlike voice. She approached the front of the chapel and placed her hand in his. Frederick isn't here yet, thought Edward. I must convince them to wait. His pulse was racing, and he tried to turn to speak to the pastor, but the wedding was already over, and they were out on

the steps of . . . wherever they were, alone.

"Edward, where is the coach?" asked Melissa. "There was supposed to be a coach." She sat down on the top step in a rustle of organdy, her skirts a crimson stain on the weathered stone.

"I don't know why Frederick doesn't like this color," she commented absently, smoothing the fabric with her hands.

"Melissa!" Edward realized with horror that she was bleeding. A stream of blood ran down the steps and pooled on the sidewalk below. A passerby looked up curiously at Edward, who discovered he could not find the breath to shout for help. Melissa was pointing at the blood and laughing.

Where was the coach? Edward bent to lift Melissa, to carry her down to—

Then he saw the raven hair of the woman in his arms. It was Claire.

"No!"

Edward sat up in bed, his heart pounding in his ears and his breath coming in ragged gasps.

"Edward?" He felt his wife's hand on his shoulder.

"I'm . . . I'm all right."

"You were shouting," Claire said. She lit the candle on her nightstand. "Shall I get you some brandy?"

" 'Twas only a dream."

"An evil sort of dream, I think."

"Yes." The small flame was a comfort and Edward stared at it until he felt his pulse slow. Claire sat up, her hair tousled and glowing in the candlelight. She was clutching the sheet to her chest, and Edward realized they were both unclothed. Oh, yes, they must have fallen asleep immediately after—

"You called out Melissa's name," said his wife.

The tendrils of nightmare which had faded with Claire's touch, curled again around Edward's heart. "Yes," he said, hoping she would ask no more about it.

"Will you be all right?"

"I am fine, thank you," he said, a bit curtly. He was not a man to tolerate weakness in himself. The Earls of Ketrick did not succumb to such evils as nightmares.

He reached for Claire, and she blew out the flame. They sank back into the bedding and lay nestled together, Edward content to merely hold his wife. He was beginning to drift back into sleep when he felt her stir.

"Edward?"

"Hmm?"

"How did Melissa die?"

He forced himself to speak. "She died in the miscarriage of a son."

"Oh, Edward, I am sorry. Was it after Frederick's death?"

"No. A few months before."

There was silence between them for some time. It was only much later that Claire would learn anything more about the death of Frederick's wife, and even then, as Lady Pamela could have told her, she did not hear the whole of it.

After that night Claire began to see less of Lord Tremayne in the evenings. The midsummer days were long, and she took walks down to the river after supper, hoping he might join her. The water flowed golden, lit by the setting sun, and all manner of creatures crept to its shores for their evening's drink. Her heart might break, Claire often thought, and still the beauty of Wrensmoor would be some solace. She refused to feed the geese, considering them sassy and plump enough already, but sneaked occasional handfuls of cracked corn to the peacocks and quail. She wandered along with the earl's two hounds for company and wondered if her husband ever saw her from his study window.

Edward often remained closeted there until after she had retired to bed, drinking, if Claire was any judge of it, copious amounts of brandy. He would then come to her bed in the middle of the night and, without a single word spoken, throw back the bedding and cover her body with his. As his passion became ungovernable, he would cry out and then moan her name over and over. Claire. Claire. Claire.

Claire awoke alone. She was fastening the ties to her morning robe when Constance brought in tea.

"Thank you, Constance. I'll have it out on the balcony."

"Oh, milady, t' early morning air's no good for you," said Connie, scandalized at the thought of her mistress drinking tea while out of doors. "Just lie back down, and I'll leave the teapot on your nightstand."

"Nonsense. It is a beautiful morning. I'll be perfectly fine. "

She opened the doors to her balcony and stepped out into the cool air. Mist rose from the river. Small white smudges on the opposite bank showed where the sheep grazed, and as Claire watched them, she saw someone riding over the crest of the hill.

She knew of only one horse at Wrensmoor that black and that big. It was Achilles, and Edward had ridden out again this morning without her. She sighed.

"Milady?"

Claire turned to see Constance hovering nearby, still hoping, Claire supposed, that her mistress would return to bed. "Yes, Constance?"

"Um, 'is lordship says as to warn you that the rector'll be payin' a visit today, 'im and 'is wife. And they allus come powerful early, you know."

"Oh, good heavens," said Claire, "that's right. Well, I trust his lordship will be back in time from his ride. Connie,

166

will you please send Flora in to help me dress?"

"Yes, milady."

"Good day to you, Lord Tremayne. And my lady." The rector bowed over her hand, and Claire resisted the impulse to snatch it away before he bestowed his usual smacking kiss.

"Mr. Redmonds, Mrs. Redmonds." The earl's face was blankly polite; only Claire knew how much he had wished the rector and his wife would postpone their visit. A year or two from now wouldn't have been too soon, according to her husband, but that had been too much to hope for. It was customary in the village for anyone who was anyone to pay at least one courtesy call on the earl when he was in residence—especially now, with his new bride!—and Mr. Redmonds was not one to neglect the courtesies.

It wasn't quite fair to paint the wife with the husband's tar, thought Claire. She liked Bessie Redmonds well enough, and so, she suspected, did the earl. The rector's wife was a plump, amiable lady of perhaps fifty years, who dressed quite fashionably for her position in life, and who sported a pair of enormous dimples whenever she smiled. Mr. Redmonds, on the other hand, was an entirely different matter, and Claire had given up trying to find words to describe the man. *Fawning, obsequious,* and *insincere* all came to mind, but none quite did justice to his oily, sycophantic nature. Apparently he had been rector at St. Andrew's for as long as anyone could remember and had remained a great favorite of Edward's father until the end of the old earl's life. Now that was a mystery, indeed.

They moved into the drawing room, Mr. Redmonds prattling the entire time. The windows of the church seemed much on the rector's mind today. Claire had already heard about "our glorious fenestrations" during a previous visit to the rectory, and her poor husband! How many times he had listened to this same speech?

"And, Lady Tremayne, the stained-glass windows are, as you know, the finest in Kent, and all due to his late lordship's kindness. I'm sure there is no luckier parish than ours for the prodigious care taken by our noble patrons—"

"How does the Lynch family fare these days?" interrupted Edward, addressing Mrs. Redmonds. Claire already knew of this large and extended family, which was notorious in the village for its loutish, heavy-drinking men and its slatternly women. Apparently the earl and Mrs. Redmonds had engaged for some time in a gentle conspiracy to tempt some of the younger children to school and the older girls into service at the castle. At least in that way they would be fed.

Edward had never told her about his efforts on behalf of the various Lynch children, but Constance was one of the family's older girls, and she had been lavish in her praise of Lord Tremayne. "Saved my life, he did," Connie had told her, and after hearing Mrs. Redmonds's description of the family, Claire was inclined to agree.

"Old Jinks broke his leg in a fall," Mrs. Redmonds was now telling Edward. "Which is a blessing for Meg, as he'll not be beating her 'til it heals."

"Goodness," said Claire, startled at this piece of information. She was growing used to thinking of Wrensmoor as an idyllic place to live, but obviously it wasn't so for everyone. "Can't someone assist the poor woman?"

"I could take Jinks out one of these days and show him the other side of a fist," suggested Edward.

Claire looked at him in alarm. "But if you strike him, will he not be that much more likely to take his anger out on his wife?" she protested.

"Oh, not to worry, my lady," said the rector. "His lordship

couldn't get Jinks to stand up long enough to knock him down, even when he *had* two good legs."

This comment met with general agreement.

Tea arrived, and the conversation turned to Wrensmoor. The rector took a strong lead in rhapsodizing over the castle's happy existence: its favored location, its wonderful furnishings, the beauty of its windows, *et cetera,* until Claire thought her eyes would cross. Once she thought she saw Edward wink at Bessie Redmonds, and the woman did try to deflect some of Mr. Redmonds's more effusive comments.

"I'm sure Lord Tremayne is quite relieved to have your approval," said Mrs. Redmonds tartly, after the rector had commented favorably on the moral lesson to be gained from the scene depicted on one of the larger tapestries. "No doubt there are any number of young people who have been led astray by rugs and tapestries of poor character."

"Indeed, my dear, indeed."

Sarcasm was apparently wasted on the rector. Still, there was no real harm done until Mr. Redmonds changed his focus from the castle to its new mistress.

"And let me add, my lord," said the rector, "that you are the most fortunate of men to have found Lady Tremayne! She is, if I may say so, almost the *image* of our beloved Melissa."

Claire's eyes widened in shock, but she was spared the need of making any comment when this proved too much for Mrs. Redmonds. "Melissa! William, what on earth can you be about?" she exclaimed, almost bouncing off the chair in her indignation. "They look not the slightest bit alike!"

"Oh, of course, my dear, not on the surface," rejoined her husband. "But good breeding will always tell, you know. The refined demeanor, the delicacy of Lady Tremayne's constitution—they are precisely the same."

Edward was staring at the man.

"You, my lord, appreciate the similarity, do you not?" continued the rector, who was by now unstoppable in his praise of Claire's weak nature. "A personage of such rank as the Countess of Ketrick, well, such ladies are not meant for the usual employments but to adorn our lives with their fragile grace."

"Indeed," was all Edward managed to say, and it was fortunate that the Redmonds left soon afterwards, or Claire might have risked her fragile hands in a punch to the rector's nose.

The house party had gone on for weeks, but Edward had just come down from Oxford the evening before. He loved his brother—heaven knew he enjoyed Frederick's company more than he ever had his father's—but, somehow, he was finding more and more excuses to avoid Wrensmoor. His brother's friends were the cause, he supposed. He wondered how Melissa could stand the lot of them mooning around, accosting every female in the castle and drinking up crate after crate of Frederick's brandy. He'd nearly stepped on Cecil Drere last night, passed out in the hallway.

But Melissa smiled and smiled and never uttered a word of complaint. Edward found Frederick somewhat deficient in appreciation for the saint-like forbearance of his wife. After all, was it not almost common knowledge that she was breeding?

Claire watched her husband mutter and shift uneasily in his sleep. These restless episodes had been occurring more often during the past week. She wondered if she should wake him, or if she would soon be startled by another fierce nightmare's cry.

Claire remembered the one time Edward had called out Melissa's name in his sleep. She didn't know what to think.

Was it his sister-in-law's death that her husband relived in his dreams, or something else? She had seen the portrait of Frederick's wife in the long gallery, and knew that Melissa had been a tiny woman. The Tremayne men looked to be big, so a death in childbirth—well, it was a sad thing, but hardly unheard of. Who did not look at *une femme enceinte* and wonder if she would survive her labor?

It is fortunate I am tall and strong, thought Claire. I will not be afraid.

He woke up the third morning to find Frederick gone. Boggs could not tell him why, and Melissa, when she finally appeared early in the afternoon, dismissed the subject with a laugh.

"Some silly piece of business in town," she said, giving him her enchanting little pout. "I'm sure I don't know a thing about it."

"But—" Edward was furious. How could Frederick leave when his wife was in such a condition?

"Oh, don't worry, dearest brother," said Melissa. "He'll be back. And can I not always count on you?" She fixed wide eyes on his face and stepped close to him, running her hands up his arms. Edward felt the discomfort that had recently been his fitful companion when he was in the company of his sister-in-law. He knew that what he felt was the stirring of desire, and he despised himself for it. How could he dishonor his brother—and Frederick's beautiful, trusting bride—with these debased thoughts? He was the worst, the foulest kind of cad—

She could not sleep with Edward turning and tossing so. Claire rooted around in the sheets for her chemise, blushing to remember how it came to be at the foot of the bed instead of on her person. Her husband had taken her that evening with an almost frantic urgency, and Claire would not be surprised if she found the chemise in tatters.

Not that she didn't enjoy their lovemaking as much as he did.

Oh, here it was. She pulled the thin cotton shift over her head and rose quietly. It was a warm night—Claire walked out onto the balcony, and stood for a while, watching the twinkling starlight reflected in the river below. Wrensmoor was beautiful beyond dreams, and she realized that her deepest wish was to share it with children of her own.

Frederick returned three days later and immediately informed his guests—to their general astonishment—that they would all be leaving early the next morning. The house party was over, in short, and the host avoided the ensuing uproar by retiring to his rooms for the remainder of the day. Edward found him in his study later that evening, quietly getting drunk.

"Welcome, brother," said Frederick, draining half a glass of brandy in one gulp. "How runs the estate? And my dearest wife— has she been treating you with all hospitality?"

Edward heard these words with dismay, thinking that his brother somehow knew of his disgraceful response to Melissa's innocent touch. But how could that be? He had done everything possible to hide his reactions.

"We have been very well here," he replied. "But I will confess that I am not sorry to see the rest of them go. I am happiest with family, you know."

"Oh, indeed, family!" Frederick snorted and stood up, splashing brandy on the carpet. "Let me tell you, my dear brother, about the merits of family!"

"Frederick . . ."

"And I do believe, yes, I am quite certain, that the only thing better than family is friends. *"*

Edward was by now aware of two things: first, that his brother was drunker than he had ever seen him, and second, that Fred-

erick was speaking with a bitterness that Edward would have thought alien to his very nature. His thoughts returned uneasily to Melissa, and he wondered if he should confess his shame to Frederick or simply leave Wrensmoor altogether. Edward was still a young man and had, as yet, little experience of casual flirtation with women.

Frederick was pacing unsteadily about the room. Edward tried to guide him to a chair, only to be pushed roughly away.

"Don't need any help," muttered his brother. "Nothing you can do to help."

"What has happened?" cried Edward, now truly alarmed. He had never known Frederick to be anything other than carelessly cheerful. "What is wrong?"

"Oh, little brother," said Frederick, "let me give you a piece of advice."

"Advice? What do you—"

"Never marry a woman you love," said his brother. "Better yet, never love a woman at all."

Edward frowned and was about to ask more, when they heard a commotion in the hall, and Melissa's dresser burst in.

"Lord Tremayne, you must come immediately. Milady is terrible ill!"

From this point, Edward's memory was scattershot. He knew that he and Frederick had run upstairs to Melissa's rooms and burst through the door.

After that, all he could remember was the blood.

Chapter Twelve

Claire had another week's grace, a respite from the storm that even now was descending on the Earl of Ketrick and would soon drive him back to London. But the grace was incomplete. Edward had stopped seeking his wife's bed and was now avoiding her even during the day. This afternoon had been a good example. Claire had harassed poor Boggs into letting her into the earl's study after lunch, and she sat in the window seat for an hour, becoming sleepier and sleepier in the warm sun, waiting for her husband. Finally the door opened, and he strode over to his desk.

"Oh," said Edward when he saw her. "I won't disturb you."

And he had turned on his heel and walked back out.

"Edward—wait," she had called, but the door was already closing behind him.

Claire combed out her hair in front of the fire and thought how much emptier her bed looked now that she was the only person who ever slept in it. She knew that it was Lord Tremayne's right to conduct himself in whatever way he pleased. As he had made clear to her on more than one occasion, he had no obligation to stay at Wrensmoor at all.

But if he did not wish to bed her or to spend any time in her company at all, for that matter, why was he still at the castle? Claire sat on the rushing in front of the fire and puzzled over this. She was convinced that her husband was troubled by something. He had received several letters from Justin MacKenzie recently, and he'd seemed in a worse humor with each one. Was it something involving her? worried Claire, who had reviewed her last real conversations with Edward time and again, searching for something she might have said to disturb him.

Claire frowned and tossed back her hair. The whole situation was very frustrating. It was not in her nature to beg for her husband's attention or to complain that she did not receive enough of it. But how could she discover why her husband continued to avoid her, if they were never in the same room together? She arose earlier each morning, only to be told he had already breakfasted. Of late, the only times she had seen Edward were at the evening meal, and his conversation there was distant and formal, limited to pleasantries concerning her day and his.

"Would you care to join me in the library after supper?" she had asked him just that evening, finally deciding that she must be more forward in her address. He had looked at her bleakly and, to Claire's eye, with total lack of interest.

"Ah, no. No, there is business I must attend to. . . ."

"I see. Yes, of course."

But she did not see. Business! This supposed business from what she could tell, consisted entirely of glass after glass of brandy. Edward's eyes were bloodshot now more often than not, and the hollows in his cheeks appeared more pronounced by the day.

He will be gone to London at any time now, thought Claire, feeling a sudden chill even in front of the fire. I may not even know it until supper arrives and he is not there. What if he is planning, even now, to be gone before daybreak? The idea took her breath away. There can be nothing more to lose, she thought, and resolved that another night would not pass without serious conversation between herself and her husband.

But how to accomplish this? Claire rose and paced the thick carpet for a few minutes, finally sitting down on the bed to consider the situation in detail. Edward would not breakfast with her or ride with her or even kiss her. Perhaps this was not the time for subtlety, thought Claire, and, despite everything, she smiled. The new Countess of Ketrick was an exceedingly practical woman and not one to ignore her own strengths. She called for Constance and asked the girl to prepare her bath.

A wave of dizziness came over him, and Edward swayed, barely managing to remain upright. He clutched the railing of the staircase, thankful that he had talked himself out of that last decanter of brandy. Perhaps he could sleep tonight without drinking himself into unconsciousness, although—

He groaned as a vision of Claire lying beneath him flashed through his mind.

—it was hopeless.

He sat down on the stairs for a moment, head in hands. He thought about returning to his study and the oblivion of drink. He would find rest no other way—

If you can call it rest, came the insistent thrumming voice within him, the voice that had been tormenting him night and day.

"Shut up," he muttered.

Just take her, it answered, unrepentant. She's your wife. Take her, take her, take her.

"Shut up."

He staggered to his feet and resumed his wobbly climb. At least he wouldn't be repeating last night's fiasco, when he had awakened at some cheerless, black hour to find that he had passed out on the floor in front of his wife's door. Aghast at the thought that one of the servants might have seen him lying there in a drunken stupor, Edward had sworn to himself that he would take no brandy this night. Although he had not kept that vow, at least he had exerted enough self-control to be able to find his own rooms.

At last. The door to his bedchamber opened as he fell against it, and he managed the few steps to his balcony. He stood there for a long time, feeling the night's breeze against his overheated skin, and eventually his head felt clearer.

He needed to sleep. Strong as he was, he could no longer keep up the schedule he had set himself of late: up at dawn, a frantic spate of activity during the day, followed by drinking far into the night. And none of it had managed to drown out the yammering voice in his head.

Take her. Take her.

Edward shuddered as desire washed over him, and he stepped back into the room. This was idiocy. He should leave for London soon, find a bed-partner and be done with it. He'd seen the gleam in Chedley's eye when he'd mentioned being in need of a mistress. No doubt by now the viscount had a list as long as his arm of applicants for the post. And Gerald's taste was impeccable, running to exquisite, shapely blondes.

Edward groaned, and flopped down on the bed. He was fooling himself and he knew it. No matter how desperately he craved the relief that a mistress might provide, he found himself unable to leave Wrensmoor.

Ha! came the chiding voice, changing its tack. You've never had any trouble leaving the castle behind before, have you? The woman has bewitched you.

Then, a new voice. Frederick's. *Never marry a woman you love—*

Edward would have returned to the study, if the thought of negotiating the stairs again hadn't seemed insurmountable. He undressed slowly and lay down, hoping to sleep sometime before he heard the castle peacocks announcing the dawn.

Claire held her breath and opened the door to the short passageway between her rooms and Edward's. The massive door swung easily and silently on its hinges. Well-oiled, she suspected, at her husband's behest, during the time when he was coming to her at all hours of the day and night. She crept along the passage, seeing a faint glimmer ahead. She realized the door on Edward's side must be ajar and the tapestry not quite enough to block the light entirely. That was lucky—

She came to the door which was indeed partially open and stood still, listening. She heard night sounds from the river, the crackling of the fire—and then footsteps, heading, as far as she could tell, to the bed. Edward wouldn't be able to see her very easily from that vantage, and Claire risked a peek around the edge of the tapestry, feeling the stirrings of a mischievous excitement. Her husband was in this room only a few steps away, and she was about to go to him, to seduce him.

The earl was standing with his back to her, removing his shirt, which was, to Claire's blushing distraction, the very last item of clothing he wore. She stared at his body, the strong muscles of his back and legs outlined in firelight, and wondered if she would be able to follow through with what she had planned. Perhaps she should just creep back to her own bed.

No. No, it was time to force the issue. If he no longer wanted her, if he no longer desired her in the way he had seemed to so urgently desire her only a few weeks ago, then it was time she found that out. Perhaps he would think her wanton, but during the past few days Claire had decided it would be better to be thought a wanton than not to be thought of at all.

Edward climbed into the bed and blew out the candle. Darkness settled over the room, and Claire waited for her eyes to adjust. She untied the sash of her wrapper and took a deep, steadying breath as it fell off her shoulders and slid silently to the floor. She smoothed the silk of her nightgown with trembling hands. This was Madame Gaultier's most daring confection and the fabric was almost transparent. The neckline was deeply cut and she had never before summoned the nerve to wear it.

"Edward?" she whispered.

The small sounds of a body shifting in bed ceased. She guessed that he was listening intently, unsure of what he might have just heard.

"Edward?" she whispered again, stepping into the room. She heard her husband's sharp intake of breath, and smiled. It was time.

His wife's body was outlined in perfect, erotic detail by the firelight. Edward at first thought she was wearing nothing at all, but then realized she was clad in a diaphanous nightgown that clung to her every curve. Her nipples were clearly visible at neckline, and Edward's body responded immediately with furious, urgent demand. He couldn't have her. He *had* to have her.

"Edward?"

She smelled of roses. Edward pushed himself up to a sitting position, the bedding clenched in his hands, and tried to form a coherent reply.

"What is it?" he heard himself say, his voice sounding

ragged and harsh to his own ears. What could she mean by coming in here dressed like that? If she came any closer she would be sure to notice how his body had responded to her—

Take her, take her, came the drumbeat voice, so deafening that for a moment Edward was not sure if Claire had spoken and he had simply failed to hear.

She sat on the edge of the bed and gave him a half-smile. "My lord?" she said. "Did you ask me something?"

"What are you doing here?" he managed to rasp, aware of how ridiculous he must sound.

"Mmm," she said, and reached to stroke a fingertip down the line of his jaw. She laughed softly as a muscle jumped under her touch, and he fought to keep his breathing even.

"Did you wish something from me?" he asked, trying to gain some control over the situation. His eyes felt trapped by the sight of her breasts, full, rounded, pressing against the filmy silk of her gown.

It was the wrong question. He had meant to be intimidating and brusque, but his wife nodded. "Yes," said Claire, and she scooted next to him on the bed. "I do. In fact, I *need* something from you." She sounded impossibly composed. Edward, whose mind had been fixed on the tormenting pressure in his loins, was taken aback for a moment. What was she talking about? What was it that she needed to come to him at night, dressed like—like—

She'd tried to talk to him this afternoon, in his study, he remembered. And later, too, at dinner. Perhaps there was a problem that he had been ignoring. From now on it was of the utmost importance, Edward decided, that he allow conversation between them during the *day.*

He felt a little calmer at this thought, although his need for his wife did not abate in the least. It had obviously been a mistake to try to avoid her altogether. He would find out what she wanted now, and in the future—

"I find I miss our . . . lovemaking," said Claire, looking at him in innocence, as if she had just remarked on the weather. "I'm not terribly experienced yet, as you know, but I believe what I am feeling is the need for your touch."

He stared at her, unable to move.

"It's a very strong feeling," Claire continued, "somewhat like an ache inside. Do men feel this, too?" She fixed her large, silver-grey eyes on him, and her lips parted slightly as she ran the tip of her tongue over them.

Edward was edging past the point of coherent thought. "Yes," he said. It came out as a croak.

"But you no longer feel this way for me?"

Was the wench blind? "Ah. Well, yes, but—"

"And, Edward, I do not believe I am breeding yet. Perhaps before you leave for London, we should continue to—"

Even at this moment, with his self-control in shreds, Edward told himself he was only going to kiss her. Just a small, chaste kiss. He leaned toward Claire and touched his lips to her cheek. She smiled at him.

"Perhaps, if you are not feeling . . . well . . . *ready,* I could—" Claire slid a hand under the bedding.

"Claire, don't—"

Her eyes widened. "Dear me," she said.

"Claire," Edward groaned.

It was the last intelligible thing he was able to say for some time.

Claire awoke an unmeasured time later in her husband's bed. The sky was still black, so she decided it couldn't yet be much past the earliest hours of the new day.

She felt the solid bulk of her husband lying next to her, felt

181

the slight movements of his breathing.

Her attempt to seduce Edward had been successful beyond imagination.

He had been almost too aroused at first. Frantic, fumbling, he could hardly contain his need as he took her. Claire stifled a giggle. It was a good thing the castle walls were thick; otherwise Edward would have been heard all the way down to the stables.

The second time had been slower but no less passionate. Claire stretched and wiggled her toes. Every single part of her felt sated, and she mentally chided herself for having allowed her estrangement from Edward to have lasted as long as it had. A single night was too much to spend apart from such delights. Certainly now he would realize how much he needed her, and how much she needed him. Perhaps true love *was* just romantic nonsense. Perhaps she and her husband would have no need of such foolish sentiments to continue their enjoyment of mutual interests and pleasures.

Edward stirred and rolled over onto his back. The planes of his face, the high cheekbones and the strong line of his jaw, were sharply defined even in sleep, and Claire thought he looked tense. They had engaged in very little . . . talk during the night, and she was no closer than she had been before to finding out what was troubling her husband.

The bedding had been rumpled, tangled, and finally tossed aside during the night's activities, until it now shielded very little of her husband from Claire's sight. Edward Tremayne would never really look vulnerable, but this was as close as he came, and she indulged herself in a long and careful scrutiny of the body that had recently pleasured her so well. The skill of the earl's tailor had never obscured the muscles of his shoulders and back, but she was still enthralled by the sight of the strength and hardness of his naked form.

Claire felt a prickly warmth begin to coil inside her. She reached out her hand—then hesitated, thinking that he looked too exhausted to wake. But it mattered not. Before she had risked even the softest touch, Edward's eyes opened.

In all the nights of loneliness to come, she would never forget the look he gave her at that moment of first waking. The mixture of anger and desire, bitterness and . . . and something else. Despair? Claire was unsure. For a fraction of a second an elusive truth blazed from her husband's blue eyes, and just as quickly it was gone. Edward's features resumed their usual cast, with the cool detachment she had begun to dread seeing.

"Well, my lady," he said, his voice soft, "I see you're still here."

The gall of the man! But Claire had come too far to be intimidated by his manner, and besides, she knew one important fact: the Earl of Ketrick still wanted her. Let him pretend indifference all he wished; she knew better.

"Aye, my lord," she told him, running a light finger down his chest. "I'm still here."

He grabbed her wrist in one strong hand and held it still. "Don't do that," he told her, and then, "It's time you should go."

"Certainly, my lord." She pushed herself up in the bed. "Can you help me find my nightgown?"

Edward muttered something in a strangled tone as Claire leaned over him to root around in the bedding for her gown. She sensed that her husband was once again very aroused. Why was he so determined to torment himself with hunger? she wondered, and decided that she wasn't about to make things any easier for him.

"Oh, never mind," she said, and swung her legs over the side of the bed to stand. "Edward, I can barely see—"

Events after that seemed to happen very quickly. Edward
lit a candle for her, and, still unclothed, she began to make
her way back to the door behind the tapestry. Halfway across
the room she heard a sudden rustle of bedding and quick
footsteps, and Edward's strong arm grabbed her around the
waist. The candle fell, guttering, and Edward kicked it into
the fireplace. Then he took her on the carpet, moaning in his
need, as ravenous as if he'd bedded no woman for months.

Claire slept deeply and was finally awakened by another
family argument among the geese. She sat up in bed and experienced the disorientation she used to feel during her first
days at Wrensmoor. Where was she? How had she gotten into
this strange bed?

The night's events rushed back into memory, and she
looked around for her husband, not really surprised that he
wasn't in her bed. He had carried her back to her room afterwards, but from the way light was streaming into her window,
she had slept much later than usual. Edward had probably
breakfasted by now. Still, Claire experienced a brief rush of
hope. Perhaps if she hurried, she could catch up with him,
and they could ride together this morning.

There was a scratch at the door, and Flora came in with
tea.

"Oh, milady, I'm sorry. I didn't know if you were awake."

"That's all right, Flora," said Claire. "I just woke up this
minute. Do you know—has Lord Tremayne breakfasted already?"

Flora looked up from preparing the tea, and from her
glance Claire somehow knew what had happened. No! she
wanted to cry. No! I didn't ask that question—don't answer!
Give me another few minutes of peace—

But it was too late.

"Lord Tremayne?" asked Flora, clearly confused. "But— milady—he left for London this morning. 'Afore the birds, 'e was."

"Oh," said Claire weakly. "Oh, yes. I'd forgotten he intended to leave today." She smiled brightly at the girl. "Thank you, Flora. I'll dress myself this morning."

" 'Is lordship told us how we was t' give you every consideration whilst he was gone," said Flora, clearly impressed by the mandate. "I'll stay t' help you dress."

There was nobody more dogged in her position than a Kentish-born lady's maid, but Claire had a sudden, urgent need to be alone. "No, thank you," she told Flora. "I'll call you if I need you." She almost pushed the poor girl out the door, and leaned against it for a moment after it closed.

Gone. To London. Early this morning.

Claire closed her eyes against the shaft of pure pain that stabbed through her. What did you expect? a voice cried from deep inside. What did you expect? Lovemaking changes *nothing* for a man, nothing! He can get *that* from his mistress!

"Oh, shut up," said Claire to the voice. She straightened and, taking a deep breath, went to drink her tea.

Chapter Thirteen

Claire slid down from Athene and looked back towards the castle. She never tired of the view from this spot. The hall seemed to rise from the middle of the river itself, the water sparkling in the early morning sun, and the sheep were fuzzy white spots on the green sward below. Through some happy circumstance of the land's incline, you could usually hear their soft bleating from this hill but never the raucous cackle of the castle geese. She peered in the direction of the road leading to Wrensmoor, telling herself that she, as the castle's mistress, was merely observing the activities below, that she had no special interest in *who* might be riding up to the draw-bridge.

Or who might not be. The road was empty of travelers, as usual.

"Hallo-o!" she heard and saw her brother flying up the hill on Artemis. Jody possessed a remarkable ability to find his sister whether or not she was in the mood to be found, and recently he seemed to think she couldn't be left alone for a minute. Claire sighed. She had never courted pity, and solicitude from a fifteen-year-old boy was no easier to take when the boy in question was one's own brother.

Quit fussing, she reminded herself, as she did every time her thoughts threatened to veer in this direction. You can be happy in the present situation, or you can be unhappy. It is *your* choice, and the Earl of Ketrick has no power over you in this matter. She waved at Jody and led Athene down to meet him.

Her brother had arrived at Wrensmoor almost two months ago, a week after the departure of Lord Tremayne. Jody had not written her of his plans to leave London but had simply appeared at dinner one night, as rested as if it were no more than an hour's journey between town and the castle. She knew she would be glad of his company.

Patience wasn't a virtue to a fifteen-year-old boy, so after a quick hug her brother had come immediately to the point.

"What happened? Why did Lord Tremayne leave Wrensmoor? He didn't say anything to me about it. He hardly talked to me at all!"

The words tumbled out in a rush and Claire smiled. She'd missed her brother. But as to answering his questions—well, she didn't understand Lord Tremayne's actions herself.

"I don't know why he left," she'd said.

"How can you not know? Claire, what did he say? Didn't you talk to him? Didn't he tell you when he was coming back?"

Claire sensed that her brother was half-minded to believe that *she* was the cause of the earl's change of address, and she could tell, too, that Edward's brusque replies had hurt Jody. Well, it couldn't be helped.

"He didn't give me a definite time that he would be back at Wrensmoor," she told Jody. That was true enough.

"But, Claire—!"

"Jodrel, I really don't know. He didn't ask for my sentiments when he left."

"Are you . . . ?" Her brother hesitated and turned red, and

despite the depressing subject of this conversation, Claire nearly laughed.

"No, I'm not increasing," she told him, fairly sure that this was the case.

"Then, why—?"

Claire sighed in exasperation, afraid that she would not hear the end of this inquisition for days. What could she tell her brother? That during the last few weeks Edward had been at the castle he had generally shunned her company, had bedded her like a man starved for one tempestuous, feverish night, and then left before dawn the very next morning?

No. She could hardly tell him that.

Her brother had been nothing if not persistent.

"Jody, I just don't know—" It seemed she had answered him with those words a thousand times before he finally gave up asking about Lord Tremayne. A fortnight's argument, at least. Then, gradually, they resumed old, familiar ways, Jody frequenting the kitchen, and when he wasn't eating cinnamon rolls, helping Finn McLeevy with repairs. They played game after game of piquet and bézique in the library after supper, and on most mornings she and her brother rode in the warmth of the waning English summer. Jody was as charmed as she by the Kentish countryside, and Claire was glad of it. Whatever pain her marriage might have brought her, their situation at Wrensmoor was so much better than their life at Cheltdown Manor that she could have no real regrets.

This was, after all, what Edward had intended all along, thought Claire. The imprint of the first weeks of her marriage was fading, and the more she tried to cling to her memories, the faster they seemed to slip away. Already, it seemed almost ordinary to wake up alone. To sleep alone.

She wondered what Edward was doing and if he was with his new mistress. He must be, she decided. She would not think about it. She refused to think about it.

Jody had finally caught up to her, and his mare greeted Athene with a friendly nicker. They let the horses graze and walked through the tall grass for a while, picking wildflowers, while Jody treated her to a description of the newest tiff between Flora and Constance. The two girls had just barely managed to keep apace with their duties during the past few weeks as Constance vied with Flora to capture Jody's attention. Claire, who knew where a flirtation between a pretty lady's maid and "the young master" was likely to lead, had kept an eye on the proceedings, but so far neither girl had made much headway with her brother.

Apparently Jody was a bit too young to really enter into the spirit of the contest, although that, Claire knew, could all change in the course of even a few more months. Sixteen wasn't just fifteen plus a year. What if Flora and Constance were still making doe eyes at Jody when he discovered girls? Then what would she do?

It would certainly help to have a man's advice in this, she thought, sighing. Lord Tremayne would know how to guide her brother through the trials of late adolescence.

"What's wrong?" asked Jody, alert as always for any change in his sister's state of mind.

Claire laughed. "Nothing easily helped, I'm afraid."

"Claire—"

"Let's race," she told him, and they ran back to Artemis and Athene.

Lady Pamela watched the Earl of Ketrick as he danced

past her, and she frowned in dismay. Danilla Hansfort! It could hardly be worse.

"Is she his mistress yet, do you think?" asked Lady Detweiler, accurately gauging the direction of Pamela's interest. "I believe there's a wager going at White's about whom he'll finally choose."

Lady Pam shook her head. "Danilla? She's only been out of mourning a fortnight."

"A fortnight! That's as good as a year for her," said Amanda. "The lovely Danilla isn't going to waste time when it's the Earl of Ketrick in the offing."

"I'm afraid you're right," said Pam. "Damn! Why does she keep getting invited everywhere?"

"Entertainment value, I should think," was Amanda's comment.

Pam snorted. Danilla Hansfort wasn't good *ton*—not very good *ton*, anyway—but she was a widow, and widows were subject to fewer constraints in society than either wives or unmarried girls. Especially rich widows, which Lady Hansfort most assuredly was. Danilla had made no secret, from the earliest days of her mourning, that she would be in the market for a special . . . relationship as soon as she was out of her greys.

With a rich man, of course, but money wasn't everything Lady Hansfort was in the market for. Pamela remembered the sound of the woman's husky contralto as they had chatted in Lady Jersey's salon. "Darling, it's been almost a year! Who cares about boring old jewelry? What I need is a man in my *bed*." And Danilla had laughed, as if daring Lady Pam to be shocked. They didn't know each other very well, of course. After a lifetime among the *ton*, Lady Pam didn't think anything could shock her.

True love, she thought suddenly, smiling wryly to herself.

True love might just do the trick.

Danilla's crop of red hair was hard to miss, so Pamela and Lady Detweiler caught frequent glimpses of the earl and his partner as they continued around the ballroom, the unmistakable sound of Lady Hansfort's laugh floating across the parquet from time to time.

"She'll play the slut well, will she not?" asked Amanda.

Pam snorted again. It was hard to miss Danilla pressing herself hotly against Edward as they waltzed. Lady Pamela was not a prude, but the amount of bosom displayed by that particular gown was alarming. She made a sudden decision. Edward had sought out her hand in dance repeatedly during the last two months. She had refused him every time, but tonight—

Tonight she would make an exception.

"Amanda?"

"Hmm?" responded Lady Detweiler, still craning her neck in the direction of the waltzing pair.

"I need a small favor."

Jody sat with his sister and tried with little success to read Pindar as she concentrated on her needlework. It had been a trying day, between a call from the rector, who prosed on and on about the windows in the church until Jody thought he could scream from boredom, and a letter from Lady Gastonby, proposing a visit.

At least that danger had been averted. His normally polite sister had simply said, "No, I won't do it," and had written the earl's aunt an immediate reply, bidding her wait until her nephew was in residence. Subtlety, said Claire, was wasted on Lady Gastonby.

Jody turned the pages in his book from time to time but continued to glance covertly at his sister. Lord Tremayne was her husband! Didn't she even miss him? She must miss him. Jody was sure Claire was hiding her true feelings about the earl, but during the two months he had been at Wrensmoor, his sister had remained seemingly content. It was very frustrating.

"Ouch!" His sister yelped and popped a finger into her mouth.

Jody snickered. His sister was hopelessly inept at needlework. Why did she even continue in the attempt? Perhaps, he thought, she is trying to keep her mind off the earl.

He should be glad that Claire wasn't pining away for lost love. Still, if she insisted on being happy it was going to be a lot more difficult to persuade her to return to town. Jody had considered his options at some length during the past few weeks. He'd been quite excited by his first idea, which was to forge a letter from the earl, asking Claire to join him in London. Jody had even written a trial draft or two, but looking at the smudgy, ink-smeared sheets, he knew his sister would never be fooled. Besides, she surely knew Lord Tremayne's handwriting a lot better than he did.

And arguing with Claire simply hadn't worked. "This was the arrangement we agreed upon," she told him every time he broached the subject. "Lord Tremayne lives in town, and I live here. No more arguments!"

Maybe she *is* happy, thought Jody. Maybe I should leave well enough alone.

Lady Detweiler had played her part well, and the second waltz with Lord Tremayne now belonged to Pamela Sinclair instead of Lady Hansfort. As Pam danced away with Edward, she could see the annoyed widow out of the corner of her eye. Danilla was almost stamping her foot in frustration, with Amanda glued to her side, the picture of sympathetic innocence. Lady Detweiler was chatting away at top speed, talking to Danilla about . . . whatever it was that Amanda had insisted she *must* talk to her about.

Edward smiled down at Lady Pam. He was a marvelous dancer, and she felt herself gliding effortlessly across the floor. Pamela remembered the many waltzes she had shared with this man, and indulged a small pang of nostalgia. It really was a shame they had never managed to fall in love.

Edward was smiling down at her. "I'm glad you changed your mind," he said.

"Changed my mind? About what?"

"Dancing with me."

"I decided it was time we discussed your love life," Lady Pamela told him.

"Pam, no—" said the earl, a clear note of warning in his voice.

"Don't cut up snappish with me, young man," she said, and Edward laughed.

"I don't *have* a love life at the moment," he told her.

"You have a wife. Why are you not at Wrensmoor?" demanded Pamela. She felt the sudden tension in Edward's hands and saw the color that appeared on his cheekbones. Just a faint flush, of course, but she knew him too well to be fooled.

"I never planned on staying there. You knew that," he told her.

"Fustian. I know that's what you told me you *intended*," she said to him. "It was nonsense then, and it's nonsense now. You have an intelligent, beautiful wife. Why aren't you with her?"

The earl wouldn't meet Pam's eye. "I . . . can't," he finally said.

This was a start, at any rate. But men seemed to have an

inordinate lack of common sense when it came to their emotions. "You can't what? Be there? Be with Claire?"

"Yes to both," said Edward. "Pam, let's not discuss this."

"Ah! What would you prefer to discuss, my darling? The virtuous Lady Hansfort?"

He stared at her, then broke into a laugh. "Careful, Pam, I might think you're jealous."

"I," said Lady Pamela, "am not your *wife*. I am merely curious. Claire Tremayne"—she saw him wince at the name—"is not only prettier than Danilla Hansfort, she is also better bred, better spoken, and has some integrity of character."

"Pam—"

"Be careful what you throw away, Edward," she told him. "You might some day wish for it back."

They danced on in silence, Pamela judging that for now she had said all she dared. As the last strains of the waltz faded, Edward asked if she would like to join him for a stroll in the gardens. Fresh air was a relief after the stifling ballroom, and they walked along the raked gravel paths, listening to the sounds of the city in the distance. Several times the earl seemed about to speak, and Pam waited.

"You're right," he said at last. "I don't want Danilla Hansfort on my hands. I'm not sure why it ever seemed like a good idea."

Still she said nothing.

"Chedley has been throwing one woman after another at me for a month now," he added. "I couldn't—none of them—" He sighed. "But it's time, Pam," he said. "I need to return to my old life."

"Why?"

"It's who I am."

Pamela shook her head. A few yards away was a square of knotted herbs, and their clean scent perfumed the night air.

194

She found a clipped hedge of rosemary and bent to pick a sprig.

"I don't think it's who you are at all. And if you were happy with your old life, why did you bother to marry?"

"We've discussed this. I'll need an heir eventually, and Claire de Lancie solved that problem quite neatly. I'm sure she'll be a wonderful mother."

"Is Claire increasing yet?"

"No," said Edward, put off balance by the question. "No, I don't believe so."

"Well, then—"

"Pam . . ."

She turned and walked away, annoyed with Edward for his stubbornness and feeling guilty for her own part in his marriage. She could have ignored Edward's interest in finding out about the girl. But she had been so sure it was right, so sure that Claire de Lancie was the one for him. Had she been mistaken? Was *true love* still in wait, somewhere, for the Earl of Ketrick?

Perhaps it was, but she doubted love's name was Danilla Hansfort.

Cecil Drere and the viscount were still at White's when Edward arrived, although Cecil may not have been conscious. It was difficult to tell.

"Well, old man, how was the scrumptious Danilla?" asked Chedley. "Surely you've not conceded so early in the night? I'd always heard she was quite . . . demanding. Not to mention athletic."

The earl scowled and called for brandy. The viscount laughed and took a healthy swig from his own glass.

"Oh, come now, dear boy, this won't do. I simply will *not* believe that the lady wouldn't have you. It strains credulity."

Edward made a suggestion concerning the viscount's credulity. Chedley was unfazed.

"We had high hopes for your association with the widow Hansfort," he told the earl. "The wager in the betting book has crept up to five hundred pounds, you know."

"*What* wager?" growled Edward.

"Oh, don't tell me you haven't heard. Quantity is the contest, my dear boy, quantity! The wicked widow and the Earl of Ketrick are ripe for the prize, I'm sure. Nobody ever came close to you and the Huxley chit, even riding Pardy's best. And with the delectable Danilla to keep you pointing skyward—"

"Danilla Hansfort is a whore," Edward said suddenly, a little surprised at his own vehemence. Even the viscount seemed taken aback. Cecil stirred to life and sat up.

"A whore? Of course she is, old m-man," hiccupped Lord Drere. "Good heavens, what do you think you've been looking for this past month?"

As summer crept into autumn, Jody became convinced, despite himself, that Claire was content to live at Wrensmoor without Lord Tremayne. Her appetite was good, she laughed often, and she never complained. In fact, his sister rarely even alluded to the existence of a husband. So life at the castle was comfortable and easy, and they might never have gone back to London at all, had he not noticed Claire doodling one day at her writing desk.

She wrote regularly to her husband, Jody had discovered, although, to his disappointment, these letters were devoted almost exclusively to estate business. Claire was concerned about making expenditures for the castle without the earl's permission, a scruple which seemed absurd to her brother. He suspected that Claire could have purchased an entirely new stable of horses, and the gilt-covered carriages to match, without Lord Tremayne's lifting an eyebrow.

The earl never answered Claire's letters and, as far as Jody knew, she'd had no word from him since the day he left Wrensmoor. If he was my husband, thought Jody, *I'd* complain.

He found his sister in her study that morning, writing another short letter to be sent off to London. 'Twas the tapestries in the great hall this time, Jody learned. They'd been cleaned, but several of the oldest and most valuable ones needed repair. It was a dicey business, repairing old fabric, and this time Jody didn't blame his sister for wanting to check with Lord Tremayne before arranging to have it done. Noble families tended to get puckish about their tapestries.

Afterwards, however, he noticed her staring pensively out the window, scrawling absentmindedly on a sheet of blotting paper. Jody waited until she left the room, and hurried over to the desk.

Edward, Claire had written. *Edward. Edward. Edward.*

That was enough for Jody.

"Mmm, darling," Danilla was saying, "this is so cozy." The earl's carriage had plenty of room for more than the two people currently occupying it, but Lady Hansfort was almost sitting in Edward's lap. "Don't you want to come in for . . . tea?"

"No, thank you. Danilla—"

"Or you could have your man drive us somewhere." She was running light fingers up and down the taut fabric of his breeches, tracing the muscles of his thighs. "I find the motion of the carriage ever so stimulating, don't you?"

"No. Danilla—"

"Mmm." Lady Hansfort's voice remained light and seductive, but inwardly she sighed. What would it take to get the man into bed? Or into carriage, as it were. Danilla didn't mind where the Earl of Ketrick took her, as long as he did so, and she was running out of patience. She knew Lord Tremayne's reputation as a lover of great vigor and stamina, of course, it was one of the reasons she had chosen him for her first *affaire de coeur* after her husband's death. But the earl's legendary abilities *en rapports sexuels* would do her no good if he wouldn't respond. . . .

He *must* be responding, she decided. This absurd, frustrating man had to be responding, and was just trying to hide it from her. Lady Hansfort found this a perplexing state of affairs. She was offering herself to the Earl of Ketrick as an energetic and talented bed partner, no strings attached. Why, it would be most men's dream. Certainly he couldn't be worried about his silly wife, idling away in the wilds of Kent. What nonsense! If *she* had him to herself in some draughty old castle he wouldn't leave the bedroom for a month. The girl must be a positive antidote.

This is the end of it, she decided. She would give the earl another chance to seduce her and then look elsewhere. Lady Hansfort was choosy about her partners, but not impossibly so, and there were plenty of strong, male fish in the London seas.

Good heavens. Claire came to her feet, trembling, and stared at the heavy sheet of vellum in her hand. She shook her head to clear it, but the words remained obstinately the same, slanting across the page in Jody's careful hand.

Ma cher soeur,

It is no use. I have tried and tried to forget her, but I cannot.

198

She is all I ever wanted, and I must prove myself worthy of her name. I have gone to London to seek my fortune and I will not rest until I have made her my wife.

Do not search for me. I am sorry, dearest sister, to cause you pain, but I am sure that when you finally see her you will understand everything.

-J.

She didn't know whether to laugh or cry. The thought of her brother, whose main interest only this past summer was seeing how far he could spit grape seeds, in the throes of a *grande passion*—oh, it was too much. Claire forced herself to take several slow, deep breaths. Perhaps she should simply let Jody get this out of his system. A flirtation in London might be better, come to think of it, than ending up in the hayloft with Flora or Constance. The girl must be from a good London family—

But even as Claire considered the matter, she realized the situation could not be that simple. It was, in fact, potentially quite serious. As far as she knew, Jody had attended only a few entertainments in London. How had he met this girl? And what girl of good family would be allowed to keep company with a fifteen-year-old boy who claimed no fortune? Even as the Earl of Ketrick's ward—for that, in effect, was Jody's position—he was hardly of an age to be courting.

Oh. Goodness. Another possibility came abruptly to mind, and Claire's blood flowed icy in her veins. What if this girl was some . . . some creature of the demi-monde? What if Jody was being used, somehow, to extort money from Lord Tremayne? She wasn't sure why this possibility now struck her so forcibly, but she was suddenly terrified that her brother might, at this very moment, be in considerable trouble, and a cause of embarrassment to the Earl of Ketrick. She must stop this immediately. She must go to London.

If she couldn't find Jody herself, surely Lord Tremayne would help.

The Earl of Ketrick was a desperate man. How had he ended up escorting Danilla Hansfort home from one more dreary, interminable ball? He could barely endure the woman's company another moment. Lady Hansfort's hands were moving up and down his thighs, and she had somehow adjusted her bodice so that he could see practically the whole of each breast.

It would be so easy. So easy to have her, here and now, in the carriage. Edward tried to imagine himself on top of Danilla, pressing her down into the cushions of the coach, pushing her skirts aside with one hand, loosening the buttons of his breeches—

He imagined her face looking up at him, passionate, trusting—

Claire's face. Edward swore out loud.

"Darling?"

Women! A pox on the whole tiresome sex! Why not just take her now and be done with it? Tomorrow he could visit Gaston's, make some arrangement with Pardy, and never again need to see the same female twice. Yes, thought Edward. Gaston's was definitely the answer.

Can't you just hear Chedley laughing? came that obnoxious little voice, his constant companion for the last several months. Edward Tremayne, the Earl of Ketrick, resorting to whores! The viscount would surely see to it that no patron of White's remained uninformed of the earl's activities. If word ever got back to Claire—

Claire. But of course! said the little voice, mocking him. *You could always go return to Wrensmoor. Your wife is* there, remember her? You could bed her any time you pleased.

Edward groaned and swore again, louder. It was fortunate that the carriage had now stopped in front of Lady Hansfort's house, because the woman was relentless in her pursuit and the earl was nearing the end of his tether. Another ten minutes inside the coach and she would be unclothed. He grabbed suddenly for Danilla, who blushed prettily and cooed, "Oh, Edward, I never—"

Shouting for his driver, he flung the carriage door open and pushed her into the street, sticking his head out of the coach only long enough to ensure she had landed upright.

"Edward!" shrieked Lady Hansfort.

"Drive on!" yelled Edward.

Chapter Fourteen

Claire stepped out of the carriage and looked up at the lights of Tremayne House. She was exhausted from the drive, worried about Jody, and deeply apprehensive about seeing her husband again. There had been no time to warn him of her arrival, and she hoped *that* interview could be put off until the morrow.

The earl probably wasn't at home now, anyway. There are many things to keep one busy in London in the evenings, reflected Claire, with a tired sigh. So many ways for a man to occupy himself with a mistress. She started towards the steps, the front door looming above her. The thought that she would be knocking on that door as an unwelcome guest was oppressive.

Could Edward be at home? And if he was—

Oh, heavens, he wouldn't have *her* at Tremayne House, would he? Claire hesitated on the first step. What if, at this very moment, the earl and his mistress were . . .

Well, it couldn't be helped. She needed Edward's assistance, and, for Jody's sake, she would have to ask for it. Claire had faith in the essential goodness of her brother's nature. She didn't believe he would do anything intentionally hurtful, but there were too many ways in London for a naive boy to call down disgrace upon his head. And Jody's relationship to the Earl of Ketrick would make things worse, instead of better, if there was to be scandal.

She hated the possibility that the de Lancie name might involve the earl in gossip. Still, the sooner the matter was dealt with, the better. Jody had been gone only a day and a half, surely he couldn't have done anything irreparable yet. She mounted the steps, squared her shoulders, and lifted her hand to knock, remembering that with Boggs at Wrensmoor, the under-butler was now in charge at Tremayne House. What was his name? Oh, yes. Lodge.

Lodge opened the door, looking not the least bit surprised to see the Countess of Ketrick standing on the steps.

"Ah, your ladyship. I'm glad you've arrived safely."

"Ah . . . yes. Thank you, Lodge." Claire was confused. Who could have told the household that she was arriving? And if they knew, certainly Edward knew, too. Oh, dear.

"He's waiting for you in the library, my lady. He said you'd probably be tired but to please have a word with him first."

Lodge took her traveling cloak and was giving instructions to her driver as she pulled off her gloves. Claire, assuming they would take her things to the bedroom she had used before her marriage, did not pay much attention to what the butler was saying.

"Thank you, Lodge," she repeated, heading towards the library with heart pounding. She would have preferred a night's rest before facing Edward, but there it was.

The door to the library was ajar, and she could hear the crackle of a warm fire. Stopping briefly to take one deep breath, she stepped into the room to face—

Jody.

"Here, milady, let me take you to your rooms."

Claire looked up to see one of the maids—Sally?—standing at the library door. Jody must have rung for her after he left, thought Claire. How long had it been? How long had she been sitting here, staring into the fire?

"Thank you, Sally," she said, the words coming automatically to her lips. She followed the girl upstairs, her head aching with fatigue, too wrung out by the dispute with her brother to think coherently. First, some sleep, Claire told herself. And stop this fretting. No one has been injured, there will be no scandal, and you can sort out everything else in the morning.

The room Sally brought her to was not her old bedroom, but Claire was in no state to argue or even care. It was clean, the bed-linens were fresh, and she allowed herself to be undressed and tumbled into bed, asleep before her head reached the pillow.

The Earl of Ketrick was nowhere near as drunk as he would have liked to be. Brandy was the only way he could manage sleep lately, but he'd been partnering Cecil Drere at four-hand Casino all evening, and the cards had been flying too fast for drink. For his part, Edward would have been happy to lose the money and get back to the brandy, but he had Drere's finances to think of as well as his own. And, in truth, it would have been embarrassing to show up at White's more inebriated than his current partner. A man had to draw the line somewhere.

Edward had always been fascinated by how Cecil could remain perfectly sober at the card table. Lord Drere was consistently underestimated by his opponents, to the detriment of their finances, because everyone seemed to have difficulty thinking of him as anything other than a drunk. He and Cecil had won a tidy sum that evening.

And considering the substantial amounts that he knew Drere had won over the years, Edward reflected, perhaps the man is sober rather more often than one tends to think.

Edward wasn't sure how long he had been asleep or if he had slept at all, when he heard footsteps in the bedroom next to his. The countess's rooms—

Soft footsteps, as if someone was trying to creep unheard through the house. Edward heard the balcony doors open, and he was out of his bed swiftly, knife in hand, throwing open the door to the adjoining suite. It was a cloudy, moonless night, and he could barely distinguish a figure on the balcony. Edward was behind him in a moment, his knife at the man's throat—

And his hand brushed against soft skin, delicate bones, the pulse a quickened thrumming under his fingertips before he realized that the intruder was a woman, not a man and then, in confusion, that it was his wife.

She hadn't made a sound, but she put a hand to her throat, and Edward realized, to his stunned horror, that he had drawn blood.

"Dear Lord—lie down—I'll call the doctor at once—"

"Don't be ridiculous," came his wife's voice, sounding strangely calm. She was looking down at her fingertips. "It barely qualifies as a scratch. There might be a drop or two of blood all told."

Edward wasn't about to waste time arguing. He swept Claire into his arms and carried her to the bed. After lighting a candle he realized, with a wave of relief that pounded through his veins and left him weak, that she had been right. A tiny nick on the side of her neck had bled for a moment but was now stopped. He left to get a clean cloth and water from his own rooms, and by the time he returned, Claire was sitting up in her bed.

She smiled at him wryly. "Such a dangerous place, London. First I'm shot, and now my own husband has knifed me."

It was meant as a jest, but it was a poor one, and Edward had just had the scare of his life. Fear and relief had destroyed any self-control he might have otherwise mustered, and the words poured out of him with no thought to their effect.

"What are you doing here? You are never to come here! You are to stay at Wrensmoor! I believe I had made that perfectly clear!" he thundered.

"Edward—"

"How dare you come to London! I thought you were a thief! I could have killed you!"

"My lord—"

"And don't ask me if I'm quite through yet!" roared Edward. "No! I am *not* through!"

This was enough for Claire, who was now as angry as her husband. She swung her legs over the side of the bed and stood, tearing at the ties to her nightgown.

"Get back into bed at once!" shouted the exasperated earl. His mind flashed back to the moment he had held the knife at his wife's throat, and he shuddered and felt something threaten to break loose inside him. He could still see a delicate tracery of blood on her skin. . . .

She ignored him. Marching to the wardrobe, she pulled her nightgown off and chose her warmest day dress from the wardrobe. She started to put it on over her chemise.

"What do you think you're doing, you little idiot!"

"Leaving!" Claire yelled back at him. She was too upset to think where she could go in the middle of a London night. But if he thought he could stand there and *shout*—

The earl was in front of her in two long strides. He ripped the dress out of her hands, picked her up, and slung her over his shoulder.

"Let me go!"

She kicked and pounded with her fists to no avail. He

tossed her onto the bed and neatly sidestepped a flailing foot. The earl looked around for her nightgown; he found it, and threw it at her.

"Put this on! Now!"

She glared at him mutinously, but, feeling acutely vulnerable in her thin chemise, she donned the nightdress. It gave her a few moments to collect her wits, and the more she thought about her husband's behavior, the madder she felt.

She looked up from fastening the ties to see him sitting in a chair and staring at her, his expression unreadable. His next words, however, were clear enough.

"What the hell do you think you are doing, coming here?"

"If you'd given me the chance to explain," she informed him, "I would have told you. And don't swear at me."

Edward scowled. "You are my wife, and I'll speak to you any way I please. Now, what are you doing in London?"

Claire hesitated. She had known this question was coming, of course. She'd sat in the carriage all the way from Kent preparing her explanations, planning to ask the earl to help her find Jody.

Now what could she say?

The truth, she decided. It might make Jody seem flighty and irresponsible, but her brother was going to tell Lord Tremayne the entire story, anyway. If she told him first, perhaps he would have a chance to cool down before confronting Jody.

She searched for Jody's note and held the sheet out, wordlessly, to Lord Tremayne.

"What is this?" He scowled again, and took the vellum from her. She watched her husband's face as he read Jody's letter, seeing first puzzlement, then amusement. Finally, he burst into laughter.

"Who is she?" he asked Claire between chuckles. "He's a

handsome lad, of course, but I would have thought that at fifteen—"

"She doesn't exist," Claire told him. "Jody made it all
up."

"What?"

"It was just his way of getting me to come to London."
Then she told Edward the entire story, ending with Jody's
successful attempt to convince Lodge that this was all a grand
surprise to please the earl.

"Which explains why I didn't even know Jodrel was in the
house these past twenty-four hours."

"Yes. I believe he's been living in the kitchen on Mrs.
Huppins's fried apple tarts."

"Ah."

Silence fell between them. Then—

"It's freezing in this room," said Edward. "Why were you
out on the balcony? And why is your fire not lit?"

"I don't know," Claire told him. "I was so tired after arguing with Jody, I just went to bed. I don't remember waking
up, but I must have gone out to the balcony thinking I was at
Wrensmoor."

"This is the countess's suite."

"Ah."

The earl's last words hung in the air between them. These
were "the countess's rooms," Claire noted, not "your
rooms." But then, what did she expect? Lord Tremayne had
never planned on seeing her here.

"I am very tired, my lord," Claire said finally, as the earl
showed no signs of moving from his chair. "I should like to re-
tire."

"Yes. Of course," said her husband.

And he left. The Earl of Ketrick slept very badly that
night.

Claire found her brother at breakfast the next morning. "I'm going home," she told him, without preamble.

"What? Not *today!*" Jody looked at his sister in consternation. She couldn't leave! Not after all the trouble he'd gone to in getting her to London! Jody was about to voice further protest when he glanced again at his sister and saw the droop of her shoulders, the pain in her eyes. She seemed thoroughly exhausted, and although he had been waiting for months to see her look heartsore, now that his wish had been granted he felt ashamed.

Why couldn't he have left well-enough alone?

"No, I couldn't face another long carriage ride today," Claire was saying. "But I'll leave first thing tomorrow morning. I'm sure you're welcome to stay in London, by the way. I don't believe Lord Tremayne's prohibition extends to brother's-in-law."

"His prohibition—!"

"You know what I mean. I'm not supposed to be here."

"Oh, Claire, I am sorry," said Jody.

"It's all right," she told him. "It was so easy to be content at the castle, maybe I didn't appreciate Wrensmoor as much as I should have. Now, when I go back, I'll know enough to be happy there."

And Jody had to be satisfied with that answer, as his sister would say no more on the subject.

Claire had fully intended to leave town on Wednesday, as she had told her brother, but events conspired against her. After breakfast she received, to her surprise, an invitation to a *musicale* the next evening at the house of Edwina, Lady Kensington. How anyone had managed to find out so quickly that she was in town, Claire could not imagine, nor why Lady

Kensington would invite her to a *musicale*. She'd never even met the woman.

When Edward heard about the invitation, he understood the mystery immediately. But then, he knew something his wife did not: Edwina Kensington was Amanda Detweiler's niece. Lady Pamela's sources of information were impeccable, as always, and she worked fast.

The thought of taking Claire to the Kensington affair left Edward with curiously mixed feelings, which he preferred not to examine. Squiring his wife rather than a new mistress around town should have been anathema to him. It *was* anathema, he told himself—yes, everything was in a wretched muddle.

But, on the other hand, one evening could hardly signify, since he would make sure Claire returned to the castle within the sennight. He *had* held a knife to his wife's throat last night, after all. This might be a good way to make amends and to ensure they were still . . . friends . . . before she returned to the country.

Friends.

Unbidden, his mind returned to the events of the previous night, Claire standing in the countess's suite, shivering in that filmy chemise, her eyes blazing with fury. This would never do. One *musicale* was the absolute limit. Then he would lock his recalcitrant wife into a carriage, if need be, and pack her off to Kent.

Claire refused to spend the day trapped in the countess's rooms. After enjoying the freedom of Wrensmoor, she found it difficult to stay indoors for even a single morning, and by noon she was rummaging through the wardrobes for a walking dress. Fortunately, she had planned for a longer stay in London and had brought a selection of clothing. Although now that she thought of it, no formal dress. Perhaps she would have to forego Lady Kensington's *musicale* after all.

The thought was depressing. Although Claire had not come to London with any idea of society entertainments, she realized she had been looking forward to tomorrow evening. Music was one thing that Wrensmoor lacked. And Edward had said he would escort her.

There must be a way she could manage to attend the event. Claire went back to the selection of clothing she had brought from Wrensmoor, determined to find something that might, with some alteration, serve as an evening *ensemble*. The maid had arranged her things in the wardrobe, and as Claire looked through them she found a beautiful gown of emerald-green silk, obviously unworn. She had no idea how it had gotten there. Claire laid out the dress on the lace counterpane of the bed and sat down next to it, wondering if it belonged to Edward's mistress. Was the woman having her new outfits delivered directly to Tremayne House? And delivered straight to the *countess's* rooms? Of all the nerve!

Who was she? Would Claire see her while she was in London, even—oh, heavens—at the *musicale?* Claire wondered what the etiquette was for that situation. Would they be introduced? Would Claire know it was she? Would people be laughing and talking behind her back—?

The gown must belong to his mistress, she decided, noticing that the *décolletage* was rather daring. It was hard to tell for certain without putting the garment on, of course. Claire smoothed the green silk under her hand. Surely the woman couldn't be a blonde. A blonde would look dreadful in this color, whereas *she,* on the other hand, could wear it nicely.

Well, it would not do for a walk in St. James's Park, and that was where Claire was going now. Putting the gown back in the wardrobe, she drew out a serviceable wool and dressed quickly. The sun was shining and she needed to feel the grass under her feet. She slipped downstairs and out the door with only a footman in attendance, thinking that Edward would probably disapprove. Well, it was just too bad. If he didn't want her in London in the first place, he could hardly have much interest in where she spent her time while she was here. She set out at a brisk pace for the park.

"Where is she!"

Jody bit his lip. "I don't know," he admitted. "Claire seemed a little dispirited this morning. Perhaps she's gone for a ride—"

"I already checked the stables. She hasn't taken a horse." Edward was beside himself with fury. This, *this* was why the woman would have to stay at Wrensmoor. He had things to do today, business to attend to, and he didn't have time to be chasing a flighty, hare-brained female around London. It would serve her right if he just left her out there to be accosted by the first foot-pad that came along, or to be dragged into some fetid alleyway by a sotted lecher. But when he thought about the number of ways that his lackwit wife could get into trouble in town, his blood ran cold. Edward knew he wasn't going to leave Claire on the streets of London. In fact, he knew he wouldn't have a moment's rest until his wife was back at Tremayne House. Curse it all.

"Jodrel, where would she go?" the earl asked, worried that he already knew the answer.

"To the parks, I suppose," said the boy.

"For the love of—she was *shot* at in the parks!"

"But . . . but that was just an accident," stammered Jody, clearly confused by the earl's anger.

Blast and damnation, he was surrounded by infants.

Lord Tremayne forced himself to speak calmly. "Indeed," he told Jody. "Well, St. James's Park is closest. Let's start there."

Claire took a deep breath and felt her cares dissolve as the sounds of city life faded into the distance. Even deep in the park there were too many people to pretend that one was in the country, but here the smells of grass and leaf mold prevailed over London's ever-present odors of coal dust and horse manure.

As she walked along the edge of a meadow, enjoying the season's last bits of color in the drifts of autumn crocus, Claire considered her situation as dispassionately as she could. She knew she was at least half in love with her husband. That was a pity, but it couldn't be helped.

So what do you really want? she asked herself.

To live with Edward. Preferably at Wrensmoor for most of the year, but if it has to be London, then London it is.

But how could this be achieved? If she threw herself at him, tried to make a more substantial place for herself in his life, perhaps he would take her in disgust. She couldn't stand that. And did she really need to force her presence on him? She wasn't with child, so if Edward wanted an heir, they would need to spend more time together at some point. Eventually, he would come to her.

So. Go back to Wrensmoor, a quiet, obedient wife, and leave well enough alone. The arguments in favor of this were indisputable, but at some deep, almost wordless level, Claire resisted them. She could see where her happiness dwelt, now, and it was not in her nature to wait for it to come to her. How could she leave London as if her husband's company meant nothing?

At least, she thought, at least I can attend the *musicale* with

Edward tomorrow evening. In that emerald silk gown, if I have to.

And tonight?

She blushed as an image came to mind of what she was hoping for that evening. Her husband didn't seem to be terribly difficult to seduce.

Yes, said a little voice, but that was in the country, without his mistress. Here, he can just leave you and go to her.

Her pace had quickened with these thoughts, and she found herself nearing a gravel path with a glint of water seen in the distance beyond the trees. She moved from the path and sat down with her back against a smooth-barked oak. The quiet here was not like Wrensmoor's, to be sure, but it would do. The smell of crushed grass comforted her with its familiarity, and she closed her eyes, hoping to be unnoticed by the other park denizens. Imagine, the Countess of Ketrick sitting on the ground! And in a public park, my heavens! London society was ever alert for the possibility of scandal, and she supposed this would do, if nothing better came along that day.

For the moment, she didn't care. She ignored Edward's footman who had stopped a discreet distance away.

It was a warm day for early fall, and she must have dozed off. The next thing she was aware of was the sound of approaching hoofbeats. Claire opened her eyes and her heart identified the rider even before her mind made the connection.

A tall man on a huge black horse.

"Claire!"

What was her husband doing in the park? she wondered.

Achilles thundered closer, and she could see that Edward was scowling ferociously. Claire stood and brushed bits of grass off her skirts. Bother the man! She was staying out of his way, why couldn't she be allowed a few minutes of peace?

"What in heaven's name do you think you are doing?" Edward shouted. He had jumped from Achilles and was striding towards her. His riding crop was in his hand, and for a fraction of a second Claire had the absurd notion that he was going to use it on her. She resisted the impulse to cringe and, instead, went forth on the attack.

"I am taking the air, my lord!" she replied, her voice as tart as she could manage. "I should think you would be happy, as it means I am not occupying space at Tremayne House."

"You," said the earl, "are not supposed to be in London at all. But while you are here—"

"While I am here, my lord, I intend to take every opportunity to enjoy what the city has to offer."

"There seem to be no end of things I must make clear to you," said Edward, his voice ragged and harsh. "You are not to set foot outside Tremayne House while you are in London without my escort or my express permission."

"I shall set foot where I please."

"I am not in an arguing mood, lady wife." Edward grabbed Claire's hand and started dragging her towards Achilles. He waved a dismissive hand at the footman, standing a useless dozen yards away. Even the knowledge that Claire had had the sense to take a footman did nothing to lessen his fury.

Physical resistance would have been futile, and Claire didn't bother to attempt it. She muttered imprecations as he threw her up onto the stallion's back and mounted behind her. She felt his broad chest against her shoulders and, as Achilles surged forward, the hard iron of his forearm locked around her waist.

They made their retreat to Tremayne House without another word exchanged, and Claire had to be content with the obvious signs that the earl was as uncomfortably aware of her body as she was of his.

When Claire entered the dining room that evening she discovered, to her horror, that Lady Gastonby was also in residence. Jody could have warned her, but having found his sister a rather prickly companion that day, he was haunting the kitchen.

The threesome of herself, the earl, and Lady Gastonby was not a felicitous combination on any occasion, but Claire smiled graciously, determined to act as if she belonged at this table. To her surprise, she soon discovered that Penelope Gastonby was, wittingly or not, an ally. Of sorts.

" 'Tis past time you brought your bride to town, nephew," was her opening salvo. "And clearly she's not breeding yet."

"Aunt Penelope—" began the earl. Claire stared into her soup.

"What ails you, boy?" continued Lady Gastonby, relentless. "You left her in the country with no babe? She ought not be out of her bed! Nor ought you!"

"Aunt, this really isn't—"

"Lady Gastonby, I am sure that—" began Claire, but immediately realized that it was a mistake to enter into this conversation. The aunt's attention was now turned toward her.

"And aren't you a sorry little excuse, rattling around in a huge castle all by yourself! Most men can only dream of posting paid to a figure like that, and you married to the randiest lord in Christendom!"

"Penelope," said the earl. Claire had never heard that particular note in his voice before.

Lady Gastonby remained undeterred. "Why, any fool can see the man's trousers swell every time you walk into the room," she continued. "Whatever possessed you to—"

Claire, who was unaccustomed to the considerably earthier conversation of Lady Gastonby's youth, had flushed red to the roots of her hair. She fought off the urge to flee. "Lady Gastonby, I don't care to pursue this conversation," she said, deciding to stand her ground. The earl's aunt had chased her out of enough rooms in Tremayne House already.

"Nor do I, Aunt. Claire—"

"What twaddle," said Lady Gastonby. "I don't know about you, young miss, but unless my harebrained nephew has taken a whore—"

That was enough.

"Claire." Edward pushed back his chair.

But he was too late. Claire was out the door and up the staircase to her rooms before he had a chance to stop her.

Edward was furious.

"What ails you, madam?" he said to Lady Gastonby. "This isn't the eighteenth century anymore! One does not speak that way in front of gently bred females!"

"Bah," said his aunt. "These modern misses! A bunch of namby-pamby sucklings, if you ask me."

"I didn't!"

"And the men are no better! What you need is a good dose of plain speaking, nephew," continued Lady Gastonby.

"I very much doubt I need any such thing."

"So I suppose you'd prefer to continue this mad pretense that you don't care enough about your new wife to get her with child?"

"Well, of course I care about her—"

Lady Gastonby stood so suddenly that her chair almost tipped over. The footman rushed forward to rescue it. She thumped her cane on the carpet.

"You most certainly do not!"

"Aunt, I assure you—"

"You do not," said Lady Gastonby, "merely 'care' about your wife. You are clearly besotted with her, and this absurd separation between the two of you must come to an end."

She thumped her cane again and marched out of the room.

Edward sank back into his chair and put his head in his hands. Finally he raised his gaze to the footman.

"Samuel?"

"My lord?"

"Please tell Mrs. Huppins to send the remaining courses to the countess's and Lady Gastonby's rooms."

"Yes, my lord."

"I'll be dining at the club tonight. And Samuel—"

"My lord?"

"Stop smirking."

"Yes, my lord."

The footman turned and left—still smirking, Edward had no doubt.

In love with his wife! What nonsense.

Claire pushed shut the door to the countess's suite and leaned against it, breathing hard. The woman was unbelievable! Apparently no subject was so delicate that Lady Gastonby was unwilling to tromp right into the middle of it. She was probably, even now, quizzing Edward on the particulars of his bedroom activities—

This particular thought was too much for Claire's composure. She collapsed on the bed, giggling, remembering her husband's face as Lady Gastonby had rung him a peal.

Claire's laughter continued for several minutes and then, abruptly, she began to cry.

Chapter Fifteen

The evening of Lady Kensington's *musicale* arrived before Claire saw her husband again. She didn't think Edward had slept in his rooms the night before, although the door connecting the two suites was locked from his side, so she couldn't be sure.

Would she have gone to him again, in the dark of the night? Perhaps not. Claire imagined herself creeping into her husband's chamber, all lace and scanty *négligé,* only to find his bed already . . . occupied.

Who *was* she? Claire imagined a stunning beauty, her golden hair cropped in the latest style.

But her mind wouldn't proceed much further than that. Would she see her husband's mistress at the *musicale* tonight, with everyone else already knowing who she was? It was probably too much to hope that Edward had simply returned to Lady Pamela. Deciding to make a particular effort with her *toilette,* Claire turned her attention to the mirror.

An elegant lady in green silk, her large silver-grey eyes heavily fringed with black lashes, stared back at her. The face, although a trifle pale, was accented with full, red lips, and the *décolletage* seemed, to Claire's unjaded eyes, to be fairly spectacular.

As it happened, Sally had informed her that the emerald-green gown was indeed Claire's own, a creation of Madame

Gaultier's that had been delivered to Tremayne House in her absence. Claire ran a hand along the smooth silk, adjusting the bodice. The deep neckline, combined with the tiny cap sleeves set low on her shoulders, exposed more of her bosom than was her custom, but Claire decided she liked the effect. She took Edward's wedding gift out of its case and fastened the heavy necklace around her throat. The emeralds were stunning with the green silk of the gown, and she hoped that Edward would not think to wonder why she had brought them on what was to be a mission of rescue. Claire had kept the necklace and its matching earrings on her bedstand each night the earl had been gone from Wrensmoor, the glittering gems a reminder of her husband.

'Twas a poor substitute, she knew.

Sally arrived to arrange her hair, first piling raven curls on atop her head and then threading them through with a fine gold chain.

"Ah, milady, 'tis lovely," said the maid, and Claire, normally indifferent to her own beauty, was inclined to agree. At the least, the *ton* would have no reason to believe that the Earl of Ketrick kept his wife in the country because he couldn't bear to look at her.

Edward stood next to the carriage and watched his wife descend the front steps of Tremayne House. He could not have explained the pain he was feeling at this moment, but pain it certainly was. Iron bands seemed to constrict his heart, leaving him frowning and short-tempered.

"My lady," he said to Claire, and handed her up into the carriage with a curt nod. She smiled at him.

The devil's knees, the evening was just beginning, and Edward had no idea how he was going to survive through to the end. He could not now remember why he had agreed to escort his wife to this blasted *musicale*—damn Pamela Sinclair, anyway! What did she care if he took another mistress or twenty of them! He'd had a plan, a carefully thought out plan. His wife and children at Wrensmoor, himself free to pursue entertainments in town—

What could he have been thinking, to escort his *wife* to this ridiculous affair? He understood better than Claire what the presence of the Countess of Ketrick in London would signify once word had spread among the *ton*. Tremayne House would be besieged with invitations—high teas, *soirées dansantes*, balls. It would never end.

Are you happy, Pam? thought Edward, knocking a clod of dirt from his left boot with a vicious swipe. Happy to see me forced to order Lady Tremayne back to Wrensmoor? He entered the carriage and sat down opposite Claire, glaring at her. There was a moment of sharp satisfaction as he saw the smile fade from her face, and then the pain returned in treble force.

His wife. What was he going to do?

Claire sat stiffly in the chair and listened to the soaring notes of the *aria*. Apparently Lady Kensington took her music seriously, for Madame Cavalietta was a fine soprano, her voice pure and with a melancholy edge that made Claire want to cry. She blinked rapidly and dragged her attention back to the *aria*. She would not cry. She *could* not cry, not here, in front of what, even to Claire's naive eye, was obviously the cream of the *ton*.

She'd been a fool to come, a fool to think that Edward would find pleasure in even a single London evening in his wife's company. He sat next to her, unmoving, his legs stretched out in front of him, and again his body seemed to intrude on her space, his lungs using up all the air in her vicinity. They had not spoken a word to each other since the introductions, and the only thing currently raising Claire's spirits was the warmth of Edwina Kensington's reception. Edwina had promised to introduce Lady Tremayne to *everyone.* Claire was pleased, thinking that if her husband wouldn't talk to her, perhaps someone else would.

A movement to her right caught Claire's eye. Good heavens, was that very well favored young man ogling *her?*

Edward's scowl deepened. To whom was Claire talking now? His wife had been in the middle of a crowd of admirers almost before the last notes of Madame Cavalietta's *chanson* had stopped echoing in the air, and now she was chatting with that whelp Radleigh. Radleigh! Edward's fists clenched at his sides. Benjamin Radleigh, heir to a dukedom, rich, charming and one of the handsomest men in the room.

Unmarried, too! came that small, irritating voice. *Radleigh could be talking to any female in the room, but he chose your wife!*

Edward felt someone's gaze on his back and looked around to see Amanda Detweiler watching him. She smiled and turned away, but not before Edward experienced a moment of perfect, uncanny communication.

Be careful, Lord Tremayne, Amanda's eyes had said, as clearly as if the words had been written before him in pen and ink. *Be careful. One man's throw-away—*

—is another man's treasure. How well he ought to know it.

Claire was experiencing a novel sensation, which was exciting at the same time that it troubled her. Men of every age and station of life had flocked around her at the conclusion of Madame Cavalietta's performance, and now—

Now, she was being *courted.* By the Marquis of Leddsfield, no less, the very handsome and charming Benjamin Radleigh.

He had taken up station at her left hand and showed no sign of being willing to give way to any other admirers. It was . . . flattering.

Lord Radleigh was a younger man than the earl, more her own age, in fact, and Claire was quite taken by the quiet sincerity of his manner. He was dressed fashionably, but not as a dandy, and his warm brown eyes seemed ever full of laughter. Unlike her husband, there seemed to be no underlying dark currents to his spirit, no banked fires ready to flare up at the slightest provocation. The marquis was, to give the long and short of it, very pleasant company, and Claire wasn't silly enough to claim that she didn't enjoy the attention.

"Tell me about Wrensmoor," said Lord Radleigh. He seemed genuinely interested as she described the castle. Just minutes ago he had taken her gloved hand and kissed it, a gesture so evidently heartfelt that Claire—although she felt no answering tingle, no shiver running to her toes—had given him a wide smile.

"Leddsfield."

The deep voice of her husband, almost in her ear, startled Claire.

"Ketrick," said Lord Radleigh. The young man seemed undaunted by the earl's glowering presence, and Claire's estimation of him rose. "I've just been asking your lovely countess for the pleasure of her company tomorrow for a ride in the park."

Claire stared at him. What was Lord Radleigh talking about?

"My wife does not drive out much," said the earl, and Claire felt his grip tighten on her elbow. As Edward steered her away towards the buffet table, she risked a look back at the Marquis of Leddsfield.

Benjamin Radleigh grinned at her and winked.

"Good heavens."

Claire opened the door to the sitting room the next morning to find every possible inch of table or mantel space taken up with flowers. Her husband stood in the midst of it all, scowling, and Claire had the odd impression that he had just thrown something into the fire.

"You seem to have made quite an impression on Lord Radleigh," he told her, his voice tight. "Half of these seem to be from him."

"Goodness."

"Indeed," said the earl. He slit open one of the many envelopes of crisp vellum scattered among the flowers, and Claire heard him snort in disgust.

"What is it?" she asked.

"The Duchess of Lincolnshire writes to remind me that the duke's ball is only three days hence. 'We had not thought to see you,' " the earl read aloud, " 'but since your lovely countess is now in town—' "

He snorted again. "A pox on it! We shall have to go."

"The Duke of Lincolnshire's ball . . . Isn't that the one—?"

"Yes," said her husband. "The one out-of-season ball that everyone *must* attend. In bejeweled herds, like the well-trained sheep that we are."

"If you mislike it so much, why bother?" Claire asked, trying to keep her voice cool and light. "I leave first thing tomorrow morning, anyway, so it has nothing to do with me."

"Unfortunately, it does," said Edward, a turn of phrase that did nothing to improve Claire's mood. "As of yesterday, everyone knows you're in town. If you were to leave now, only days before the Lincolnshire ball, it would be much remarked. It might even be considered a snub."

"I see. You do not wish to be in the briars with your fellow sheep."

Edward threw down the invitation and advanced towards her. Claire stood her ground against his obvious anger. "It is not my reputation at stake here. It is yours. Snub the Lincolnshires, and you will be cast out of London society without a further thought."

"Ah, yes," said Claire. "London society. It would indeed be a great loss to me if I were unable to go about in *London* society."

Edward reached for her arm, but Claire twisted away.

"I will not have your name bandied about, one more item of stupid *ton* gossip, whether you are willing or not!" the earl snapped, almost snarling. The much-vaunted coolness of the Tremayne temper seems to be missing lately, Claire thought. It didn't improve her own mood.

"I will not go," she told him. "I have no gown."

"Madame Gaultier can be here within the hour."

"I will not go!" she cried. "It was your choice to banish me from town. Take your mistress to this ball and be done with it!"

She moved to leave the room, but this time Edward caught her. He took her by the shoulders and Claire looked up to see the muscles tensing in his jaw. For a nameless moment she thought he was about to kiss her, then abruptly, he thrust her away.

"I will hear no more about this," he said. "We will attend the Lincolnshire ball."

He left the room, and Claire, rooted in place, listened as the sound of his angry footsteps faded away down the hall. After a moment she regained her composure and flopped down on the nearest sofa.

"Blast the man!"

In the few days that remained before the ball, the Earl and Countess of Ketrick received a small blizzard of invitations for various society events. Claire left her husband to deal with them. She spent a great deal of time with Madame Gaultier in the mornings, rode twice in Regent's Park with Lord Radleigh, and saw very little of Edward at all. He had chosen to remain absent from her bed, and she assumed he was spending nights with his mistress. Whoever she might be.

On the few occasions that she did see Edward in passing, Claire sometimes thought she detected a flicker, a spark of something in his eyes. But his temper was generally so ill that she simply let things be. If he chose to ignore her—well, then, he chose to ignore her. She would be returning to Wrensmoor soon, and she was going to be happy.

Claire awoke sometime in the middle of the night, a prickle of fear running down her spine. What—? She knew she had been asleep, but still, hadn't she heard a cry?

She slid to the side of the bed to stand, and her heart leaped into her throat as she saw the pale figure on the other side of the room.

Oh. She laughed shakily. It was only her new gown. Madame Gaultier had delivered it that afternoon, a full twenty-four hours before the ball. It hung against the wardrobe, a ghostly presence, with its silver netting glinting in the moonlight.

But—what was that? This time Claire knew she had heard a cry, and she realized it came from her husband's bedroom. She padded softly toward the connecting doorway, thinking it must still be locked. Closer, she realized the door was ajar. One of the maids must have left it that way, she thought. She reached out to push it open—

It suddenly occurred to her that a man or woman in the throes of . . . passion might cry out, and she stilled her hand. But the sound had not seemed to be *that* sort of sound and, hearing a third cry, she realized that Edward was having another nightmare. Entering his bedroom, she made her way quickly to the side of his bed.

Lord Tremayne slept uneasily, the bedding thrown aside, his brow covered with a sheen of perspiration.

"My love," he muttered.

Claire's breath caught in her throat.

"No!" said the earl. It was a cry of despair.

She leaned forward to smooth the hair from his forehead. "Edward," she whispered. "My lord, wake up."

His eyes flew open but did not appear to focus. He reached out and pulled her down to him, clinging to her passionately. He's still half asleep, she told herself, her own desires embarrassingly quick to surface.

"Claire," he said, his breathing ragged. "Claire."

"Are you awake now, my lord?" she asked, trying not to surrender completely to her own emotions. " 'Twas but a nightmare."

Abruptly she felt Edward's body go rigid. His eyes focused, and he sat up.

"What are you doing here?" he demanded.

"You were having a nightmare," she said. "I heard you cry out—"

"Get out!"

"Gladly, my lord!" Claire answered, stung by his tone. She rose to her feet and smoothed her nightgown. "I shall disturb you no longer—"

"And you are never to enter this room again!" Edward hissed.

"Oh!" cried Claire, and she stomped back into her own

rooms, slamming the door behind her.

A few minutes later she heard Edward's door open, and close, and his footsteps descending the staircase.

I suppose a mistress is accustomed to being awakened in the middle of the night, thought Claire tiredly. It was a long time before she slept, and she was not to see her husband again until he waited to hand her up into the carriage on the way to the Duke of Lincolnshire's ball.

Edward lay in bed, his ears alert for the slightest sound from the countess's suite. But after the reverberations from the slammed door had died out, there was nothing.

Why had he pushed her away? He'd no reason to behave so discourteously as his wife's presence in London was hardly her fault. And he could hardly deny that she cut a fine figure among the *ton*. Edward had seen the envious glances directed his way at the *musicale*. His wife had proved herself a worthy countess in every respect he could name. Beautiful, intelligent, an enjoyable companion. . . .

Edward closed his eyes and, immediately, images from his nightmare returned in vicious force.

Melissa—no, not Melissa. It was Claire in the arms of another man.

A gold locket glittered in the hollow of her neck. She was waving good-bye, and Edward felt a blinding anguish. He called out, pleading with her to stay.

Claire laughed at him. "I'll gladly stay at Wrensmoor, my lord," she taunted. "Without you!"

She took the arm of her paramour and walked away without a backward glance.

Edward sought out Frederick for comfort, but his brother only shrugged.

"Let her go," said Frederick. "You are far better off alone."

Edward was once again on the steps of St. Alban's. Claire stood beside him, smiling, her hand in his.

No. No! She fainted, and once again Edward saw the blood.

None of it made any sense. Edward *knew* it made no sense. His wife was chaste. Why he should think otherwise, or why he should imagine Claire as he had last seen Melissa . . .

It was only a dream. But the man in the dream had felt a pain that Edward had no wish to ever again feel. He remembered Teddy Alnwick's drunken speech at White's—

Love is the end of a man's life.

He would not let it be the end of his.

Unable to sleep, he rose from his bed and dressed, deciding that this was an opportunity for a late night foray to White's. He slipped quickly through the darkened streets, oblivious to everything but his own thoughts, and as his distance from Tremayne House grew his breathing calmed and his mind seemed to clear. By the time Edward reached the club he had decided that he had been right all along. Claire would return to Wrensmoor Park, and he would remain free, and at his ease in London.

Lady Pamela watched Lord Tremayne and his countess enter the ballroom. Claire's dress became her well, thought Pam, satisfied to think that Madame Gaultier, her own *modiste* as well, had managed to turn out such a beautiful gown in under three days' time. The silver gauze of the overskirt was a particularly nice touch.

"Good heavens, what is *she* doing here?" asked Lady Detweiler.

Lady Pamela turned her attention from the Tremaynes

and looked around to see the unmistakable figure of Danilla Hansfort on the arm of—

Basil Edgecombe?

"The man must be nearly eighty!" Amanda was saying. "She'll kill him!"

Pamela frowned. Lord Edgecombe had a comfortable fortune, but he certainly didn't have the special male . . . talent that Danilla had declared to be her primary interest.

On the other hand, mused Pam, he did have *entrée* into every house of the *ton,* something Danilla Hansfort assuredly did not.

Lady Detweiler had come to the same conclusion. "I bet Lincolnshire didn't invite the little widow," said Amanda. "I wonder how long it will take her to unload Basil and find new prey." Pamela sighed. She saw Danilla look around the ballroom, saw the widow fasten her eyes on Lord Tremayne. Oh Edward, thought Pam. If you're going to encourage that absurd woman again, I may just have to wash my hands of you.

The Marquis of Leddsfield was a fine dancer, although perhaps not so polished in his steps as the Earl of Ketrick. Claire whirled around the room in his arms, and felt, for the moment, anyway, like the belle of the ball.

"You are the loveliest creature here," Lord Radleigh had told her, insisting on the first waltz. She had noted her husband's frown as Radleigh spirited her away from a group of admirers and had felt his gaze on her back. But now . . .

"Who is the woman Lord Tremayne dances with?" she asked her partner. She felt his hesitation.

"Lady Danilla Hansfort," said the marquis, finally. "Widow of Lord William Hansfort this year past."

Claire raised her eyebrows. The lady in question was spectacularly well-endowed, and her *décolletage* was so low—

"Do they ever fall out?" she asked Lord Radleigh, and then blushed hotly. "Oh, I beg your pardon, I can't imagine how I came to say that."

The marquis shouted with laughter. "I believe that on one occasion 'they' did," he told her. "It was reportedly a memorable episode, but I regret to say that I was not among those present." Lord Radleigh was still chuckling.

"Dear me," said Claire, still blushing. "I hope you don't imagine that I am usually so . . . so indecorous."

Lord Radleigh gave her a long, warm look. "Oh no, my lady," he said. "I wouldn't believe that of you at all. What I *do* believe, however," continued the marquis, "is that your husband is a fool."

Claire stared at him. The dancers swirled around them, and her feet moved in the proper time as the waltz continued, but she no longer heard the music over the beating of her own heart.

"Oh Harry," said Amelie Clarence, "isn't this ball simply delicious?"

The young man at her side was disinclined to agree. Harry Rutherford never felt comfortable at any ball, let alone a crush such as this, and he was forcibly aware that he was invited only because of the Clarences. Heaven knew how his father had convinced Lord Clarence to sponsor him, he was gangly and awkward and always seemed to say the wrong thing.

He hated crowds. Looking around for means of escape, Harry noticed a tall, raven-haired woman surrounded by admirers—

Good gracious.

"What is it, Harry?" asked Amelie. "You look as if you've

seen a ghost!" The girl tittered, a sound that never failed to set his teeth on edge.

"Harry?"

"No," her partner said, "not a ghost. Just someone I didn't realize was still in town."

Edward had not expected to see Danilla Hansfort in the Lincolnshire ballroom—the duchess had rather definite ideas on who qualified as *haut ton*—but there she was, leading poor Basil Edgecombe around by the nose. The man was a fool, with a besetting weakness for large-bosomed females, and Danilla's breasts were certainly on display tonight.

Edward could see the widow surveying the room and decided it was time to take steps to evade her notice. But his height made him an easy target in a crowd, and he soon realized that it was too late, that Danilla was already edging towards him through the crush of people. Why she would even speak to him after their last meeting, when he had practically pushed her out of his carriage, was beyond his understanding.

Well, no, it wasn't. He knew what Danilla really wanted, and he was aware of what aspect of his own reputation continued to intrigue her. Edward scowled, thinking he had suffered enough at the hands of demanding females. It was time to visit Gaston's, to make his arrangements there. Lady Hansfort would need to contain her disappointment this evening, because he wasn't about to—

The sea of waltzing couples parted for a moment, and he saw across the ballroom to where his wife turned and glided on Leddsfield's arm. She was laughing, noticed Edward, laughing and smiling the wide, blinding smile that always took his breath away.

"Hmm," came a familiar, sultry murmur at his elbow. "I

see Lord Radleigh is collecting your castoffs."

"Damn you, Danilla, shut up," said the earl.

Lady Hansfort laughed. "My, my, so touchy! Shouldn't I be the offended party? After our last encounter—"

"Ah, yes. My apologies, Lady Hansfort. I can't imagine what I was—"

Danilla gave an airy, dismissive wave. "Apologies are boring," she said, adding, "Come waltz with me, my lord."

The earl frowned at her.

"Oh, don't worry! I have no long term designs on your virtue, I assure you!"

"Danilla—"

"Just one waltz," she said, moving very close to him. "I find myself growing bored with the *haut ton* tonight, my lord."

"And I suppose you have a better idea for our entertainment?"

"Well, one idea, at least. Come, Lord Tremayne," said Danilla, almost whispering now, her fingertips running lightly up his arm. "Surely we can find you something better to do than watching the countess dance."

Edward saw Claire's dark hair in silhouette against the marquis's fair. He grabbed Lady Hansfort and swung her out onto the floor.

"Not Claire de Lancie, silly, it's Claire *Tremayne*," said Amelie. "You know, the Countess of Ketrick!" Another titter.

Harry set his jaw and forced a smile.

"Everyone is talking about her! She hasn't been to town in ages, you know, they say the earl has to practically force her to visit London, she refuses to go anywhere with him, and Gladys said that . . ."

The girl prattled on while Harry's mind—never noted for its quickness of understanding—tried to grasp this new information. Claire de Lancie . . . Tremayne. Back in London.

Earlier, Claire's husband had informed her that they were obliged to have at least one dance together. "Otherwise people will talk," he said. Claire wasn't sure if she was looking forward to the event or not, but Edward was nowhere in sight, so for the moment she could put it out of mind.

Dancing was tiring work, Claire decided. She cried off her next engagement of a roundelay with some blushing viscount by claiming fatigue and sat down in the most inconspicuous corner she could find.

Such heat! The crush of people in the duke's ballroom was overwhelming, the hothouse atmosphere enhanced by the enormous quantities of flowers imported for the occasion. Claire felt sure she wasn't the only member of the assembly now regretting His Grace's passion for gardenias. And the jasmine—such an odd combination of scent. She fanned herself and wondered—

Where was Edward?

A cool breeze at her back lifted a few tendrils of hair, and Claire looked around to see that an overheated soul had opened one of the doors to the outside terrace. It would feel wonderful to have a breath of fresh air.

Once out on the terrace it was but a few steps down to the gardens, and Claire couldn't resist a short stroll. For old times sake, she told herself, although Jody wouldn't be hiding in some out of the way corner tonight to spirit her over the wall. The duke's *parterres à la française* were famous, and even though the blooms were obviously not at their best this time of year, Claire could see the design of the beds quite clearly. A slight breeze tonight carried the fragrance of evening primrose, and the familiar scent made her homesick for Wrensmoor. She continued to wander for a few minutes, until she found herself in taller grass.

Ah, well. Claire turned around and wandered back to the ball.

One couldn't accuse Lady Hansfort of being coy, thought Edward. She had spent the waltz whispering encouragements into his ear and then at its end, had insisted on stepping out into the garden. Danilla had found a convenient bench and was now clinging to him, leechlike, her hands attempting to explore places that Edward would prefer left untouched.

It was having its effect. After his last experience with the widow, Edward had thought himself immune to her charms, but a man would have to be dead not to respond to a woman as eager as Danilla. She had somehow found her way into Edward's lap, and was pressing against him, murmuring into his ear.

"Mmm, Edward," moaned Danilla. "I can't wait." She began pulling up her skirts.

Even as his body threatened to respond to Lady Hansfort, Edward began wondering about Claire and the Marquis of Leddsfield. Was his wife still in the company of the marquis? Was she dancing with him again? Or were Radleigh and Claire perhaps even now sitting on a bench such as this, the marquis's hand attempting . . .

Anger raced through his veins. How dare she? the earl raged to himself. How dare she encourage that puppy? Well, he would have a thing or two to tell the marquis, and as for his wife—He started to stand, and Danilla uttered a little shriek, the hem of her gown caught on his heel. Sitting back down, the earl began to disentangle himself.

"What are you doing?" Lady Hansfort hissed, but Edward

didn't bother to reply. It was time to find his wife, to have his waltz with her, and go home.

There was the sound of footsteps on gravel. Edward looked up to see Claire, her face blank with shock. He heard Danilla's laughter, and before he could say anything his wife had turned and walked away.

"Blast and damn!" said Edward, burying his head in his hands.

Lady Hansfort continued to laugh.

Harry watched the raven-haired figure as she took her leave. The earl wasn't in the company of his wife, he noticed—perhaps this was an opportunity he should exploit. He was in no hurry now that he knew where she lived, but it would be enjoyable, all the same, to see his cousin Claire again.

Chapter Sixteen

Claire didn't try to sleep that night. She spent her few remaining hours at Tremayne House packing, pacing the floor, and listening—despite herself—for sounds from her husband's bedroom.

Nothing. She supposed that Lady Hansfort was the earl's mistress and that he was spending the night with her. *You knew he had a mistress,* Claire reminded herself. *You* knew. It was just the reality of seeing them together that has shaken you.

She tried to cling to that reasoning, but even as she did Claire knew that one aspect of the situation gnawed at her more than any other. It wasn't only the memory of her husband embracing Lady Hansfort that hurt so much, it was the feeling of—

—of disappointment.

She's your mistress? Claire had wanted to shout at Edward, as she stood frozen in the Lincolnshire gardens. *You came back to London for* her?

In her mind's eye she had pictured Edward with someone much like Lady Pamela. Someone she wouldn't mind sharing him with . . . or at least, not mind so much. But the thought that Lord Tremayne preferred the woman Claire had seen tonight, that he could withstand his wife's charms but found that blowzy, half-dressed female irresistible—

Well, it was mortifying. Claire dragged a last walking dress from the wardrobe and threw it into her trunk, then sat down at a window to wait for dawn.

Edward settled deep into one of White's armchairs and ordered another brandy. None of Frederick's old chums were at the club tonight, a circumstance for which he was profoundly grateful. He was in no mood for cheerful company.

Damn Danilla Hansfort! Claire hadn't said a word to him in the Lincolnshires's garden, just stood there for several endless seconds, her face expressionless, before turning and walking away. Lord Tremayne had jumped up to go after her, but Danilla, of course, picked that moment to fall into strong hysterics. He was tempted to leave the widow on that cursed bench, screeching, but in the end he couldn't take the chance that a vindictive Lady Hansfort might seek out Claire to cause a scene. He spent several minutes calming Danilla, and by the time he returned to the ballroom, Claire had already taken her leave.

Go home. Talk to her, said the little voice.

The earl groaned. The little voice had been saying this all night, and he was growing heartily sick of its advice. It was nonsense to even consider apologizing for his behavior when he had nothing to reproach himself for, nothing. A mistress was a normal perquisite of a gentleman's life. His fortune was more than adequate to support one of these creatures and as he had informed Claire from the very beginning—

Don't be such a bore, the voice told Edward. *How many times have you given this speech, and just whom do you think you're fooling?*

Edward sighed and took a long swig of brandy. How galling that Claire had seen him with Danilla Hansfort! His wife probably thought the woman was his mistress, and if he told her that no, Lady Hansfort wasn't his mistress, then she would want to know who *was* his mistress—

He could see no satisfactory end to that particular conversation, and there was also the matter of the arrangements he'd been about to make with Gaston's. He certainly wasn't going to mention *that* to Claire.

Go talk to her.

She shouldn't have even been in town, he told himself again. She knew I would have a mistress—I have nothing to apologize for. An incident like this is precisely the reason I wanted Claire to live at Wrensmoor in the first place. It's not my fault!

Around and around it went, and eventually Edward dozed off, waking sometime in the early morning with a single thought in mind. He needed to talk to Pamela Sinclair.

Harry crept through the alleyway to the back of the Tremayne stables. It was a perfect plan, he thought happily. Lord and Lady Clarence rarely left their beds before noon. He had hours before they would miss him, and that would be more than enough time for what Harry was planning. It would be short work to discover Claire's London schedule, and he was confident that she still went walking in the parks—

A light female voice caught his attention, and Harry ducked back into the alleyway. He peered cautiously around the corner and could hardly believe his luck. Lady Tremayne was talking to one of the stablehands. Harry held his breath and listened intently to his cousin's instructions.

The Tremayne stablehands were up and about almost as early as the cooks. Claire found a boy to bring down her trunk and went in search of one of the younger groomsmen. She had no doubt that Lord Tremayne would allow her to use a carriage if he was asked, but right now she wasn't in the mood to wait for his return. One of the earl's more experienced men, however, might want to delay until his lordship was informed of her plans.

As it turned out, she had no problem in arranging for someone to take her to Wrensmoor. The head groomsman was off on an errand, and her small trunk was quickly packed in one of the traveling coaches while earnest, red-faced Darby Jones hitched a team.

Darby had seen no reason to question the request from his lordship's beautiful countess, who had smiled so nicely at him, and said that she knew she could rely on Darby to see that they were out of the city before the chaotic traffic of a London mid-morning.

It was true! All true! thought Darby happily. He could get 'er ladyship to the castle safe and sound, he could, and wouldn't the boys be snortin' jealous when they found out the countess'd wanted Darby Jones!

Humming softly, he secured the final ties of the hitch, careful each strap was as perfect as ever could be, and then he had a few choice words to the team about behavin' themselves. The beautiful lady was inside, he was ready to jump—

Darby hardly felt the swift blow to the back of his head, and he dropped without a word. He lay dreamlessly on the packed dirt of the stables as a few moments later, the carriage rattled away into the early morning fog.

Edward didn't remember when he had left White's, or how long he had been walking the streets of London, but he could tell from the smell of coal fires starting up for the day, that a semblance of morning had finally arrived.

Pam would strangle him if he showed up this early, thought the earl, turning in that direction anyway. The street peddlers were setting up, and he caught their looks of surprise as he walked past. The quality were seldom about at this time of the morning. Hawkers tried to catch his eye with their wares, but Lord Tremayne barely noticed. He walked faster and smiled to himself, feeling, despite the disaster of the night past, a sense of anticipation.

He needed to talk to Lady Pamela. The earl wasn't at the point of acknowledging, as he strode along, just what it was that he needed to talk to Lady Pamela *about*.

Good heavens. Claire held her breath as the carriage lurched around another corner, and she wondered if she had made a serious mistake in choosing her driver. She would have thought any of the Earl of Ketrick's men would be competent, and she certainly didn't want to get Darby Jones into trouble, but—

Oh! Good grief, they almost hit that poor woman! Claire thought about signaling to have the coach turned around, but they would still need to travel several busy streets to return to Tremayne House, and what if banging on the roof startled the young coachman? Surely once they were out of the city, he would have an easier time of it, and she reminded herself, it wasn't as if Darby Jones was the only bad driver in London.

Edward hopped over Pamela's back garden gate and made his way to the side door. A few servants would be up at this hour, but he doubted any of them would blink to see the Earl of Ketrick en route to Lady Sinclair's bedchamber.

He stopped in front of her door and listened quietly for sounds of activity within. Nothing. He pushed open the door and was surprised to see Pam already sitting up in bed.

She brushed a few tendrils of hair back from her face and sighed. "I'm not sure I want to hear this," was her comment.

Edward sat down on the edge of the bed and put his head in his hands. "I think I need some advice," he muttered reluctantly from between his fingers.

"I dare say you do," remarked Lady Pamela.

To Claire's relief, Darby Jones managed to maneuver the team through central London without running over anyone or overturning the coach. Once he made the turn onto the Great Dover road, the traffic quieted and she was able to relax, the fatigue that had accumulated with each day in London taking her over. She looked at the low chalk hills rolling by in the distance, feeling her eyelids grow heavier and heavier, until she finally stretched out on the plump cushions of the earl's coach and fell asleep.

She didn't know what awoke her. The carriage seemed to be rattling along much as before, but as she pushed herself upright she had the memory . . .

Why was her heart pounding? Stop being such a ninnyhammer, she told herself. You're in the earl's coach, on your way back to Wrensmoor. What could possibly be wrong?

. . . the memory of the carriage making a turn.

"I don't want to live apart from her any longer," Edward was saying. "Even if we do have a marriage of convenience, it just seems more . . . convenient . . . to live together."

"Ah," said Lady Pamela. "Have you told Claire this?"

"Well, no."

"Edward, I don't see the problem. You like her. She seems

to like you. So what if it wasn't what you planned? Be happy. Make babies. "

"I didn't think I'd end up . . . caring about her as much as I do."

"Heaven help that you should care about your own wife!" Pam was exasperated.

"You don't understand. Melissa died because of her baby. It was horrible, Pam, all that blood—"

"Women die in childbirth, Edward, it *does* happen, but Claire is strong and healthy. Just because Melissa had problems is no reason to think—"

"I saw her face, she looked up at me as she was dying. Melissa was such a child, such an innocent. And to die like that—"

Pamela rolled her eyes, but Edward didn't notice. He was remembering the whiteness of Melissa's skin against the sheets, the sound that a man's boots made walking across the wooden floor, each step sticky with blood—

Such an innocent.

Pamela had started to pace the room in agitation. Edward stood and looked at her, frowning. "What is it?" he asked. "I know it doesn't make sense. And I know you were never fond of Melissa, but—"

Pamela stopped him with an annoyed wave of her hand. Years ago she had made a promise to herself, but she had had enough of Edward's misplaced devotion to Melissa, and to think Claire was suffering because—

"Pam?"

"Melissa Tremayne was a *slut!*" she told him, seeing shock flood Edward's face, feeling something break free inside. "Oh, a darling, sprigged-muslin little slut to be sure, but—"

Edward raised a hand to slap a woman for the first time in

his life. All movement stopped as Pamela looked up at him, in anger and in love, refusing to turn away, to raise a hand to ward off the blow.

He lowered his hand.

"How . . . how could you say that?" he breathed. "Frederick's wife was hardly more than a child."

"A child? You cannot possibly have been that blind!" Pam cried. "She slept with everyone, Edward, *everyone!* Chedley, Lord Drere—"

"That can't be true!"

"—*both* the Alnwick brothers—"

"Stop!" said Edward. He was breathing hard.

"—and probably a footman or two if nobody else was around. No, I won't stop! And it is true! She would have slept with *you* if you'd given her half an opportunity! You must have seen what she was doing!"

Edward looked stunned and Pam was almost crying, her voice hoarse with the effort to make him understand. Who had she been trying to protect all these years, Melissa or Frederick? Or Edward? But the dam was breached now, and the words tumbled out.

"She wasn't sure about the baby, Edward," Pam continued. "Do you understand? She didn't know if the baby was Frederick's or not, she'd been sleeping with Trevor Fitzjohn all that summer—"

Edward's breath caught in his throat.

He took Frederick's hands, to kiss them—

Something glittered in his brother's left hand.

It was a woman's gold locket and chain, finely wrought. He stared at it for untold minutes, certain he had never seen it before, unable to look away. Inside was a lock of hair, and an inscription: Until I am in your arms again. TF.

"She didn't *want* the baby. Melissa never wanted children

at all. The doctors told her that she would have difficulty if she didn't stop—well, all the things she was doing, but Melissa just didn't care.

"You know it's true, Edward. You must. At the end, even Frederick knew."

Claire banged furiously on the roof of the coach with her parasol. When the carriage showed no signs of slowing down, she stuck her head out the window and yelled.

"Darby! Darby, stop! This is the wrong road!"

What was wrong with the man? He must be able to hear her—

"*Darby!*" she shouted, wondering if there was any other way to get his attention. How fast was the carriage traveling? Would he even notice if she threw herself out onto the road?

This was ridiculous. Claire took a firm grip on her parasol and leaned out the window as far as she dared.

"Stop!" she shouted again, banging on the side of the coach with the parasol and hoping she wouldn't spook the team. After a minute or two she heard the coachman yell and felt the horses slowing. Finally! she thought.

"Darby! We have to go back! We're on the wrong road!" The carriage was still moving slowly forward, but a face now peered down from the top of the coach.

Not Darby Jones's face.

"Frederick knew?" Edward asked Pam. "There was a locket—when I found Frederick, he was holding a locket—"

Lady Pamela sighed, her anger spent, and sat down on the bed. "Not at first. You know Frederick. He walked away from things he didn't want to see."

Edward nodded.

"Melissa used to laugh about wanting to make him

jealous. It wasn't easy. He could overlook an occasional tumble between friends, I guess, but when she starting sleeping with Fitzjohn at Wrensmoor, practically parading it in front of his face—"

Edward remembered the house party at the castle, his brother angrier than he had ever seen him.

"Fitzjohn must have given Melissa the locket," he told Pam, "and Frederick had it with him when he died. I didn't want to admit what it meant. I threw it away."

They sat in silence for a time. The maid brought in Lady Pamela's morning chocolate and—to Edward's amusement—his usual cup of strong tea. News traveled fast belowstairs.

"Edward," said Pam, finishing her chocolate. "I'm guilty, too. I knew what was happening, and I never told Frederick. Sometimes I think that if he had known sooner, if he'd had a chance to adjust to the truth before she died—"

"No—"

"But it's too late. I can't help Frederick now. Neither can you. Spend your love on the living, Edward. On Claire."

The earl sighed. "That's just the problem, Pam. Melissa may have been unfaithful, but I still cared about her as a sister. I can't look back on it and think she deserved to die that way—"

"What does that have to do with Claire?"

"Nothing, I suppose." Edward threw up his hands in agitation. "I know, none of this makes sense. But Frederick was so angry, so distraught, and then Melissa died, and—"

He hesitated. Pam said nothing.

"I don't think . . . I don't think I could stand to be hurt so badly by someone—" Edward stopped.

"By someone?" Pam echoed.

"—someone that I loved."

Chapter Seventeen

Darby Jones had been lying in the dirt for only a few minutes before one of the other stablehands found him, but it was a while before they managed to wake him up, and even then Darby wasn't too clear about what had happened.

A discussion ensued. Big Jerry opined that they ought t' stick the lad's head in the drinking trough again, but Darby said no, that wouldn't be necessary, that he was sure he was starting to remember.

Big Jerry said as what Darby'd just be tryin' to get out of doing a good day's work. Darby said that if Big Jerry'd done a good day's work in his worthless life he sure never'd seen it. Matters were starting to go downhill—Darby's skull felt like the cats were havin' a go inside of it, and he didn't really care to have Big Jerry pounding on him—when the head groomsman returned.

"Cor!" bellowed the man. "Have the lot of you run mad? Where t' hell is the carriage?"

Edward took his time walking back to Tremayne House. He needed to think, and he knew that once he saw Claire again, thinking wouldn't be easy.

I don't think I could stand to be hurt so badly by someone that I loved.

Strange that he had entered into a marriage of convenience, only to fall in love with his wife. Strange that it took a conversation with his ex-mistress to realize the truth.

He loved Claire. He would never willingly live apart from her again.

Edward looked around him, startled at what a difference joy could make to the senses. The grass of the park looked greener than usual, the sky bluer. Even the street noise of London sounded like a symphony.

He turned in the direction of Tremayne House and lengthened his stride. If he was lucky, Claire would still be asleep.

Jody wondered how early he dared call upon Lady Pamela. He had snuck out of Tremayne House before sunrise, although not before helping Mrs. Huppins light the ovens and extracting a promise for a batch of apple tarts, and was now hunched at the edge of the St. James's pond, watching the geese.

Silly creatures. Jody was out of sorts with the world this morning, having put all his hopes for a reconciliation between Claire and the earl at the Lincolnshire ball, only to discover that his sister had returned home early last night, and alone. Then there was her note to him this morning—

Mon cher, his sister had written. *It's very early, and I'm sorry I won't be able to say good-bye. I'm certain that Lord Tremayne will send you to Wrensmoor whenever you wish, but Jody—give me a few days.*

And that was all. Claire was returning to the castle immediately and the earl was remaining in London. Something must have happened at the ball. He was angry with Lord Tremayne, angry with his sister. Why did everyone keep treating him like a child? Claire wouldn't talk to him, the earl wouldn't talk to him—he didn't need to be protected, for pity's sake, he was almost sixteen years old!

Indeed, he knew exactly what the problem was, and he knew it wasn't going to be solved, not one little bit, if his sister and her husband continued to live separately. But did anyone ask for his advice? No, they did not.

Jody stood up to relieve his cramped muscles and shooed away an old goose who thought breakfast was being served. He hadn't seen Lady Pamela since those few days after Claire was shot, but he couldn't think of anyone else who might be willing to listen. He decided the morning was advanced enough to risk a visit, and walked swiftly in the direction of Lady Pamela's townhouse.

The head groomsman wasn't looking forward to telling the earl he had lost one of his lordship's carriages. Lord Tremayne was a fair man and a good employer, but—

Sighing, Mr. Andrews looked at Darby Jones and decided to try one more time. He kept a kindly expression on his face, thinking that the lad looked confused and a bit worse for wear.

"Now, you say you don't remember how you ended up lying on the ground?"

"No, sir, Mr. Andrews," said Darby. "But my head hurts terrible, sir, and I think someone must' a hit me."

"And stolen the carriage."

"Yes, sir."

"With the horses."

"I . . . I suppose so, sir."

Darby knew as well as Mr. Andrews where the difficulty lay with this story. Someone hadn't just taken a carriage. Someone had taken two large geldings—and the earl's cattle didn't take well to strangers—and the proper strappings for those particular horses, *and* hitched them to a carriage. It would have taken a fair bit of time.

"His lordship didn't ask you to ready a carriage, did he?"

"No, sir, I don't think so." Darby screwed up his face with the effort to remember. Lord Tremayne hadn't asked for a carriage. Lord Tremayne wouldn't talk to Darby Jones, anyway, he'd ask Justin MacKenzie, who would tell Mr. Andrews, who would—

"Oh! Oh, Mr. Andrews!" exclaimed Darby Jones. "I remember now! I did hitch 'em up! But it weren't for his lordship! It was her ladyship what asked me for the carriage!"

"Don't be a rattlebrain, lad. Her ladyship's not up in the wee hours of the morning, asking for the likes of you to ready her a traveling coach."

"No! No, sir, she did! She was going to Wrensmoor!"

A truly frightful thought had come to Mr. Andrews, and he felt the chill breath of calamity at his neck. Had they lost a carriage—or his lordship's wife?

It was turning out to be a busy morning for visitors.

"Monsieur Jodrel de Lancie to see you, ma'am," informed the butler, with only the slightest lift of an eyebrow.

Jody? What was this about? Lady Pamela barely had a chance to put down her hairbrush before the boy burst in.

"Claire's gone back to Wrensmoor! Today! I just know something awful happened last night. She and the earl went to the ball together—you know, the Duke of Lincolnshire—but Claire came home alone and it was early—not even midnight—and she wrote me a note and now she's gone!"

"All right Jody, all right. Sit down for a moment," soothed Lady Pamela, "and I'll call for more tea."

"But she's gone! And he won't talk to her, I know he won't, he never even wrote her the whole time he was in London!"

"Jody," said Pam firmly, "sit down. Let me think."

Claire had left Tremayne House? Lady Pamela chewed on her lower lip and decided that she had a pretty good idea why. Before Edward left an hour ago, he had told Pam about the rather unpleasant scene in the Lincolnshire gardens. Listening to Edward's description of his wrestling match with Lady Hansfort, she had been torn between laughter and the desire to hit him over the head with the nearest heavy object.

"Danilla Hansfort? Out in the gardens? What on earth were you thinking?"

"I wasn't . . . thinking," said Edward. *"I saw Claire waltzing with Lord Radleigh, and then Danilla was there, and I didn't know where Claire had disappeared to, and—"*

"You were jealous."

"No! No, of course not, I just—"

"Oh, stop," Pamela had told him. *"I don't want to hear any more."*

Bother it all. She had thought it would all be sorted out when Edward returned to Tremayne House that morning. But if Claire had already left for Wrensmoor . . .

"Jody?"

Despite her requests, the boy was pacing frantically around the room. "I'm sure he's done something to hurt her feelings! Claire doesn't deserve this, Lady Pamela, she loves him, I know she does. I'm going to call him out!"

Call him out? Jodrel de Lancie was going to challenge Edward Tremayne to a *duel?*

The hairs on the back of her neck stood up. Lady Pam had grown up with an older brother and numerous male cousins, and she knew all about the level of common sense to be expected from an adolescent male. This must be stopped at once.

"Jodrel, no. The earl is not going to duel with a fifteen-year-old—"

"I'll be sixteen within the fortnight."

"It wouldn't signify if you were twenty-six. Lord Tremayne will not shoot his wife's brother. If you somehow manage to force a duel, he will delope. Then what will you do?"

"I . . ." Jody hesitated.

She persisted. "The person who will be hurt the worst is Claire. Do you think she wants you involved in a duel? Or her husband shot?"

"No, but—"

"Jody, Lord Tremayne was here earlier this morning."

The boy looked up at her, miserable and hurt.

Pam laughed. "The earl and I are no longer associated in that way, Jodrel. You should know that."

"Oh." Jody sighed his relief.

"He came here to discuss Claire. He loves your sister and no longer wishes to live apart from her. He told me so this morning, and when he left he was going straight back to Tremayne House to tell her the same thing."

"Oh!" For once speechless, Jodrel de Lancie grinned at Lady Pamela, hugged her, and then burst into tears. "But she's gone! What are we going to do?"

"Don't worry, Jody. It might take a little longer than I thought, but Lord Tremayne will find his wife."

"What did you say?"

At that moment, Mr. Andrews wished himself anywhere other than standing in front of the Earl of Ketrick, looking at the fury and disbelief on his employer's face.

"It weren't Mr. Andrews's fault," said Darby Jones. "Her ladyship asked for t' carriage, and I was hitchin' the bays—"

"Darby," interrupted the earl, "let me feel the back of your head."

"Ow!"

The lump on the back of Darby Jones's head suggested a blow hard enough to have felled any man, and Edward no longer had any doubt that Claire had been kidnapped.

Sandrick Rutherford, thought Edward.

I'll kill him.

"Have Achilles saddled immediately," Edward ordered Mr. Andrews.

"Bein' done as we speak," the man replied.

Chapter Eighteen

"What in heaven's name do you think you are doing? And where is Darby Jones?"

"We're going to Cheltdown Manor! Get back into the carriage! Get back!"

The horses stomped and snorted uneasily.

"I'll do no such thing!" Claire's heart was pounding, but with anger rather than fear. She was livid. Of all the ridiculous, idiotic things that could have happened—

"I'll tie you up if I have to!" her cousin barked, his voice high-pitched and frantic.

She gave him a fierce glare and gripped her parasol tightly, refusing to move.

"I've got a pistol! I'll use it! I swear I'll use it!"

He wasn't bluffing, Claire realized, seeing a flintlock suddenly appear in his hand.

Good grief.

"Harold Rutherford, don't be a ninny." He couldn't possibly mean to harm her, thought Claire, and she moved forward to push the gun aside, ready to talk some sense into her cousin.

"Get away!" Harry jerked back and lightning flashed from the muzzle of his gun.

Lord Tremayne arrived at Cheltdown shortly before

noon, having ridden Achilles hard through the outskirts of London and Lewisham borough. The stallion was lathered and blowing, but it couldn't be helped. He threw the reins to a startled yardboy. "See to my horse," he shouted, and took the front steps of the manor two at a time. He was of half a mind to burst through the door without knocking, but here a note of caution crept in. Sandrick Rutherford seemed a man likely to panic when events moved swiftly against him, and his panic might be dangerous for Claire. Edward knocked, loudly.

Would the cursed butler never come?

"I need to see Lord Rutherford immediately," said Edward when the door opened.

The man looked doubtful.

"*Now,* damn your eyes!" said the earl.

"I beg your pardon, my lord, but I'm not sure—"

"Let him in, Harper," a voice rasped from within the house.

Edward heard the faint tapping of a cane against the floor, followed by a spate of violent coughing.

"Very well, my lord."

The butler stepped aside just in time to avoid being knocked over by the earl, who looked up to see—

Death, thought Edward, appalled. Death was standing on the staircase.

Sandrick Rutherford clung to the banister with one hand, a cane clutched in the other. His eyes were sunken and bloodshot, the skin pulled so tautly over the bones of his face that the effect was skull-like.

The butler supported him down the last few steps and to a foyer chair.

Rutherford waved feebly in Edward's direction. "I . . . apologize that I must receive you in such infelicitous . . . surroundings," said the man, with some effort. "I'm afraid the . . . the vestibule is as far as I venture, these days. Now, how can I help you, Lord Tremayne?"

Time slowed. Claire tried to move, to run, but her legs remained rooted where she stood. She felt, almost more than heard, the deafening *crack!* of the flintlock. A rush of air past her cheek, the oak tree behind her erupting in a flurry of bark fragments—

She saw Harry's eyes widen, and she turned, every movement still agonizingly slow, to see a jagged hole in the trunk of the oak. Her hands moved to her stomach, then to her chest. She looked at her fingers, almost surprised to see no blood on them.

"Oh," said Harry, looking at the tree. "Oh." He looked panicky and sick.

This was the outside of enough. In the last twenty-four hours she had been humiliated by her husband, kidnapped, almost killed traveling the streets of London, and now *shot* at. Again. Claire realized she was still holding her parasol.

"Claire, no! I'm sorry! I didn't mean—"

Harry backed away, flintlock in hand. Claire didn't know much about pistols, but she was fairly certain they fired only once without reloading. She swung the parasol.

"Claire!"

"I am tired of being shot at!" she yelled. She swung again, hard.

"Ow!"

"And look what you did to that poor tree!" This time she connected solidly with Harry's left shoulder.

"Ow! Claire, that *hurts!*" Harry was trying to back away, but she followed him. There was now a large rip in the flowered cambric of the parasol.

"And I suppose you think a bullet wound is painless? Well, it's not!"

"I'm sorry! I'm sorry! Claire, *stop!*"

"Put down that ridiculous pistol!" She raised the parasol once more.

Harry threw the gun aside. Claire stood in front of him and glared, her breath coming in gasps.

"Now, what—" she began, and paused for a deep breath. "What happened to Darby Jones? And just why were you taking me to Cheltdown Manor?"

"How can I help you, Lord Tremayne?"

Edward had planned a number of rescue scenarios during his ride from London, but none of them involved an adversary too ill to stand without assistance. The difference between this ravaged, shrunken man and the man he had bullied into signing away Jody's guardianship was shocking. The pox, realized Edward. It is taking him quickly. Still, Rutherford must have abducted Claire, for who else could it have been? Perhaps he had hired a thug for the actual kidnapping—an idea that caused Edward's blood to run cold.

"Where is my wife?"

"Claire? You are asking after my niece?"

"My *wife*. Where is she?"

Sandrick Rutherford started laughing. It was a horrible sound, and quickly turned into a fit of coughing that seemed to last forever.

"Yes, indeed, my lord, your *wife*," he said, when he finally managed to breathe. "Am I to understand that you have lost her?" Another fit of coughing ensued.

Edward glared at him. "No, she is not *lost*. She has been *kidnapped*. One of my stablehands was assaulted, and the carriage Lady Tremayne was riding in has been waylaid and taken. Are you saying you know nothing of this?"

Lord Rutherford shook his head weakly. "Don't . . . don't be a fool, Ketrick. Do you think one of my . . . men could manage to get one . . . foot inside Wrensmoor Park?"

"She wasn't taken from Wrensmoor. She was taken from London." Edward grew angrier as he spoke. They were wasting time! Where was Claire? He would drag the truth out of Rutherford, ill as he was. But even as these thoughts flashed through Edward's mind, he felt a nagging worry. The man sitting in front of him, struggling for breath, didn't strike him as having the energy to plot an abduction.

"London?" Rutherford turned—if it was possible—an even sicklier shade of white. "Did anyone see the assailant?"

"One of my stableboys saw a young man in the alleyway earlier. Curly blond hair, rather thin. But we don't know that he—"

Another fit of wracking coughs, and Edward wondered how many more such episodes Claire's uncle could survive. The man wheezed and choked, and the butler arrived from nowhere with a glass of water.

Rutherford waved the butler away. "Harry," he whispered to Edward between gasps for air.

They sat on the grass beside the carriage, talking.

"Oh, Harry," sighed Claire. "What am I going to do now?"

"I'm sorry," said Harry Rutherford. He hung his head. "I was at the ball, you see, with the Clarences, and I saw you and realized that you were back in London, but I didn't know for how long this time, and I thought . . ."

Claire sighed again. This was the impulsive, unpredictable cousin that she had known at Cheltdown.

"I guess I wasn't thinking too clearly," Harry finished lamely.

"You certainly were not. Now you are going to turn this carriage around and take me right back to the crossroads, and—" Claire stopped. What was it Harry had just said? He'd realized she was *back* in London?

"Harry. Did you know where I was before? In London, I mean, before I was married?"

"Sure. Jermyn Street. You and Jody used to walk most days in Green Park."

"How did you find us? And what were you doing in London, anyway?"

"Father . . . father thought it was time I acquired some town bronze. I know he can't—doesn't go into the city, but Lord Clarence agreed to sponsor me, and so there I was. I hate London," added Harry. "Everyone pretended to like me, you know, for the Clarences' sake. But they didn't, not really. I spent as much time as I could in the parks, and one day . . . well, you were there."

"Oh. I see." A horrible thought entered Claire's mind. It was crazy, but—

"Harry . . . Harry, by any chance did you *shoot* at me in Green Park?"

Her cousin burst into tears. "I'm sorry! I'm sorry!" he said between sobs. "I never meant to *hit* you! I only wanted to scare you, but the first time I tried Jody just looked around and you didn't even notice, so I thought I needed to get a little bit closer! But I'm not a very good shot," he concluded glumly.

"Why did you want to scare me?" asked Claire.

"So you'd go back! I thought you'd take fright of London and go home!"

"Home?"

"To Cheltdown!" Harry was babbling. "Father was furious when you left! There was nobody to talk to and he wouldn't tell me where you and Jody went, and I was . . . I was lonely—and worried about you, Claire!"

She stared at him, shocked. In all her plans for escaping Sandrick Rutherford, she had never considered the possible effects on Harry.

"I thought that if you would go back to Cheltdown that Father would let me come home, too," her cousin added.

"Oh, Harry." Claire sighed and closed her eyes for a moment. "Why didn't you just tell me? You knew where we lived. Why didn't you pay us a call?"

Harry looked at her, his eyes sad. "I was afraid you wouldn't talk to me. You left without a note, without even saying good-bye."

"Oh, Harry." Claire flopped down on her back in the grass and considered what she should do next. There was a scruffy sort of inn only a mile or two from the crossroads. She could try to hire a new driver there, but what would she do with Harry? Nobody at Wrensmoor was expecting her today, so she supposed there was no real hurry. Nevertheless—

"Come on, Harry, let's drive back to the inn and have something to eat. I'm sure if we put our minds to it, we can sort things out."

"Harry?" repeated the earl.

"The young man your stableboy saw. Blond . . . curly hair. My son," gasped Lord Rutherford. "In London this past half year . . . or more. It's difficult to . . . to remember how long. I didn't want him to watch me die like this."

"What would he want with my wife?" asked Edward, his voice gaining volume. What the hell kind of family was this?

A spark of life showed in Sandrick Rutherford's eyes for the first time. "For the love of mercy, Ketrick, don't harm him!" he said. "Harry would never hurt Claire. He's a good lad, but not . . . not bright."

Edward clenched his fists in frustration. He was no closer to finding Claire, and his impulse to do violence to someone—anyone—was being thwarted at every turn.

"He might . . . might be bringing your wife here. I told Harry . . . that I wanted to see her . . . one last time. Once he gets a notion in his head—"

"Why?" said Edward. "Why did you tell him you wanted to see Claire?" He was anxious to continue the search for his wife, but if Rutherford's benighted son was bringing her to Cheltdown—

"To tell her . . ." Rutherford trailed off, and for a moment Edward thought the man had passed away right then and there. But his head lifted, and his voice was a little stronger as he continued. "To tell her I was sorry."

"Oh, I say," said Harry, "this is really quite good."

Claire rolled her eyes as he chewed his way happily through a second rasher of bacon. Her cousin seemed to have quickly recovered from any feelings of shame attached to his recent activities. After having assaulted the stablehand and abducted her—not to mention shooting at her on several occasions—one might think he would be more subdued. But that was Harry. He was short-sighted, well-meaning, and desperate to please his father, whose affection for the boy Claire had never questioned.

To please his father. Claire wondered how abducting her would have accomplished that. Something else about Harry's story was bothering her, but first—

"Harry, are you sure Darby Jones wasn't badly hurt?"

"I told you, he's fine! I hardly touched him!"

"All right."

Did the earl know what had happened to her? she wondered. Was he worried? Claire realized she was half-expecting to see Lord Tremayne burst through the parlor door of the Blue Duck at any moment, a knight riding to his damsel's rescue. But that was ridiculous. Edward would have no idea who had taken her or where she was.

Claire sipped her tea and looked around the room. The Blue Duck barely qualified as a respectable establishment, but it was quiet in the morning hours, and the food was enough to recommend the place to her cousin. She had some time—while Harry worked through a plateful of potatoes and sausage—to consider what needed to be done.

Should she return immediately to London? She'd need a driver, but a man-at-hire ought to be easy enough to find in a place like this. Of course, if she went back to Tremayne House, she would simply have to turn around the next day and retrace her steps. Besides, if she returned to town, she would see Edward, and she would have to explain . . . things. Her uncle's name would obviously enter into the conversation, and her husband would know she'd been less than truthful with him.

Maybe Edward would decide he didn't want an heir by the niece of Sandrick Rutherford. But she didn't want to think about that. The idea of continuing on to Wrensmoor was much more appealing, decided Claire. They could take Harry to Cheltdown first, then—

But at that thought, her mind rebelled. Whatever she did, she wasn't going to Cheltdown Manor.

"I say," said Harry, interrupting her thoughts, "are you going to finish those biscuits?"

She handed him the plate.

Her first priority, no matter what else she did, was to inform the earl of the whereabouts of his carriage, his horses, and his wife. And the quickest way to accomplish that was to send a rider with a message to London. Claire wondered if the Blue Duck's proprietor was aware of such modern conveniences as paper and ink. She gazed once more around the room—

Of course, she hardly knew what to write. How could she possibly explain about Harry Rutherford? Oh, why had she never told the earl about her uncle? Her husband would have good reason to never trust her again.

Bother it all. A communication of some sort needed to be sent immediately, and Claire—excusing herself from the table—found a small dilapidated writing desk away from Harry's eye. She made her message short, deciding that everything else could be sorted out later.

My lord husband. Despite the recent unfortunate occurrence in your stables, the carriage, the horses, and I are perfectly safe and unharmed and continuing on to Wrensmoor. I shall write at more length when I reach the castle.

Claire.

Let him make of that what he would.

Harry had almost finished his breakfast. Claire regarded him thoughtfully from across the table, trying to ignore the less-than-pleasant odor now wafting in from the stableyard. Something kept nagging at the back of her mind—

"Harry . . . you said you were trying to frighten me into leaving London."

Her cousin nodded, taking one last forkful of sausage.

"But what about now? Taking the carriage? Didn't you

think Lord Tremayne would notice I was gone?"

"Oh, I wasn't going to keep you," said Harry. "I'm just taking you to Cheltdown to see Father. It will only be for a few days—"

Claire shivered. "I am *not* going to the manor with you."

"—and then you can continue on to Wrensmoor—"

"No." Was her cousin even listening?

"They'll just think you stopped at an inn—"

"*No*," repeated Claire. "I am not going to Cheltdown."

Harry slammed his fork down on the table and Claire jumped.

"Yes, you are!" His voice, suddenly shrill, echoed in the Blue Duck's dining room. The proprietor glanced in their direction with a cocked eyebrow.

"Shh!" she hissed at Harry.

"You have to come! I'll make you!" A stage whisper this time, which did nothing to improve Claire's mood. She sat back in her chair and stared at Harry, realizing that perhaps she didn't know her cousin very well. At Cheltdown Harry had always seemed so innocuous. But the young man of only a minute ago—cheerfully demolishing his breakfast—was now glaring at her, red in the face. He had been pleasant enough as a boy, Claire remembered, but always a little volatile. And perhaps the months spent amid the chaos of London had done him no good.

She felt the first glimmerings of fear.

No. I refuse to be afraid of Harry Rutherford, Claire thought. She gave her cousin a cool glance and spoke as calmly as she could. "I am going on to Wrensmoor. I am *not* going to Cheltdown with you."

The glare continued, but then—suddenly—Harry's face seemed to collapse.

"Well . . . all right," he said glumly. "But Father said he

wanted to see you one last time, and I thought—"

"One last time? What are you talking about?"

"My father is dying. I think he wanted to say good-bye."

Chapter Nineteen

"I didn't see him," said Edward suddenly. He was pacing in Lord Rutherford's front hall.

"Your pardon?"

"I didn't see the carriage on my way here. If Harry took her, where are they?"

Rutherford managed a weak chuckle. "Well, I know Harry, and I know Claire. I wouldn't be surprised if she browbeat him into taking her home."

Edward shook his head. Not back to London—he would have seen that, too—and what if Claire's kidnapper wasn't Harry Rutherford? What if even now, as they spoke—?

Damn! He couldn't stay here a minute longer. He had to search for his wife.

"My horse—"

"Lord Tremayne, I would venture to guess that you . . . wasted no time riding here. Your horse must be spent," said Rutherford.

Edward swore explosively. It was true.

"I have a fine stallion . . . good chest, a strong runner. Take him."

The earl nodded. "I will."

"You will visit, won't you?" said Harry.

Her cousin was standing in the yard of the Blue Duck,

talking to Claire through the open window of Lord Tremayne's carriage.

She shook her head. "I promised to write your father," Claire reminded Harry, "but I can't promise to come to the manor."

"But, Claire—"

"I would have to inform the earl, and—you know, Harry—he might not be very happy about any trips to Cheltdown after our excursion today."

"I suppose you're right. But—"

Claire felt her patience eroding. "Oh, Harry—I'll try. It would only be a short visit."

He gave her a sad smile. "That doesn't matter. Whatever Father has to say won't take long."

The carriage lurched, and Harry moved to give Claire a quick peck on her cheek—thought better of it—and settled for a wave. As the driver maneuvered the earl's coach out of the yard of the Blue Duck and onto the road to Wrensmoor, Claire leaned back into the cushions with a long sigh.

It was time to go home.

All things considered, she and her cousin had parted amicably enough. Once Harry realized that Claire would not willingly accompany him to Cheltdown—but would consider a later visit—he had calmed down and become almost reasonable. She had even come away with an improved opinion of Harry's character, having concluded that his efforts, foolish as they were, had been largely inspired by the wish to comfort his father.

"Just don't shoot at anyone anymore," Claire had told him.

He had promised not to.

"I'm not going back to London," Harry had added. "I don't belong there, and I never should have agreed to leave my father in the first place. Please—come and see him—"

Claire took a deep breath and held on to the seat as the coach rattled across a bumpy log bridge. A visit to Cheltdown? She would worry about that later.

In the meantime, her cousin was making his way back to the manor alone, and with any luck and a skilled driver, she should still arrive at Wrensmoor before dark. Presumably Lord Tremayne would soon receive her message and leave her in peace at the castle. Perhaps she could manage a way to avoid mentioning the Rutherford name.

Well, no, Claire admitted. That wouldn't be possible. She needed to accept the fact that the earl would soon find out exactly who he had married. She should have told him long ago. For better or for worse, there would be no further deception in her marriage.

As time wore on, Claire slept fitfully, waking up on occasion only long enough to assure herself that the carriage was still on the right road. As they proceeded farther into Kent, the countryside began to look more and more like Wrensmoor Park. Claire felt her spirits lift.

Let him stay in London, she thought. Let him trade balls and soirees and drunken evenings at his club for the hills and meadows of Kent, and the castle, and the river, and—and even the stupid geese. Let him be a fool.

These thoughts eventually occupied Claire to the point that she no longer slept. So she was sitting upright when the carriage overturned.

If I were a foolish young man, thought Edward, riding hell-bent back to the crossroads on Rutherford's stallion, and I'd just abducted an . . . an equally foolish, headstrong, *disobedient* young woman, where would I be?

Part of him was insisting that he should return to London

immediately. What if Harold Rutherford was not Claire's kidnapper? What if, even now, she was being held prisoner in some seedy London rowhouse?

But why? He had no real enemies that he knew of, and as for Claire—

No, Harry Rutherford was still the most likely culprit. If the uncle was right, Claire had probably convinced Harry to take her to Wrensmoor. Perhaps someone at the Blue Duck would have seen them, or at least have seen the Ketrick carriage. Edward usually avoided the inn—home as it was to half the shady characters between here and Dover—but as a source of information, it was hard to improve on the Blue Duck.

In the end, the accident could have been blamed on the deer—or on Harry.

It was midafternoon, and Claire had reached the point where she never wanted to see the inside of a traveling carriage again, no matter how well-upholstered it was. At least they were closer to Wrensmoor. She felt the happy anticipation of journey's end and wondered how long she could delay writing Lord Tremayne with the details of her day's adventure.

Ahead was the sharp turn which Claire remembered as being only a mile or two from the castle. The driver didn't slow until the last minute and, as it happened, a family of deer burst from a copse of trees just then, leaping and skittering across the road.

"H'ya!"

The geldings—well-trained animals, but in unfamiliar hands—broke stride for a moment, the traces sagged, tangled briefly under-hoof—

—just as the road turned sharply left and dipped. The

right wheel caught a side rut, and the carriage skidded sideways into a sickening lurch, tipping to the side.

Claire hung on to the straps with quiet determination, trying to anticipate which way the coach might overturn. She didn't think it would help the driver to hear her yelling, and indeed he seemed to be bringing the horses under control. Perhaps—

They reached the bottom of the hill at a precarious angle but still upright, the geldings maintaining an even stride as they slowed, and Claire had started to breathe again when the right wheel—which had received a bad knocking about earlier that day in London, under Harry's guidance—splintered and gave way. Over they tipped in a halting, slow-motion fall, the driver jumping free and Claire, bracing her feet against the side cushions, shaken but unhurt.

The abrupt silence was eerie, and then Claire heard footsteps.

"Milady! Milady!" The driver's face peered down at her through one of the carriage windows.

"Yes, yes. I'm fine," she told him. "See to the horses, please. I'll get myself out."

The face disappeared, and after taking a few moments to collect herself, Claire looked around for a means of escape. The door was now underfoot, she realized, which meant climbing out one of the carriage windows. Oh, drat it all anyway. What other disasters could this day produce? She began the slow, clumsy process of hoisting herself up and out, losing a number of hairpins in the process. Her skirt caught on a large splinter of wood and, annoyed, she ripped it free.

Where was the driver? Claire wondered, hearing the nickers of the horses. Oh, this blasted skirt! Cursing modern fashions—and the entire male sex—under her breath, she hauled herself through the window and tumbled a few feet into the dirt.

"Bother." Claire stood up and brushed at her dress, thinking she was going to make a pretty picture arriving at the castle in such disarray. She looked around, puzzled that she wasn't hearing any activity. The horses had been unhitched and were grazing quietly nearby. There was no sign of the driver—

She finally spotted him, fifty yards down the road.

Of all the—

"Driver!" she yelled.

The man looked back briefly, then took off at a run.

"Driver! Hey!" Claire stood in the middle of the road, took off one of her shoes and threw it at him. She stamped her foot in the dust as the man disappeared around a curve. Well, thought Claire in disgust, that's what comes of hiring someone from the likes of the Blue Duck Inn. She supposed she should be grateful he had stayed around long enough to find out she wasn't seriously hurt.

Retrieving her shoe, she returned to the overturned carriage. The bays were looking at her, ears pricked, and when she took a few steps towards them they snorted and moved away.

"Oh, you daft animals, don't play games with me."

Claire stepped closer to the geldings. They immediately edged away again, and she conceded defeat. She went back to inspect the carriage. It didn't seem to be damaged badly except for the one wheel, which was in pieces at the side of the road. There was nothing she could do about it now, or the two skittish geldings. Someone was bound to come along the road eventually, but Claire wasn't willing to put her fate in the hands of the next stranger to pass by. Even in these days, highwaymen were not unknown.

She was going to have to walk. Claire thought she had a pretty clear idea of where the castle was from here, and she spotted a path leading off in that direction. It would be quicker than following the twists and turns of the road, she decided, setting off at a brisk pace. After a few yards she tripped over her torn skirt and skidded down onto her hands and knees.

"Botheration!" She ripped the offending piece of fabric from the skirt and flung it aside. At this rate, she'd be lucky if Boggs allowed her in the front door of the castle. She stomped off again, cursing Lord Tremayne as if he alone was responsible for her current predicament.

"Oh, aye, my lord, I seen 'em," said the proprietor of the Blue Duck. "Pretty pair, they be, but I thinks maybe she weren't so choosy as he was."

Edward clenched his fists but refrained from striking the man. He didn't particularly want the Countess of Ketrick's name to be associated with the Blue Duck Inn, and the less the proprietor remembered about the entire incident, the better.

"And did you happen to have seen the direction they headed?"

"Oh, aye, my lord. Kent-wise, t' lady was going. Left well a'fore the noon."

"The blond-haired man was driving the carriage?"

"Ach, no." The man spit on the floor. "Don't know where he be off to. Me Eddie took 'er where she wanted t' go. Wrensmoor Castle."

The earl almost groaned. One of the Blue Duck's groomsmen. This day just kept getting worse.

It was late afternoon before Claire was willing to admit to

herself that she was lost. The endless series of rolling hills that had so delighted her on her first approach to Wrensmoor were now a source of frustration. She would climb up to the crest of one hill, certain that this time the castle would be right there in front of her, making her worries seem silly, only to find—

—one more hill.

How can it not be here? she thought. I'm sure I headed in the right direction! Panic threatened, and Claire fought the urge to take off in mindless flight. She forced herself to sit down in the grass at the top of the hill and think.

The situation was not that serious, she decided. She was sure she could find the path again, retrace her steps, and return to the road.

Of course this would all take time, and make explanations that much harder once she arrived at the hall. But it couldn't be helped. Her shoes—which had been intended for a day's coach ride and definitely not for hiking—were a hopeless mess. Claire tugged them off and threw them down the hill, followed by her stockings. That felt much better. Standing up, she decided—I'll try just one more hill. Then I'll turn back to the road.

Edward came around the sharp curve and saw the coach overturned at the side of the road, with the two bays still grazing nearby. Fear, which had been having occasional skirmishes with anger in his mind, now won an abrupt victory.

"Claire!" he shouted, spurring his mount. "Claire!"

There was no reply. An overturned carriage easily broke bones, and the thought that his wife might be lying unconscious in that wreck, or worse—

"Claire!"

When he reached the site of the mishap, however, he saw

no sign of either Claire or the driver.

Of all the idiotish things to do—she hadn't stayed with the coach! Anger staged a comeback, and Edward muttered curses as he searched the area for any indication that she might have been hurt.

No, he concluded, a wave of relief making him almost dizzy. *Doesn't she know any better than to scare a man out of his wits? When I find her*—

Edward's thoughts of how he would berate his wife were easier to endure than his previous thoughts of Claire kidnapped or Claire injured. He would find her and take her to Wrensmoor, or to London, or wherever she liked, and if she ever *dared* to leave his sight from this day onward—

Edward had remounted and was about to continue on to the castle when he noticed a scrap of muslin on the grass, away from the road. He recognized the fabric at once as a piece of one of his wife's dresses. *And she's heading down* that *path? Well, the silly chit will be good and lost by now,* thought Edward. *I'd better rescue her.*

Exhausted, her feet protesting every pebble underfoot, Claire climbed to the top of the next hill. A drizzle had started sometime during the last hour and it showed no signs of letting up. She wished she had thought to bring her parasol—water was dripping down her forehead into her eyes and she was too tired to brush it away.

No. The parasol was ripped. Remember? Claire began to feel afraid. The day was almost over, and if she didn't find the castle before dark she would be stuck here—cold and wet—for the entire night. *Quit fussing,* she told herself. *You'll manage. This is England, after all, not the wilds of America.* She continued to plod wearily upwards, slipping several times on the wet gravel of the path. Her hands were scraped raw from the falls, and as she reached the summit of another hill she prepared herself for disappointment. But, then—

Wrensmoor. The castle had never looked more beautiful. Claire felt the tears well in her eyes, and she collapsed at the crest of the hill, content for the moment simply to sit there in the drizzle and gaze down at her home.

Edward. Oh, Edward, why won't you come and live with me in paradise?

Minutes went by. Filthy, wet, and barefoot, Claire tried to talk herself into rising and walking down the hill to the castle, but it seemed almost too much trouble to move. Her hands were oozing blood from the accumulated scrapes and, absently, she wiped them on her skirt. Then, as the light continued to fade, she saw a horse in the distance. Claire's heart leaped, but—no, it wasn't Achilles. Still, the man was traveling in her direction, and she was ready to request his assistance, highwayman or no. As the rider drew closer, she recognized—

"Edward!" Claire jumped up and started to wave, but the moss and rock of the hilltop were slick from rain. Her bare feet slipped out from under her, and she overbalanced and fell, tumbling down the far side of the hill.

Chapter Twenty

Edward jumped down from Rutherford's horse and ran. He reached the crest of the hill with a few long strides and, to his horror, saw his wife lying motionless some ways below in a jumble of blood-stained skirts. A large clump of bracken had stopped her fall and Edward was kneeling at her side in seconds, his heart racing, slamming violently against his ribs.

"Claire. Oh, my love, please—"

She was bleeding. He was afraid to move her, but—she was bleeding—her skirts—

"Claire—"

"Mmm," said Claire. She opened her eyes for a moment, then shut them again.

No. Oh, no, no. Edward wanted to scream, to shake her—

"Edward?" whispered his wife.

"I'm here. I'm right here. Don't move," said the earl.

"No—I'm fine. Just a second. Help me up." Claire tried to get her hands underneath her, to push herself up—

"Lie still! You're bleeding."

"It's just my hands," said Claire. "Scraped. From falling." Her eyes were open again, and she attempted a weak smile. "Sorry—"

"Sorry!"

"I don't think I've broken anything. Really." Her voice was stronger now.

"Be quiet." Edward was carefully feeling her legs.

"Edward, really," said Claire, a bit of color returning. "I'm quite sure I'd know if I had broken my leg."

He continued his examination, ignoring her protests, but was eventually satisfied that, apart from scrapes and bruises, his wife was unharmed. He rose shakily to his feet, his emotions fluctuating so wildly between rage and relief that he could hardly speak.

"Of all the idiotic, irresponsible, harebrained stunts!" he flared, abruptly finding his voice.

"Oh!" Claire stood up and faced him, her expression mutinous.

For some reason the sight of her bare feet, dirty and with a smudge of blood, infuriated him even more.

"I ought to put you over my knee and spank you! I ought to lock you up in the tower donjon!" He was in front of her now, his fists clenched, his heart pounding. She looked up at him with silver eyes blazing.

"It was an accident!" she cried, matching his fury with her own.

"An *accident*—?"

"I checked the carriage and there was little damage beyond some scraped paint and one broken rim! I'm sorry that it happened, but it won't cost much to repair—certainly not as much as one more trinket for your . . . your floozy!"

"Repair—? A broken rim—? What in heaven's name are you talking about?" Edward was at sea. Was Claire telling him that her abduction was an accident?

"The carriage, you . . . you blockhead! We caught a wheel and overturned. Didn't you see it by the side of the road?"

"Yes, but—" Edward was silent for a moment, then took a deep breath. "Oh, *that* accident."

Claire looked confused. "What accident did you think I was talking about?"

"The—oh, never mind." Edward felt an edge of sanity return. He looked down at his wife and saw that her toes were once more peeping out from under the hem of her traveling dress. The dress itself was no longer clean, and he saw several tears in the fabric of the skirt. He held out the scrap of muslin he had found.

"I believe you lost this." He meant it as a small jest, a peace offering, but Claire glared at him and snatched the fabric out of his hand.

"Thank you!" she said. "I was doing perfectly well on my own, you know. There was no need to gallop up like some . . . like some . . ."

"Knight in shining armor?" suggested the earl.

"Exactly," said Claire. "Wrensmoor is just over this hill, and—"

Suddenly Lord Tremayne started to laugh.

"I fail to see what is so humorous," said his wife. "I saw the castle, and—"

"My floozy?" said Edward and let out a guffaw. "My *floozy?*"

Claire looked at him in indignation. "You know very well what I mean! Your mistress!"

"Claire—"

"Your doxy, your *chère amie,* your . . . well, I don't know all the words! That . . . that *woman* with the red hair!"

"Lady Hansfort," said Edward. He was still chuckling.

"Well, whoever she is. And stop laughing at me!"

"I am actually," said the earl, "laughing at myself. And Lady Hansfort is not my mistress."

"Well, who is—? *What?*" said Claire, doubly outraged. "If she's not your mistress, why were you embracing her?" She looked daggers at her husband. "Are you telling me you have a mistress *and* a floozy? Or do you just hold *every* woman who looks like her breasts are about to burst from her gown?"

"Nonsense, I'd hardly have the time. Besides, Danilla's breasts only fell out that once."

"Oh! Men!" Claire looked around for something to throw at him and then, abruptly, laughed. "Yes, I heard about that," she said. "Lord Radleigh said—"

"Lord Radleigh! How dare he discuss such a thing with—"

"Don't change the subject. Who is your mistress? You promised to tell me."

"Claire." Edward reached for her hand. She backed away, stumbled over a rock, and sat down hard. He bent and dragged her up, holding her locked against his chest. They stood there silently for a moment, Claire trying her best not to burst into tears, until the earl spoke again. "Claire."

"Mmm," said Claire, her voice muffled by his shirt.

"Claire, Lady Hansfort was never my mistress. She was a . . . mistake."

"Mmm," he heard again, this time with a distinctly skeptical note.

"Look at me," he said. He tipped her chin up until her silver-grey eyes, bright with tears, stared into his own. "I may have not been as forthcoming as you might have wished, in many ways, but have I ever lied to you?"

A shaky "No . . ."

"What you saw in the gardens was all there was to see. It never went any further, and it won't happen another time. I don't have a mistress. I'll never have a mistress again."

Claire looked at him and shook her head. "I don't understand."

"I love you, Claire," said Edward. "I want to live with you now, and forever, at Wrensmoor, or London, or—wherever you wish." He smiled. "I don't plan on having the time or the energy for a mistress."

Claire could no longer hold back her tears. Edward kissed them away, and then his lips moved to her forehead, the tip of her nose, her mouth—

"Mmm," said Edward after a while.

"I love you, my lord," said Claire.

"I love you, my lady wife. Let's go home."

They walked hand in hand down the hill to Wrensmoor, as the drizzle ceased and the sun set behind the ramparts of the castle in a blaze of scarlet and orange. Sheep bleated lazily in the distance and Claire thought how wonderful it would be to see the river and the quail and even the silly geese again. Her heart was full. From time to time she looked at her husband, who was whistling cheerfully out of tune and leading a chestnut stallion nearly the size of Achilles.

A stallion—

"Edward, where did you get that horse?"

"Ah." Her husband chuckled. "Well, that's another story. Now what's all this I hear about your cousin Harry—?"

Epilogue

It was a fine day in early spring. The grass in Green Park was at its most fresh, the meadows dotted with crocuses and daffodils. Lady Pamela rode slowly along the path, breathing in the scent of French lilacs and keeping her mare firmly in hand so as not to outpace Lady Detweiler. Amanda's seat had never been reliable, and she agreed to these occasional rides only to humor Lady Pam. "An open carriage is so much more sensible, my dear. Why should *I* be forced to steer the silly animal?" was her usual complaint.

"It's almost a shame to leave London at this time of year," commented Pam, watching the fountain spray glittering in the sunlight. "I can't imagine the Cotswolds will be one bit nicer than this."

"*Les petits horreurs* won't be in residence, will they?" demanded Amanda. "You know I adore the duke, but his children—" She shuddered.

Pam laughed. "I'm sure the governess will keep the littlest ones out from underfoot."

"Ah, the governess! But has His Grace been fortunate enough to find someone like Charles's Helène?"

"I understand that Miss Taylor is nearer sixty."

"Worse and worse."

They rode on in silence for a few minutes. Clouds scudded

across the sky in the cool breeze, but the sun on their backs was warm.

"Hmm," said Lady Detweiler, still thinking about the invitation to the duke's estate. "Darling, I'm just not sure. If Gloucester is still determined to invite some scruffy, impoverished *artiste* to every one of his house parties—"

"Just think of the possibilities. Remember the time Lady Gregory ran off with the violinist?"

Amanda snorted. "She must have seen something in him the rest of us missed. He was hopeless at the violin." She paused and reached up to adjust the tilt of her shako. "Oh, very well," she told Pam. "I suppose it might be entertaining, at that. Is the Marquis of Lidgerwood really planning to offer for that ridiculous Forsythe chit, do you suppose? Gwendolyn claims that he is smitten, although how anyone could be *smitten* with Susannah Forsythe is beyond my comprehension, I can just *imagine* what the children will look like."

"Ah . . . Miss Forsythe? Well, I'm not sure," said Lady Pamela absently, catching sight of a group of riders in the distance. She watched them carefully.

"I know he's more than desperate for the cash, but really, my dear, the child still has spots."

"Hmm." Pam's attention continued to wander as her friend chatted. The Earl of Ketrick and his family were in town for a short stay, she had heard, the first such visit since the birth of his son. She had longed to pay a call at Tremayne House and see the boy, but it would be more comfortable, perhaps, to meet them in less formal circumstances. She knew both Edward and Claire favored the meadows of Green Park.

"How is Robert's oldest?" asked Amanda. "Lady Andrews's nephew was just sent down from Oxford, you know—

something about a bull in the quadrangle—" She abruptly stopped talking, watched Pam for a few moments, and shook her head in despair. "You haven't heard a word I've said," she told Lady Pamela.

"Hmm?"

"Oh, a pox on the blasted Earl of Ketrick and his absurd infant," said Amanda. "You've been a perfect bore since the day the family set foot in London. Pottering about in the park at all hours of the afternoon, as if you had nothing better to do. Really, Pamela—"

Pam sputtered. "Lord Tremayne? What has he to do with—"

"Oh, posh. You don't fool me. Babies! Why anyone can be so besotted with the smelly little creatures is a mystery to me, they just squall and make one revolting mess after another—"

"I am merely interested in—"

"Well, there they are, anyway." Amanda abruptly nodded in the direction of the duck pond.

"Who—?" A moment's confusion, then Pam turned to see Jodrel de Lancie crouched at the edge of the water, apparently in earnest conversation with a tiny, dark-haired child.

The earl's son. Pam's mouth twitched in amusement as the toddler shook his head vigorously. A high-pitched "No, no, no," followed by a burst of giggles, wafted across the grass. Jody was pointing at something over the child's shoulder.

"No, no, no!"

There was a movement in the corner of her eye, and Lady Pamela spotted Edward and Claire walking arm in arm through the flower-strewn meadow. The earl's head was inclined towards his wife, the rich brown of his hair a perfect counterpoint to the raven black of hers. Pam saw Edward gesture wide with one arm and heard Claire's soft laughter.

True love, thought Lady Pamela. *It does exist.* She smiled.

Amanda watched her with raised eyebrows. "Oh, come now, stop looking like a moonstruck calfling. You were never really in love with him."

"I know," said Pam. "But isn't it marvelous that she is?"

Claire felt the brawn of her husband's arm securely at her side as they walked through the afternoon warmth. She hadn't returned to Green Park since the day she was shot— less than two years ago, but it seemed like an eternity. Claire sighed in contentment.

"My love?"

"Hmm. I was just thinking about the day Harry shot me. I never properly thanked him."

"Thanked him? I don't think I want to hear this."

"It was the start of everything."

"The start of everything? You heartless minx! I'd already asked you to marry me!"

"Pooh. You didn't mean it."

"Much you know." The earl took his wife in his arms and, ignoring her protests, kissed her soundly in full view of the rest of Green Park.

"Papa!"

They broke apart, smiling, and Edward knelt as, under Jody's careful supervision, Peter toddled towards them. Their son was not yet completely secure on his feet, and twice he tumbled back onto his bottom into the grass. Finally, with a small cry of triumph, he reached his father—

"Papa!" Lady Pamela heard the child's delighted giggle as the Earl swung him high overhead. "Papa!"

She heard Edward's laughter then, deep and rich. Father and son. Pam's breath caught in her throat at the sight, and her eyes threatened to fill with tears.

"Oh, heavens," said Lady Detweiler. "Enough of this fussing. Let's say hello."